RAGING SUN

A James Acton Thriller

By J. Robert Kennedy

James Acton Thrillers

The Protocol

Brass Monkey

Broken Dove

The Templar's Relic

Flags of Sin

The Arab Fall

The Circle of Eight

The Venice Code

Pompeii's Ghosts

Amazon Burning

The Riddle

Blood Relics

Sins of the Titanic

Saint Peter's Soldiers

The Thirteenth Legion

Raging Sun

Special Agent Dylan Kane Thrillers

Rogue Operator

Containment Failure

Cold Warriors

Death to America

Black Widow

Delta Force Unleashed Thrillers

Payback

Infidels

The Lazarus Moment

Detective Shakespeare Mysteries

Depraved Difference

Tick Tock

The Redeemer

Zander Varga, Vampire Detective

The Turned

RAGING SUN

A James Acton Thriller

J. ROBERT KENNEDY

ISBN-10: 1532737262

ISBN-13: 978-1532737268

First Edition

10 9 8 7 6 5 4 3 2 1

In memory of the last American soldier to die in combat during World War II, PFC William C. Patrick Bates of K Company, 3rd Battalion, 3rd Regiment, 3rd Marine Division, on Dec 14, 1945. Killed while on patrol in Guam by a Japanese sniper unaware the war was over, almost four months after the surrender of Japan. He is buried in Honolulu's Punchbowl, Section 17, Grave Number 178.

RAGING SUN

A James Acton Thriller

"The occupying forces of the Allies shall be withdrawn from Japan as soon as these objectives have been accomplished and there has been established, in accordance with the freely expressed will of the Japanese people, a peacefully inclined and responsible government."

Article 12 of the Potsdam Declaration, July 26, 1945

"As part of such advice and consent the Senate states that nothing the treaty [San Francisco Peace Treaty] contains is deemed to diminish or prejudice, in favor of the Soviet Union, the right, title, and interest of Japan, or the Allied Powers as defined in said treaty, in and to South Sakhalin and its adjacent islands, the Kurile Islands, the Habomai Islands, the Island of Shikotan, or any other territory, rights, or interests possessed by Japan on December 7, 1941, or to confer any right, title, or benefit therein or thereto on the Soviet Union."

U.S. Senate Resolution, April 28, 1952

PREFACE

On both July 25 and July 31, 1945, in the dying days of World War II, Emperor Hirohito ordered the Lord Keeper of the Privy Seal of Japan to protect the Imperial Regalia "at all costs". These ancient relics, a sword, a bronze mirror and a jade jewel, through tradition, represent valor, wisdom and benevolence, and their possession confirms the Emperor's claim to the throne.

Two weeks later, at noon local time on August 15, 1945, Japanese Emperor Hirohito was heard on radio delivering what became known as the Jewel Voice Broadcast in which he announced the Japanese acceptance of the Potsdam Declaration. Without admitting defeat, it was effectively an unconditional surrender.

Three days later the Soviet Union invaded the northern islands of Japan known as the Kuril Islands. They then proceeded to expel the 17,000 Japanese inhabitants, and in violation of the Potsdam Declaration, continue to occupy these islands. The issue remains a cause of friction between the two nations, both with significant navies in the Pacific.

On January 7, 1989, the Imperial Regalia were presented to the new Japanese Emperor, Akihito, as part of the enthronement rituals. All were covered by red brocade, the artifacts unseen, unlike during the enthronement of Akihito's grandfather, Hirohito, in 1926.

To this day, many question whether the Imperial Regalia were actually lost at the end of the greatest war to have ever afflicted mankind.

Courtyard Moscow Paveletskaya Hotel, Moscow, Russian Federation
Present Day

Professor James Acton poked his head out of the elevator and checked both ways before stepping into the hallway, his wife's hand gripped tightly—Professor Laura Palmer clung even tighter. Tensions were high in Moscow, and there was no way any sane person would be here right now, not with a war brewing off the coast of Japan.

But he had never been accused of being sane.

His life as an archaeology professor was far more exciting and far more dangerous than it should be, with more bullets, rockets, bombs, knives and vehicles thrown at him over the past few years than most soldiers experienced in a lifetime.

And it had almost got him and Laura killed on multiple occasions.

In fact, she was still recovering from a gunshot to the stomach about a year ago, she still winded easily.

She should definitely *not be here.*

"There it is." He pointed at a door to their right. Room 906. He knocked and they both listened, Acton stepping back so whoever was on the other side could see his face.

He just prayed that the person on the other side of the door was the one they were expecting.

Professor Arseny Orlov.

They had met only once, several years ago in Germany, to discuss how best to protect ancient ruins in warzones.

How prophetic that turned out to be.

1

At the time, no one could have conceived of an ISIS type group rampaging almost unopposed across the land, destroying priceless, irreplaceable pieces of history. It angered him to no end, and he wished a horrible, prolonged death for any involved, then an eternity of damnation in the afterlife.

The door opened and they both breathed sighs of relief as Orlov ushered them inside, holding a finger to his lips. They had received his desperate call only that morning, the cryptic message begging them to come to Moscow on hastily arranged visas.

A matter of life and death.

His day never went well when *that* line was delivered, even by the best of friends.

You could stop a war.

That had piqued their interest, sending them to Laura's private jet, the wealth left her by her late brother a blessing in times like these.

Orlov hugged him then kissed him on both cheeks, Acton's thoughts flashing to their crotchety old Interpol buddy, Hugh Reading.

Hugh would have decked him.

The greeting was repeated on Laura before the man finally spoke.

"I cannot thank you enough for coming!"

Acton nodded. "You made it sound like we had no choice."

Orlov smiled slightly, his eyes darting between the door they had just entered and one to an adjoining room. Acton glanced at it, noting the deadbolt appeared to be in the unlocked position.

A double-knock had Acton spinning toward the sound, Orlov raising his hands. "It's okay, it's my son."

The adjoining door opened and the young man who had driven them here stepped inside, smiling at them, his eyes lingering on Laura a little too long. She was a striking woman, and Acton sometimes forgot how he had reacted the first time he had seen her through the window of her classroom door at University College London.

She had taken his breath away.

Then helped save his life.

They had been together ever since, he finally, truly, happy.

Acton nodded at the young man who took up a position at the door, peering periodically through the peephole. Acton turned to Orlov. "Why are we here?"

"This." Orlov motioned toward a table, a cloth covering something whisked away in a flourish.

Acton gasped. "Are those what I think they are?"

"I don't know, that's why you're here. I know what *I* think they are, but I need *you* to authenticate them."

Laura leaned in without touching. "Don't you have people who can do that for you?"

"None that I can trust. Not with what is happening."

"So these are why the Japanese are so hopping mad." Acton picked up one of the three priceless relics sitting on the table. "I had heard rumors they had been lost during the war, but I had assumed they were just that."

"This is what my own research tells me," said Orlov. "Do you think they are real?"

"Where were they found?"

"On one of the northern islands of Japan that my country claims as its territory."

Acton's eyes narrowed. "Where they recently found the bodies of those Japanese soldiers from the war?"

Orlov nodded. "Da."

"Huh. If these were with the soldiers, then that means they've been lost for over seventy years."

Laura glanced up from the relic she was examining. "Do you realize what this means?"

Orlov shook his head. "No, what?"

Acton placed the relic on the table. "It means that the current emperor of Japan was sworn in with fakes, and his claim to the throne is illegitimate."

Laura returned her relic. "Not only does it mean the Japanese government and the emperor have been lying to its people for decades, but the current emperor is technically a fraud."

Orlov stared at them wide-eyed. "No wonder they're willing to go to war."

Laura looked at him. "One question begs to be asked. I can understand why the Japanese want them back, and are willing to risk everything, but why Russia? Why won't your country simply return them?"

Orlov shrugged. "Politics, I fear, but whatever the reason, they must be stopped."

A pit formed in Acton's stomach. "What's your plan?"

Orlov looked at him then Laura. "I want the two of you to smuggle them out of the country."

Tires screeched on the streets below.

Palace Castle, Tokyo, Empire of Japan
August 13, 1945

Major Hiroshi Sato cringed as the room shook, dust floating gently down from the ceiling of the bomb shelter. The Americans so far had left their location alone after destroying much of the palace during the firebombing of their city three months ago, though that didn't preclude a stray bomb from hitting them. But the gods would protect them, would protect their son in this realm.

They will protect His Majesty, and through Him, us.

He told his family every day that this was the safest place to be, though unfortunately they couldn't be here with him. Instead, much of their days spent trying to live as normal a life as possible in the dying days of this war they should never have lost, the betrayal of His Majesty by the military and government, obvious.

We would have won if everyone had committed to the cause as they should have.

His duty was his life, and his duty was to protect His Majesty at all costs, and as the days grew more dire, the American bombing almost incessant now as more bombers came into range, it was clear the end would soon be here.

Especially after the unbelievable massacres in Hiroshima and Nagasaki. He had only heard the reports, the devastation unlike anything imaginable. Apparently both cities were essentially flattened, as if the gods themselves had crushed everything for miles.

And the bodies.

Vaporized, dark outlines on buildings, charred remains frozen in time.

And worse.

The survivors, their flesh hanging off them, burned head to toe, many blinded by what was apparently an incredibly bright light. Even some here in Tokyo claimed to have seen it, though he didn't believe it. Surely it couldn't have been that massive. It would take more bombs than the entire army could muster to create something so large.

Yet there was no denying the reports.

Over one hundred thousand dead, mostly the elderly, women, children.

Not soldiers.

The soldiers were fighting.

And not a man, woman or child that remained, went to bed at night not worrying that Tokyo, or their city, would be next.

What kind of monsters could do such a thing?

The war was lost. Surrender wasn't what terrified him and his comrades.

It was occupation.

The government had filled the airwaves for years about the imperialist pigs that were the Americans, how they viciously massacred and desecrated the bodies of the brave fallen of the Imperial Japanese Army, and how, should the people fail their emperor and these round eyes set foot on Japanese soil, how they would rape and pillage their way across the country in a bloodlust not seen for a thousand years.

It was his wife, son and three daughters that he feared for the most. He was perfectly willing to die, in fact, as a matter of honor, expected to. He could think of no greater shame than to survive the war, unscathed.

Except perhaps to fail His Majesty.

The door to the shelter opened, the heavy wood slamming against the concrete wall with a loud slap, startling everyone inside. "Major!"

Sato leapt to his feet, snapping to attention at the sight of his commanding officer, Colonel Tanaka. "Yes, sir!"

"Follow me!"

"Yes, sir!" He grabbed his hat off the table, the others saying nothing, all eyes averted lest they be dragged themselves from the safety of the shelter, the pounding outside showing no signs of letting up.

He pulled the door shut behind him, climbing the stairs carved into the ground, soon joining his commanding officer in what was hard to describe as fresh air. He presented himself to Tanaka and bowed, it barely returned, the man instead staring out over the city.

A city afire.

Searchlights crisscrossed the sky, anti-aircraft fire thundering away, tracer fire revealing their positions, the sky thick with the drone of heavy bombers delivering their death from above, unchallenged by a decimated air force.

His home burned.

His country cried for mercy.

A mercy they wouldn't receive. Not from the brutal Americans.

"I've chosen you for a most important mission."

He snapped to attention, sucking in a deep breath. His stomach filled with butterflies and his chest tightened with fear, but a slight flush of pride flowed through him, tempering the natural fight or flight response. He hadn't seen a day of action since the war began, though if he should be needed in these final days, he may yet regain the honor he felt he had lost by not defending his country.

"You are to handpick a team of ten men. His Majesty has ordered that the Imperial Regalia be moved from their sanctuaries to somewhere safe before the Americans arrive."

"Yes, sir. It will be my honor to protect the Imperial Regalia from the American horde. Where shall we take them?"

"To the northern islands. There are currently no enemy troops near there, nor do we anticipate any as they have no strategic value. Take your men, three month's supplies, and bury the Imperial Regalia so they cannot be found by the enemy should you be discovered. When it has been deemed safe by His Majesty, you will be called for."

"When do we leave?"

"Immediately."

He hesitated for a moment, the Colonel catching it.

"What is it?"

"Our families. If this is indeed the end…"

The colonel eyed him. "Is it not their duty to sacrifice their lives for His Majesty? Would you have their wellbeing interfere with your duty to Him?"

Sato immediately dropped into a bow of shame, his eyes squeezed tight, his arms straight and tucked against his sides. "I apologize for my selfishness, Colonel. Of course, our duty to His Majesty is of the utmost importance!"

There was a pause, the sounds of the bombs and screams in the distance the only sounds beside the rustling of the leaves of the keyaki trees surrounding them. "Your family is near here, is it not?"

"Yes, sir."

"I think your route will take you past their house, will it not?"

It wouldn't. It couldn't. It would actually be a few minutes out of the way.

He suppressed an eager smile, cocking his head slowly to the side so he might catch a glimpse of the colonel while still hunched over with his shame. "Ahh, yes?"

"It would be unfortunate if there were vehicle trouble for a few minutes in that neighborhood."

"I-it would be?"

"Yes, I think it would be. Now fulfill your duty to His Majesty!"

He bowed even deeper. "Yes, Colonel!"

Kharkar Island, South Kuril Islands, Russian Federation
Japanese name: Harukaru Island
Present Day. Four weeks before Acton's arrival in Moscow

"Umm, Comrade Lieutenant, you need to see this."

Lieutenant Markov stared up the communications tower at the white, red and blue of the Russian flag fluttering overhead in the wind, it having just been replaced, the Japanese having an annoying habit of sneaking onto the island from time to time to steal the flag, sometimes even replacing it with their own.

So it probably wasn't the government, but civilians doing it.

Teenagers. They're the same everywhere.

He had no doubt that if he went on YouTube, he'd probably find footage of them actually carrying out the deed. It never ceased to amaze him the stupidity of today's youth, and he knew from friends around the world that it wasn't just a Russian phenomenon.

They're stupid everywhere. Who posts footage of their crime on the Internet?

He grunted, taking one last glance at the flag.

I wonder why so many flags are red, white and blue.

He looked at the seaman. "What is it?"

"I, umm, found something."

Markov frowned. "Out with it, Seaman. What did you find?"

Instead of replying, the young man, part of the generation he had little respect for, turned and walked hurriedly to the southern portion of the tiny island. Markov followed, his frown deepening. He was about to open his mouth when he came upon two of his men standing, staring at the ground.

They looked up as he arrived.

"What is it?"

They all pointed at the side of a slight embankment. Markov stepped forward, it evident the recent typhoon had done a number on the already rough terrain, the communications tower not the only thing to take a hit from the storm.

His eyes popped wide.

"Are those—?"

"Bones!" cried the seaman, the others bobbing their heads rapidly.

"Someone was murdered and buried here," said another, stepping forward and pointing at a shattered skull, its grinning visage unsettling to say the least. "Look, a bullet hole!"

Markov knelt down beside the remains and leaned closer to the skull, there clearly a circular hole in the forehead, as if the person had been shot at close range, essentially between the eyes.

Executed.

He noticed something flap in the wind, just a sliver of fabric exposed by the heavy rains. He reached over and gently brushed away the dirt, exposing more of it. His eyes narrowed. He carefully yanked at the cloth, revealing what appeared to be an epaulette.

With insignia.

He leaned back on his haunches, considering the find.

"It's a Japanese soldier."

"But who killed him?" asked the seaman, kneeling beside him. "He looks like he's been dead a long time."

"He has. I'd say at least seventy years."

Shiba District, Tokyo, Empire of Japan
August 13, 1945

"Stop here."

The Isuzu Type 94 truck ground to a halt, his driver looking at him curiously then at the sky nervously. The bombing had continued over the hour that it had taken to load their supplies, though it wasn't concentrated on this area, it mostly residential and already devastated.

There's not much point in bombing homes to dust when they're already rubble.

Factories and naval yards, however, were fair game.

Over and over.

"What is it, sir?"

"Something's wrong with the engine."

The young corporal's eyebrows rose. "Sir? The engine is—"

Major Hiroshi Sato glared at him, the young man cringing. "There's something wrong with the engine. I think it will take you about fifteen minutes to repair it."

"Umm, y-yes, sir. I-I think there might be."

"Good. Get to work." Sato jumped to the ground then rounded to the back of the truck where his second-in-command, First Lieutenant Moto, joined him from the second vehicle. "Something's wrong with the truck."

"Really?" The lieutenant began to push his sleeves up, appearing eager to dive under the hood of their Isuzu built transport.

Sato held up a hand. "Your family is near here?"

A cloud replaced the eagerness. "Yes."

"Tell the men. Fifteen minutes. Anyone not here when I get back will be hunted down and shot along with their families."

11

Moto appeared confused for a moment then his jaw dropped slightly before snapping tightly shut. "A patrol of the neighborhood, perhaps?"

Sato smiled. "You'll earn that third star with thinking like that."

Moto grinned then snapped to attention, a smart salute executed. Sato returned it.

"Fifteen minutes. Tell the men."

Moto nodded and spun on his heel as Sato turned, walking briskly down a rubble-strewn lane and rounding a corner. Out of sight of his men, he sprinted toward his home, it still standing though damaged the last time he had seen it. He turned the corner and the air sucked out of him as if he had been struck in the stomach by a cricket bat.

His home was levelled.

Bile threatened to fill his mouth yet he pushed himself forward, stumbling toward his humble home, it now reduced to a single wall, the rest collapsed inward, a crater next to it where their neighbor used to live.

Their home completely destroyed.

His at least was recognizable as once being the safe haven of an innocent family, once a home where the laughter of children and the singing of his wife and mother-in-law could be heard before times had turned grim.

The laughter was sometimes still there, the innocence of children a blessing that could still bring a smile to his face even on the worst of days.

But the singing had stopped, his wife no longer a happy woman. He had told her to take her mother and stay with his family in the countryside yet she had refused.

"This is my home. No one will force me from it, not the Americans, and not you."

It was a futile argument that he hadn't pressed.

As he collapsed to his knees in what was once their front doorway, tears threatened to erupt, tears of shame in his failure as a husband to protect his wife, a father to protect his young children, as a soldier to protect these innocent civilians.

And as a man, to fail them all.

His shoulders shook and his chin dropped to his chest as he could hold back the emotions no longer. He cursed the war, he cursed the Americans, and if he weren't such a dedicated soldier, he would curse His Majesty.

But he couldn't.

And he chastised himself for even thinking it.

Though he would curse the military and the government, those truly responsible for getting them into this war, and truly responsible for its failure.

A siren sounded in the distance, the air raid over, the reprieve missed in his grief.

"Hiroshi?"

He tensed up, his hands darting to his face to wipe the tears as he pushed himself to his feet. He brushed his knees free of the dirt he had knelt in then drew a breath before turning.

He smiled slightly as he recognized his neighbor. "Mrs. Kita, it is a relief to see you are well." He nodded toward the crater that was once the old woman's home. "I had feared the worst."

She shuffled over to him as others began to emerge from their hiding places, the occupants of a bomb shelter down the road beginning to spill out into the nearly impassable street. "We are fine. We were all in the shelter when it happened."

His head dropped and he squeezed his eyes shut. "When did it happen?"

"Three days ago. It was the only bomb to hit the area. The Volunteer Fighting Core Officer said it was probably a mistake, a bomb not releasing

13

when it should, or one of the murderous Americans thinking nothing of dropping a bomb meant for a factory, instead on a house."

Three days. If only she had listened!

"Hiroshi!"

His chin lifted and his eyes widened as he heard a voice he would recognize through the shock of a thousand bombs. His wife. He peered past Mrs. Kita and spotted her, running toward him, her arms outstretched, her usually beautiful hair held tightly by a dirty bandage wrapped around her head. He stumbled toward her, numb to the reality of the situation, a moment ago the love of his life dead, and now, alive and well, falling into his arms, sobbing. He held her tight, saying nothing, his eyes shutting out the world around them as he lost himself in this moment granted him by the gods.

"Daddy!"

It was a chorus as wondrous as the most capable of choirs as four little bodies slammed into them, their tiny arms wrapping around his legs and those of their mother. He breathed a sigh of relief as he released his wife, gazing for a moment to the heavens to thank the gods for watching over his family.

"I feared you were dead."

"We almost were," said his wife. "I was getting water with the children when it hit." She stared at their home, tears rolling down her cheeks. "We should be dead."

"But you are not." He checked his watch then turned to her. "I want you to take the children, tonight, and head for my parents' place."

His wife shook her head. "No, I want to—"

He lowered his voice, placing his mouth to her ear. "The war is about to be lost. Perhaps in a matter of days. Once the Americans arrive, they will rape and pillage their way across the country. Our children will be

14

slaughtered in front of you and when they are done with you, you will beg them to kill you." His wife paled, his message at last sinking in. "You must go. Now."

She nodded, gripping her children close to her side. "What about you?"

"I'm leaving on a special mission for His Majesty. I should be safe. Once the war is over, it may take some time before I return, so do not be alarmed."

She looked up at him. "I love you."

He smiled. "I love you too."

"We love you, Daddy!"

He dropped to a knee and gave them all hugs then took his eldest son, only nine, by the shoulders. "You are the man of the house until I return. You will obey your mother, but protect her and your sisters. Understood?"

He snapped out a salute. "Yes, Major!"

Sato smiled then rose to return the salute. "As you were!"

Little arms instantly ensnarled his leg. He looked at his wife. "I have to go. I'll come find you as soon as I can."

She nodded, a final hug and kiss exchanged. "Be safe."

"You be safe."

She pried the children off him and he walked briskly away, taking one last glance at his family as he turned the corner, his children waving, his wife forcing a smile on her face, the image one he hoped he could burn into his memory until he saw them again.

But as he rounded the corner and lost sight of them, a chill ran through his body as he knew with a certainty unlike any he had felt before, that he would never see them again.

Ebiso District, Tokyo, Japan
Present Day. Three days before Acton's arrival in Moscow

"It's a matter of honor."

Jiro sat on the floor of his living room, legs crossed, hands resting on his knees as he breathed deeply, his eyes gently closed. He held it then slowly exhaled, willing his inner demons out of his body.

It wasn't working.

He couldn't meditate anymore, his troubles far too great, his discipline far too lacking. His mother was pressuring him to get married, his boss was pressuring him to put in more hours, and his landlady was pressuring him to do the chores around the property he had promised in exchange for a break on his rent.

And his stomach growled with a ravenous hunger, despite having only eaten an hour before.

I hate diabetes.

He was one of the lucky ones—and he certainly meant that sarcastically—where his body didn't work properly, his brain constantly being signaled that he was hungry, despite having just eaten a generous helping of salmon and rice. He was so ravenous, he would be tempted to gnaw at his arm if he could.

He cast his eyes down at his too round stomach.

It's all your fault.

He had abused his body for years trying to escape the pain, the pain of a childhood of teasing, of a propensity to gain weight at the drop of a hat, never to lose it unless he starved himself.

What kind of a life is it if I have to starve myself for the rest of it?

16

A tear rolled down his cheek.

No life at all.

He worked his ass off at work, easily putting in twelve hours a day, six days a week, yet it was never enough. Times were tough, and the boss wanted everyone to put in more effort.

For the same pay.

And then there was his love life.

There was none.

At least now there wasn't. He had been pining over Keiko in Personnel for the better part of two years, and had finally gathered up the courage just this morning to ask her to coffee.

The look she had given him had cleaved his stomach hollow.

He hadn't waited for the words of rejection, he had merely turned and left.

It was the giggles that echoed behind him from the others that had truly knocked the wind out of him.

He was pathetic.

With the hours he was putting in at the office, he'd never have time to find a woman to marry, so his sick mother would never get off his back, and even if he did find the time, it was obvious after years of trying he was neither appealing to the opposite sex—no matter how much his mother insisted he was—nor confident enough to approach a woman.

He would die alone, exhausted, doing the same job he had committed to during college.

His life was a prison he couldn't escape. One of constant work, little play, and now a disease he wasn't sure he could handle.

Life isn't worth living.

He opened his eyes, his grandfather's ceremonial shin gunto sword mounted on the wall. He knew how to commit seppuku, the ritual suicide—he had researched it enough over the past few months—it a painful though quick method of ending all his suffering, but it was also a terrifying prospect.

And Keiko had always been there, a beacon in his darkness, a beacon extinguished when she had stared at him, wide-eyed with horror, at his audacity in asking her out.

Perhaps it's time.

He sucked in a deep breath and rose, straightening his shirt before walking over and lifting the ornate sword off the wall, it a gift from his father to him when he had turned nine.

"That was how old I was when my father last saw us. He left on a mission for His Majesty, and was never heard from again. Now it is yours, and when your son turns nine, it will be his."

He had been in awe of the sword ever since, and of his grandfather, the brave major who in the dying days of the war had been sent on a daring mission to protect the Imperial Regalia.

A mission he had apparently failed to fulfill, though the true extent of the shame of that failure was a family secret never shared with anyone.

A shame, if it were to become known, that would destroy his family's honor for generations.

He unsheathed the sword slightly, exposing part of the gently curved blade.

It could all be over in minutes.

Compounding the shame of his family.

But at least you won't have to deal with it.

The doorbell rang and he jumped, his heart racing as he jammed the blade back in its scabbard and returned it to the wall. He crossed the tiny floor space of his far too expensive apartment and peered through the peephole, fully expecting it to be his landlady with another chore for him to do.

He gasped, it the last person he had expected to see.

Keiko!

He unlocked the door and opened it, his heart hammering, his stomach flipping, his world almost ready to spin out of control. He clamped down on his cheek with his teeth.

"Hi, Jiro. Umm, can I come in?"

He nodded hastily, retreating, pulling the door open for her. She stepped inside and he motioned toward the living room, saying nothing. She smiled awkwardly and removed her shoes, slipping her feet into a pair of sandals he kept for visitors then tentatively entered his humble abode.

She turned. "I-I wanted to apologize for earlier."

His mouth went dry, his eyes widening.

She's sorry!

But what did that mean? Did it mean she had changed her mind? Did it mean she was sorry for the giggling from the others? Did it mean she was sorry for not actually saying the words, "no thanks"?

He said nothing.

"You caught me off guard. That's why I didn't say anything when you asked."

"Your face said it all, I think," he mumbled, shocked he had the courage to challenge her.

Her face slackened, the color draining from it as she bowed deeply. "I-I'm so sorry. It wasn't because it was you. It was because of *where* you asked me. Y-you're the first boy to ever ask me out in my entire life, and, well, I guess I didn't think it would happen at my desk, surrounded by a bunch of gossiping women." She rose, peering up at him, her hands clasped low in front of her. "If we had been alone, I would have said—"

19

The doorbell rang and they both flinched, Keiko quickly curling inward, as if protecting herself from whatever was to come. Jiro didn't know what to say or what to do, his mind filling in various endings to the interrupted sentence. "Yes." "No thanks." "Are you kidding me?" "I'd rather date anyone but you!" "Why don't you go kill yourself you fat pig!"

The doorbell rang again, followed immediately by several hard raps.

"Sorry," he mumbled, turning toward the door. He didn't look to see who it was, his mind still reeling. He pulled open the door and nearly peed. Two men in military dress uniforms stood in the hall, their faces serious.

"Are you Jiro Sato?"

He nodded.

"You are the grandson of Major Hiroshi Sato?"

His eyebrows rose slightly, the temptation to glance back at his grandfather's sword almost overwhelming. "Yes."

Both men immediately bowed, the first extending his arms, presenting a previously unnoticed wood box. "Sir, I am Major Oshiro. It is with great humility that I, on behalf of the Japanese people, present to you the personal effects of your grandfather, Major Hiroshi Sato." Jiro took the presented box, not sure what to say, when he suddenly noticed Keiko beside him.

"Please come in," she said, gently tugging him toward the living area.

"Thank you, ma'am." The two men followed them inside.

And Jiro still said nothing.

"The remains of your grandfather and his platoon were recently discovered. It took several weeks to confirm their identities, however there is now no doubt as to who they are." He held out a hand and the other soldier placed an envelope in it. "These are all the pertinent details. Your grandfather is entitled to a funeral, paid for by the government. We attempted to contact your mother, but she—umm—refused us entry." Jiro smiled slightly, picturing it. "When you are ready, please contact us." He handed the envelope over, Jiro taking it with two shaking hands.

"Wh-where did you find him?"

"Their remains were discovered on Harukaru Island."

Jiro sucked in a breath, glancing over at the sword. "Then he succeeded," he whispered.

"Succeeded in what, sir?"

Jiro looked at the soldier, the family's shame of decades beginning to lift. His grandfather hadn't failed. After the war, his commander, a colonel whose name he had long forgotten, confided in his mother the nature of the mission, and how he regretted sending her husband when it had proven to be completely unnecessary. The colonel blamed himself for the failure, and for the fact the precious relics had been lost, but his family blamed their own, and a whispered confidence by his grandmother to her own mother sealed their shame, their community shunning them.

Thankfully none knew the true nature of the mission, merely that his grandfather had failed in a mission of the utmost importance to His Majesty, and only days later the empire had fallen.

Clearly his grandfather's fault, at least in part, at least in the minds of those they had once called friends and neighbors.

"If you found him then you must have found the relics?"

The major's eyes narrowed. "Sir?"

"My grandfather was part of the Imperial Guard. His last mission was to take the Imperial Regalia to safety before the Americans arrived. He never returned."

The major exchanged a glance with his partner. "I have no information on that, sir, however I am quite certain the Imperial Regalia are secure."

Jiro looked at Keiko who appeared as confused as the men in front of him. He turned back to the soldier.

"That is what you might tell the people, but my family has known different for over seventy years."

Atsuta Shrine, Nagoya, Empire of Japan
August 14, 1945

"Is it ready?"

The Shinto Shinshoku bowed, Major Hiroshi Sato returning the gesture. "Yes, Major. As per His Majesty's orders, the Kusanagi-no-Tsurugi sword has been prepared for transport." Sato rose as three elderly men entered the room, white robes flowing over their shoulders, extending to their feet, their hair high and tight, their faces expressionless. As they approached, the two flanking the man in the center stopped, the third carrying an ornate wood box on a plush cushion coming to halt directly in front of him, bowing slightly.

"This is it?"

"Yes, Major."

The cushion was held out and he reached for its contents, his hands trembling slightly as he lifted the box, the three men quickly bowing their way out of the room the moment it cleared the cloth.

"I must open it."

"It is forbidden."

"I have my orders."

This same argument had been repeated at the Ise Great Shrine when they had retrieved the Yata no Kagami mirror from their keepers.

He opened it, they gasped, he left.

And what had been, was again.

And another gasp.

The sword, seen by only a handful of mortals in a generation, sat inside the case. He had no reason to believe it was fake, nor any means to confirm whether it was genuine. He had only the honor and faith of the Shinto Shinshoku to rely upon.

He snapped it shut and bowed deeply. "Thank you, Shinshoku. May the gods protect you in these troubled times."

The shock and anger on the Shinshoku's face was momentarily out of sight as Sato stared at the floor, and it took a moment for the man to respond, bowing, though not as deeply, he clearly not pleased. Sato rose and left the room, two of his men snapping to attention then accompanying him to their transport vehicle.

"Major!"

He turned to see the Shinshoku rushing out after him. "Where are you taking it?"

"I cannot tell you that. It's classified."

"I-I realize that." The old man seemed to be hesitant to ask the question he had on his mind, and Sato had no time for delays.

"What is it, Shinshoku? We have little time."

"Forgive me, son, but what happens if you do not make it to your destination? If the Imperial Regalia are lost, there can never be another Emperor."

Sato felt his chest tighten at the words. The idea that he and his men might die on the mission had of course entered his mind on innumerable occasions, but his life was His Majesty's to take. He gave it willingly.

But if the Imperial Regalia were lost, would it indeed have ramifications that could echo for decades?

He looked at the old man.

"Pray that we do."

Ministry of Foreign Affairs, Tokyo, Japan
Present Day. Three days before Acton's arrival in Moscow

"Sir, there's somebody here that I think you should see."

Arata Sasaki glanced up from his keyboard, his recently sprained wrist forcing him to type one-handed, it a skill he doubted he'd master before it healed.

That's the last time I play squash with Goro. He's a lumbering fool!

"I'm quite busy. I have a meeting with the minister in fifteen minutes."

His assistant, Etsuko, bowed apologetically. "I am sorry to interrupt, but I *know* you'll want to hear this first."

He leaned back in his chair, his eyebrows rising slightly. The carefully chosen words suggested some news story was about to break, and the woman was right. If it were, it was best to know ahead of time so answers could be prepared, giving the impression the government was prepared and on top of it.

Even if it was only by minutes.

"What is it?"

Etsuko moved aside and an army major stepped forward, snapping to attention.

"As you were. You have something to report?"

The major glanced at the door and Etsuko closed it. "Sir, I am Major Oshiro. Earlier today I had the honor of participating in a repatriation notification—"

"One of the bodies recovered on Harukaru Island?"

Major Oshiro bowed slightly. "Yes, sir."

"Was there a problem?"

25

Oshiro took in a breath and held it for a moment. "Not a problem with the notification itself, but—" The man seemed to struggle for the right words.

"Out with it, Major. I'm a busy man, and if this information was so important that it couldn't wait then I need to know it now."

Oshiro flushed slightly, bowing a little deeper. "Yes, sir. Sorry, sir. Sir, it was something the grandson of Major Sato said. I informed my commanding officer of it after I executed my duties, and shortly thereafter received orders to report here to inform you personally of what was said."

"And that was?"

"It was about Major Sato's final mission. According to the grandson, the Major's final mission was to take the Imperial Regalia to safety."

Sasaki's head tilted back slightly as his eyes widened. Etsuko's jaw dropped for a moment before it snapped shut. "I'm sure he's mistaken."

"He seemed quite certain that not only was that his mission, but that his grandfather's commanding officer, the former head of the Imperial Guard, confirmed it after the war, and also confirmed that the Imperial Regalia had been lost during the failed mission."

Sasaki's chest tightened. "Rants of a fool. You are dismissed."

"Y-yes, sir."

The major snapped to attention then turned for the door.

"And Major?"

"Yes, sir?"

"You and your men are not to repeat a word of this to anyone."

"Yes, sir."

He stared the major in the eyes for a moment, his face emotionless. "Not—a—word."

The major bowed deeply. "Understood, sir."

Etsuko opened the door then closed it behind the rapidly retreating major. "It can't be true, can it?"

Sasaki pursed his lips as he reached for his phone. He glanced up at his assistant. "That goes for you too."

"What?"

"Not a word to anyone."

Etsuko's eyes widened. "You mean it's true?"

Sasaki pressed down on the receiver. "The minister told me after he was sworn in about this. The Imperial Regalia were indeed lost at the end of the war, and we've been trying to find them since."

"But His Majesty!"

Sasaki raised a finger. "Lower your voice!" he hissed. "I see you understand why this must be kept quiet."

Etsuko's head rapidly bobbed. "What are you going to do?"

"Move up my meeting with the minister."

Etsuko checked her watch. "But it starts in ten minutes."

"It's ten minutes we might not have to waste."

Harukaru Island, Empire of Japan
Russian name: Kharkar Island
August 18, 1945

"Here. Quickly."

Major Hiroshi Sato's men set to work digging in the hard terrain as he stood atop the highest point of the tiny landmass. It was deserted save for themselves, that confirmed by a quick circling of the island in their small boat commandeered earlier in the day. It was a civilian vessel, a fishing boat, it important there be no official record of where they had headed, the specific island chosen by him in the event the command staff in Tokyo were captured and tortured into revealing the truth.

No one knew they were there.

No one would ever know they were there.

Until the war was over.

He pointed at the hole. "Make it deep. We don't want it accidentally discovered. It looks like the seas are pretty harsh here."

His men dug with renewed vigor when his radioman came running from the boat, carrying the portable. "Sir, you have to hear this!"

Everyone stopped what they were doing, the sound from the radio becoming clearer as the young corporal approached.

"What is it?" asked Sato.

"The war, sir, it's over!"

Sato sighed, his eyes closing. Not in relief, but in shame. The mighty Japanese Empire had fallen, its armies failing their emperor, their great nation's future suddenly uncertain, except for one thing.

The Americans were coming.

It had been inevitable. The devastation wreaked upon Hiroshima and Nagasaki was a fate he knew couldn't be risked on other population centers. The Americans had won not because they were better soldiers, but because their government was more brutal than anyone had imagined.

We were too civilized in our approach.

"What does this mean?" asked the corporal as the general surrender message repeated, it apparently originally broadcast three days ago.

"It means all hostilities are over. We have surrendered unconditionally."

The men digging leaned on their shovels. "So what do we do?" asked one of them.

"We have a mission, given to us by His Majesty. This broadcast says we have surrendered and that hostilities are over. It says we are to hold our current positions until further orders. That includes us." He pointed at the abandoned hole. "Our mission is to protect the Imperial Regalia from the Americans. Now the Americans are coming for certain, therefore our mission is of even more importance."

"Sir, look!"

Sato spun toward where the lookout was pointing, his stomach flipping at the sight.

A ship, steaming rapidly toward their position, several others on the horizon.

"Americans?" asked the corporal.

Sato removed his binoculars and stared.

His chest tightened.

Soviets.

He pointed at the hole. "Hurry!"

Ebiso District, Tokyo, Japan
Present Day. Three days before Acton's arrival in Moscow

"Jiro Sato, is that you? I haven't heard from you since school! How are you?"

Jiro smiled at the sound of his friend Haru's voice, it still dominated by a distinctive nasally tone that he apparently hadn't grown out of like his mother had promised. "I-I'm fine. You?"

"Busy helping my father, you know, the same as always. The life of a fisherman is never one of leisure. But you, I hear you have a job in the big city doing big things."

Jiro grunted. "I see your mother has been talking to mine."

Haru laughed. "They do enjoy their gossip. Now you haven't called me for the first time in seven years to say hello. Something's wrong. Tell your old friend."

Jiro sighed, leaning back in his chair, his eyes coming to rest on his grandfather's sword. "I had a visit today from the government. The Army, actually."

"Really? What about? Did they draft you to fight the Chinese?"

Jiro smiled slightly. "No, they found Grandfather."

There was a pause. "Umm, not alive, I assume?"

Jiro shook his head. "Of course not alive! They found his remains on Harukaru Island."

A burst of static over the earpiece signaled Haru's shocked exhalation. "Did they say how he died?"

"The paperwork they gave me suggests he was shot in the head, they believe in the final days of the war."

"You must be happy then. He died honorably."

Jiro nodded. "Yes, it would appear so. But there's more."

"What?"

"Something I've never told you."

"Really?" He could hear the shock in his childhood friend's voice. "I thought we told each other everything?"

"We did. I didn't find out until I was sixteen, when my father figured I was old enough to know."

"Sixteen? That's just before he died, isn't it?"

Jiro's chest tightened slightly at the memory of his father's final days, a ghost of his former self, cancer having eaten away at him from the inside. "Yes."

"Well, what's this family secret?"

Jiro drew in a long, slow breath, closing his eyes. "My grandfather's mission was to take the Imperial Regalia and protect them, under orders from the Emperor himself."

There was silence for a moment. "That's quite the responsibility. He must have been trusted."

"Yeah, I guess so. But there's more."

"I'm listening."

"His commanding officer visited the family shortly after the war ended and told my grandmother that her husband had not been heard from since leaving for his final destination, and that the Imperial Regalia were still with him. We were to report to him if we ever heard anything about where my grandfather ended up."

"You mean…" Another pause. "You don't mean…"

"I mean, if they just found my grandfather on Harukaru Island then that means he made it there. If he was shot in the head then it means he fell in combat. He would never commit ritual suicide with the Imperial Regalia under his protection."

"You mean…"

"I mean that if he died with them in his possession, and his commanding officer had no clue where he was after the war, then the Imperial Regalia are still missing."

"You mean…"

"I mean that if the Imperial Regalia are missing then the current emperor—"

"Isn't legitimate!"

"Exactly!"

"That's, I mean, wow, I mean"—there was a pause—"I've got nothing."

"It took me a while to wrap my head around it too."

His mind drifted to Keiko for a moment and how they had talked for a few minutes before he ushered her out the door so he could think, she securing a promise from him to meet for coffee later that night.

The thought warmed his tortured heart, if only for a moment.

"Why are you calling me? Shouldn't you be calling the authorities?"

"I told the men who were here."

"What did they say?"

"They said it couldn't be true, or something to that effect."

Another pause. "Umm. Just to think of things from the negative perspective—"

"That's usually my job, but go ahead."

"—you just told the government that the Imperial Regalia that confirm the current emperor's legitimacy to his title have been lost for seventy years, therefore implying that the current emperor is illegitimate."

"Yes."

"Aren't you scared?"

Jiro sucked in a breath, his eyes widening. "I am *now!*"

"And so am I! Oh, Jiro, why did you have to call *me* after all these years to tell me something that could see us both killed? Wait a minute, why *did* you call me?"

"I need your boat."

"Huh?"

"I need your fishing boat."

"Why?" The word was drawn out, as if Haru was afraid to hear the answer.

"Because I want to go to the island and search for the Imperial Regalia."

"Are you nuts! That island is held by the Russians! If they catch you there you just might be joining your grandfather in the afterlife!"

Jiro nodded. "I'm more concerned with my family's honor. I want to retrieve the Imperial Regalia and return them so I can clear my grandfather's good name and erase the shame that has burdened my family for generations. And I need your help to do it."

A loud burst of air followed by a groan from his friend had Jiro wondering just how long a neglected friendship from one's childhood could last. "I'll think about it."

"You better think fast. I'm leaving in the morning, with or without you."

"You could get yourself killed."

Jiro closed his eyes. "I've accomplished nothing in my life. I have a dead-end job where I'm disrespected every moment of every day, and have never kissed a girl. If I die trying to restore my family's honor then so be it. I would die happy."

"But your mother! You know you're the only thing that keeps her going."

Tears welled in Jiro's eyes. His voice cracked. "If I die then she can finally let go and find the peace she deserves."

His friend sniffed. "Come tonight. We'll leave first thing in the morning."

Harukaru Island, Empire of Japan
Russian name: Kharkar Island
August 18, 1945

"Open fire!"

Along the ridgeline loud reports erupted from the Type 38 rifles of Sato's men, puffs of smoke revealing their position quickly swept away by the stiff wind, the cries of several Soviet troops just reaching the shore indicating at least some of their aims were true.

Yet though they had won the first round, they would lose the fight.

There's too many.

Another volley fired, more of the enemy dropped, yet more reached the shore, rushing for cover, gunfire erupting though not yet on their position, the men below clearly unprepared for a fight, this island expected to be abandoned.

He glanced over his shoulder at the men filling in the hole, the Imperial Regalia their only concern, not their lives.

This is a delaying tactic.

He took aim and fired, his target dropping to the ground with a stomach wound that would soon take him.

Something thundered from the water and he turned to see a puff of smoke from a deck gun of one of the Soviet ships indicate the eventual end of their skirmish.

"Incoming!"

He dropped tight to the ground and covered his head just as the round slammed into the hillside not twenty paces from where they lay. And it wouldn't be long before the gunners had a lock on their position, they no doubt already adjusting their massive weaponry.

There was only one way to keep this battle going.

And that was to eliminate the threat of the destroyer's weapons.

"Charge!" He jumped to his feet and rushed forward, over the ridge and toward the Soviet troops below, his men on his heels, the roar of his brave comrades swelling his chest with pride. Theirs was a hopeless cause, but today they would die like men, in service to their country, to their emperor, forever remembered as the men who died protecting the most important of His empire's possessions.

Something hit his stomach, the sound merely a thud, as if something had swatted him.

He dropped, tumbling down the embankment, two of his men turning to help. He pointed at the shore. "Go!"

They did.

He struggled to his feet, one hand pushing off the ground, the other gripping his stomach, when he collapsed again, unable to breathe. He looked at his hand and gasped, it covered in blood.

It doesn't hurt.

He had always imagined getting shot would hurt, yet for some reason he barely felt anything. He tried to move his legs and they refused to cooperate, they like playthings attached to his waist.

I'm paralyzed!

The thought scared him, the very idea of living out his remaining days confined to some chair distinctly unappealing.

He stared at the blood oozing from his stomach.

You don't have days.

He pushed himself up on an elbow to see his men, or what was left of them, reach the shore, hand-to-hand combat ensuing, they performing admirably though ultimately futilely, the last falling within minutes.

There were just too many.

But it was a glorious battle.

Footfalls behind him had him turning to see the detail that had been working on burying the relics rushing to his side. "Major, are you okay?"

"The Imperial Regalia?"

"Buried."

"And the hole?"

"The turf has been replaced. They won't see it unless they're looking for it."

"Good." He reached out a bloody hand, grabbing the young corporal by the wrist. "You know what you must do."

The young man nodded, a look of resignation creasing his face. "I do." He snapped to attention, executed a quick salute with his partner then roared down the hill, automatic weapons fire from the now prepared Soviets mowing them down before they went ten paces.

Sato dropped to the ground, on his back, staring up at the clouds above, contemplating his life. It had been a good one, shorter than he had imagined, though not much so. It *was* war, after all.

Shorter than he had hoped *for.*

That might be more accurate. He fumbled at his buttons, managing to unclasp enough to reach inside and retrieve a photo of his wife he had kept close to his heart since the day he had left for training. He pulled it out and held it in front of his face, her expressionless, formal appearance conveying none of her gentle side, though he could see the hints of it in the corners of her eyes, in the tiny, almost unnoticeable suggestion of a dimple as she had suppressed her smile only moments before the camera snapped.

J. ROBERT KENNEDY

He clasped it to his chest and closed his eyes, picturing her and their four small children, and how they would be forced to fend for themselves now that he was gone. He just prayed they had made it to his parents' place and would be protected from the rampaging Americans.

He wanted to weep for his country, for his family, for his men, but he resisted. The sounds of boots on the hard terrain were fast approaching, and the Soviets would be upon him at any moment.

And there was no way he would give them the satisfaction of seeing his pain.

Instead, he prayed for death, it the surest way to securing the secrets he held.

A Soviet officer leaned over him and kicked him in the hip, shouting something in Russian.

"What are you doing here?" asked another voice, the translator stepping into view.

"What are *you* doing here?" he gasped. "The war is over."

A spat of angry words met his translated response. "These islands now belong to the Union of Soviet Socialist Republics. You weren't supposed to be here."

The officer unholstered his pistol and aimed it at Sato's head.

Sato gripped the photo tighter to his chest, closing his eyes.

Goodbye my love.

The sharp burst ended his life.

And protected his secret.

For seventy years.

Ministry of Foreign Affairs, Tokyo, Japan
Present Day. Three days before Acton's arrival in Moscow

"Sir, I need to speak to you." Arata Sasaki lowered his voice slightly. "In private."

Minister of Foreign Affairs Yamazaki glanced up at him, a hint of surprise on his face quickly wiped away, and probably unnoticed by the others in the room, Sasaki only recognizing it after years of studying the man.

"Are we done here?" asked Yamazaki of the room, rapid acceptance of the polite termination bowed out as the table rose, everyone leaving the room in silence. Yamazaki waited until the last door clicked shut before looking at his underling. "It's unlike you to interrupt a meeting like this. I assume you have a good explanation."

Sasaki bowed deeply. "Forgive me, sir, but I do."

"Sit."

"Thank you, sir." Sasaki sat in the chair pointed to by his boss, it three places down the long conference table, the distance indicating his position in the grand scheme of things.

Peon, even if I'm the Deputy Minister.

"What is it?"

Sasaki lowered his voice. "Sir, we may finally have a lead on where they are."

Yamazaki's eyes narrowed, confusion and frustration written across his face. "Where *what* are? Out with it."

Sasaki lowered his voice further, leaning over one of the chairs separating them. "You know. *Them.*"

39

Yamazaki's frustration grew and he opened his mouth before his eyes suddenly widened. "Oh. *Them.*"

"Yes, *them.* Do you recall the remains that were discovered on Harukaru Island by the Russians recently?"

"Yes, yes of course." Yamazaki's eyebrows popped. "Please tell me the Russians don't have them."

Sasaki rapidly shook his head then stopped, his chest tightening. "I-I don't think they have them. Surely we would have heard something?"

"You tell me! You're the one that's supposed to be briefing me!"

Sasaki bowed in his chair. "Of course, sir, I apologize. At this moment, we have no reason to believe the Russians have them."

"And why do we think they might be on this island?"

"The grandson of one of the deceased soldiers informed the notification party that his grandfather's last mission was to hide the Imperial Regalia, and that his commanding officer had informed the family after the war that the soldiers, and the Imperial Regalia, were missing."

"If they are indeed on Russian territory, they must not be allowed to find them first."

"But if we try to retrieve them, and are caught, it could lead to an international incident. Perhaps even considered an act of war."

"Which is why you must go in undercover. Fishermen perhaps. The people must never know what we are doing, or why. Should word get out, the shame would be unbearable, the embarrassment to His Majesty and the government irreversible."

"Agreed."

Yamazaki looked at him then rose, Sasaki immediately bursting from his chair. "Arata, I want you to handle this personally. There is no room for failure."

"Yes, sir. I won't fail you, sir."

"I know you won't. But it is imperative that this appear to be a civilian matter."

"I studied archaeology for a time, perhaps it would be believable that we are a team that got lost."

"Archaeologists who can't read a map?"

Sasaki smiled. "The GPS failed?"

Yamazaki tossed his head back and laughed. "Make sure you bring one that's made in China."

Kharkar Island, South Kuril Islands, Russian Federation
Japanese name: Harukaru Island
Present Day. Two days before Acton's arrival in Moscow

Jiro Sato glanced around nervously, his eyes glued to the horizon, his mind split between the danger they were in and the fantastic time that had been had last night.

I'm in love.

It had only been one date, and it could barely be called that, though it had lasted almost two hours, it only ended by the fact his train was leaving for Akita and he couldn't miss it.

Keiko was wonderful.

And after years of pining for her, their conversation last night had given him a renewed hope for his future. Yesterday he had been prepared to die, here on this island, to restore his family's honor.

Which was complete garbage.

He had wanted to die here doing something noble, rather than plunge his grandfather's sword through his stomach in a cowardly attempt to end his own miserable existence.

Though with Keiko in his life, that existence would be wonderful.

They were to meet again tomorrow if he made it back—in time, is what he had told her, he not wanting to scare her. He hadn't told her what he was doing, merely that he was visiting an old friend. Though when he returned, triumphant with the lost relics, he fully intended to share his success with her before handing them over to His Majesty.

I wonder how I'll do that.

He hadn't planned that far ahead.

Maybe I just walk up to the gates and knock?

It was an idea. If he showed them what he had, surely they couldn't refuse him entry.

But what then? Did he honestly think he'd get to meet the Emperor? Did he actually *want* to meet the Emperor? His chest tightened. Perhaps it would be best to return them anonymously so they couldn't be traced back to him should they want their secret preserved.

The prow of the boat cut into the shore as Haru cut the engines. "Let's be quick about this, okay?"

Jiro shook out a nod and jumped to the ground, reaching up to take the gear Haru handed down. He lugged it up the small rise topped by a communications tower of some sort, a fresh Russian flag snapping overhead.

Bastards.

He hated the Russians. He had never actually met one, but the fact they occupied Japanese territory illegally, infuriated him, not to mention their recent habit of invading their neighbors.

Exactly what he'd expect from Russians.

"Look!" Haru pointed to some overturned terrain on the north side of the hill. "That must be where they found your grandfather."

Jiro nodded, picking his way across the uneven ground and pausing before the hastily filled in hole, it far larger than needed for one body. "A mass grave?"

Haru frowned, stepping carefully around it. "They killed them then buried them so no one would discover their treachery, then seventy years later forgot they were keeping the secret."

Jiro's lip curled slightly. "They'll pay for what they did."

Haru stared at him for a moment but said nothing. He lifted one of the metal detectors they had brought. "Should we start here?"

Jiro scanned the area. "No." He pointed toward the shore. "That's north. That's where the Russians would have come from, so that's where my grandfather would have fought them. He'd try to keep the battle as far from the Imperial Regalia as he could so they wouldn't find them."

"That still leaves half an island."

"Yes, but they also wouldn't bury it too close to the shore because the waves might erode the soil away and expose them."

"So the south side of this hill?"

Jiro shrugged. "It's where I would have put them."

Haru stepped around the communications tower and flicked the switch on the metal detector, beginning a slow sweep of the ground, Jiro activating his own.

"Got something!"

Jiro placed his metal detector down, marking his spot, and joined Haru who was furiously digging with a spade.

He hit something, metal.

Haru glanced up at him, grinning. "I think someone may want us to succeed brilliantly today."

Jiro dropped to his knees and they both carefully removed more dirt, a hint of metal appearing, then disappointment. Haru jammed his spade in and pushed it down by the handle, popping a Russian soda can from the ground. He picked it up and whipped it at the communications tower, it ricocheting off the steel lattice.

Jiro patted him on the shoulder. "Let's keep going, we don't want to waste any more time here than we need to." Haru nodded and rose, resuming his search as Jiro returned to his own detector, but before he could reach it Haru cried out again.

"Got something! Big!"

Jiro returned to join Haru in his frantic dig, this time it taking several feet of dirt before they hit something. Something hollow. Haru looked at him. "Wood?"

Jiro shrugged, clearing away more dirt, the hole finally big enough that every movement didn't rebury whatever they had found. "Definitely wood." More frantic clearing with the spades and it was obvious it was something manmade. "I think it's a chest." They quickly found the edges, trimmed with metal corners and hinges, there now little doubt this was what they were searching for.

Though when he brushed away the dirt, all doubt was removed.

"Is that—"

Jiro smiled. "An imperial seal? Yes."

Haru fell onto his backside. "What do we do?"

"Open it."

"Are you crazy?"

"We have to be sure."

A motor revved behind them and they both spun, Jiro's heart leaping into his throat at the sight of a boat, a rush of adrenaline surging through his already on-edge body.

"Russians!" hissed Haru. "We're dead!"

Jiro joined in his friend's assessment for a moment then noticed the markings. "No, they're ours."

Several men jumped ashore, rushing toward them, the man clearly in charge pointing a finger at them the entire climb. "Who are you and what are you doing here?"

Haru scrambled backward in fear but Jiro responded with anger of his own. He was moments away from restoring his family's honor, and now, these men, clearly government, were ruining everything. "Who are *you?*"

The lead man produced identification showing he was Arata Sasaki from the Ministry of Foreign Affairs. "I'll ask again, what are you doing here?"

Jiro pointed at the exposed chest. "The same thing you're doing here, I would guess."

Sasaki's eyes went wide and his jaw dropped before he fell to his knees, reaching inside and opening the chest. The adrenaline and anger of the moment was lost as everyone knelt around the hole, gasping as the hinged top revealed its secrets after all these years.

"May I?" asked Jiro, looking at Sasaki. "It was my grandfather who put this here."

Sasaki smiled slightly. "It is fitting then that one of his descendants should be responsible for returning it to our people."

Jiro exhaled, thankful the expected argument had never occurred. He reached inside and lifted the first of what appeared to be three carefully wrapped objects. If he knew his history, its size suggested it would be the Kusanagi-no-Tsurugi sword. He placed it on the ground and gently opened the cloth, revealing an ornate black case.

He opened it.

And they gasped.

It was indeed the sword.

"We've found them!" hissed Sasaki.

Jiro stared at him. "Then you knew?"

Sasaki nodded. "A few of us did. I just never dreamed I'd be the one to find them."

Haru cleared his throat. "Umm, *we* found them, not you."

Sasaki bowed slightly. "Of course, I just meant I didn't think I'd be *part* of finding them."

"That's better."

The whoop of a navy ship split through the silence and the totally engrossed men all jumped at the sound. Jiro nearly peed when he saw the Russian cruiser rapidly approaching, two zodiac style boats already in the water, filled with troops.

"What do we do?" asked Jiro, staring at Sasaki.

"We get these out of here now!" he cried, reaching into the chest and retrieving the other two relics. Jiro quickly wrapped the sword and they all sprinted for the boats when gunfire suddenly erupted over their heads, bringing them all to a hasty stop.

"They can't know why we're really here," said Sasaki. "We're archaeologists, here by mistake. We made a discovery that clearly belongs to our country and we intend to return with it and hand it over to the Tokyo National Museum."

"And us?" asked Jiro.

"You are fishermen who came to see what we were doing."

"I like that story," said Haru. "It keeps us out of this."

The troops stormed ashore, quickly surrounding them, the commander stepping forward, saying something in Russian.

Nobody responded.

He then spoke English, Japanese apparently not in his repertoire. "Do you speak English?"

Jiro stayed quiet, despite speaking English quite well. Sasaki responded. "I do, a little." Jiro had a feeling the man spoke perfect English.

"What are you doing here?"

"We're archaeologists."

"What are those?" The man motioned toward the tightly gripped relics.

No one said anything.

The man reached forward and took the wrapped case from Jiro, quickly removing the cloth and tossing it aside. He opened the case, his eyes

47

widening slightly. "Interesting. Looks valuable." He snapped the case shut, using it as a pointer as he singled each of them out. "You're thieves, stealing from the Russian people."

Sasaki stepped forward, still gripping the other two relics against his chest. "No, these clearly belong to the Japanese people. All we ask is that we are allowed to leave here with them, and we will never return."

The commander motioned at Sasaki with a flick of his wrist and two of his soldiers stepped forward, yanking the remaining relics from Sasaki's arms. "They are on Russian soil, therefore they belong to Russia."

Sasaki stepped forward. "No! They—"

Weapons were suddenly aimed at them all, the negotiations over.

Jiro's head dropped and his shoulders sagged.

His family's honor still not restored.

I really *hate Russians.*

South Kuril Islands, Russian Federation
Japanese name: Chishima Islands
Present Day. Two days before Acton's arrival in Moscow

Jiro anxiously watched the Russian boat shadowing them, risking only a glimpse from the corner of his eye, terrified if he paid them too much attention they might change their minds. Behind them the fishing boat belonging to Haru bobbed happily along, the towline taut between the larger research vessel the government officials had arrived on, and the small but proud commercial relic that had been in Haru's family for three generations.

The Russians had confiscated the Imperial Regalia, though it was clear they had no clue what they had. The government official, Sasaki, had begged them to be careful with the objects, using the word 'priceless' to give the Russians pause.

It only made the greed in their eyes more obvious.

And the doubt within grew as to whether or not the Imperial Regalia would ever be seen again, he getting the distinct impression the Russian commander intended to profit by them, perhaps on the black market.

And once they hit that, the truth will come out.

And his family's shame would be rekindled in the minds of their neighbors and friends.

And a government, and a dynasty, could fall.

And it would. The fact that Sasaki had arrived proved they knew the relics were missing. Sasaki had expressed no surprise at what was inside the chest, expressed no doubts as to whether they might be genuine. The government had been searching for them, and it wasn't until his grandfather

49

had been found that they realized where they might find them, just as he had.

But they found Grandfather weeks ago.

He walked over to Sasaki. "How long did you know?"

Sasaki looked at him, gripping the rail that ran the length of the deck. "Excuse me?"

"How long did you know they were there?"

"Frankly, Mr. Sato, we had no idea where they were until you mentioned it to the notification detail yesterday. Up to that point, we had lost all hope they'd ever be found."

"Why did you lie?"

Sasaki regarded him, it clear a debate was raging inside. Openness won. "There's no point in lying to *you*, since you're one of only a handful that know the truth. From what I understand, it was a very confusing, chaotic, shameful period. Our nation had surrendered, our crimes laid bare and our emperor forced to admit unfathomable truths. For him to admit he was a mere mortal, and then to reveal he did not possess the Imperial Regalia, it would have shaken the country to its core. We needed stability, and His Majesty provided that."

"Yes, but surely by the time the new emperor was sworn in, the truth could be told."

Sasaki shook his head. "No, by then the lie had been underway for over forty years. To admit to it then would have brought the government down, the families involved too powerful. The hope was that the current emperor would live a very long life, and by then, those who were involved would be long dead, and perhaps, with good fortune, the Regalia would have been found. At a minimum, those alive who knew, and participated in the lie, would be gone."

"Leaving their shame for future generations."

Sasaki massaged his wrist. "Your family carries the shame, doesn't it?"

Jiro nodded. "A shame only a few of us know the true extent of. When this goes public, I hope my grandfather's good name will be restored."

Sasaki shook his head. "This can never go public."

Jiro felt his heart slam hard, just a single palpitation, then a bulge rush up his throat. "This *must* go public. My family now knows the truth. My grandfather fulfilled his duty *and* was killed by the Russians. He successfully hid the Regalia as he was ordered to, protecting it from the invaders. They didn't find it until today, when *we* failed, *not* him. There was no dishonor in his mission. He died fighting, the Regalia were left safe. Seventy years of derision *must* stop. Now!"

Haru looked over at him, shocked at the outburst. Jiro ignored his friend, instead focusing his rage on the man in front of him.

"I understand, but *you* must understand that there are bigger things at play here."

"What could be more important than the truth, especially now?"

"Honor. Integrity. Tradition."

"There was no dishonor in protecting our Imperial Regalia. There was no lack of integrity in the way my grandfather fought to protect them. And he upheld the greatest of traditions by dying to protect that which His Majesty had ordered him to. The truth will only uphold those three tenets you hold so dear. What won't uphold them is the Russians selling them on the black market, and your secret getting out."

Sasaki's face froze for a moment then a look of horror flashed in his eyes. He glanced back at the Russian cruiser shadowing them. "You don't think…"

"Don't *you*?"

Sasaki swung around. "Are we in international waters yet?"

51

"Yes, sir, five minutes ago," replied a young man. He pointed ahead. "And look!"

They all turned to see two large military vessels steaming toward them.

A lump formed in Jiro's chest. "Are those ours?"

"Yes they are." Sasaki rushed toward the bridge, Jiro following. "Hail the lead vessel, and make sure the Russians can hear us."

"What?"

"You heard me!"

"Yes, sir!"

The radioman complied, and moments later handed the mike to Sasaki. "Japanese naval vessel. Be advised that we are in international waters and have been peacefully conducted from Russian claimed waters. They are in possession of property belonging to the Japanese people, confiscated at the time of our arrest. Please notify the Foreign Minister to arrange recovery of the confiscated items. Out." He handed the mike back and turned toward Jiro.

"What does that accomplish?"

"We have now made it public that the Russians have property of ours. That will force the captain of their vessel to return what was taken to Moscow, or at the very least, notify Moscow that they have something of ours. That prevents it from being sold on the black market."

"But it still leaves them in the wrong hands."

"Yes, but governments are more likely to be reasonable than rogue naval captains."

"And if the Russians refuse?"

"Then I fear the peace we have enjoyed for seventy years will be broken."

Jiro's eyes widened slightly. "Do you really think it could come to that?"

Sasaki looked back at the Russian vessel as it bore hard to port. "Don't you? The Russians now possess our country's most important relics, integral to our culture, our history, our traditions and our very way of life. Honor demands we do whatever it takes to get them back."

"But war?"

"Countries have fought for less, and I can't think of any reason more important than one's very identity." He looked at Jiro. "I fear, young man, that we could be at war before the week is out."

Ministry of Culture, Gnezdnikovsky Lane, Moscow, Russian Federation
Present Day. The day Acton arrives in Moscow

Arseny Orlov glanced up from his computer as an old colleague, Igor Krupin, entered the room, dropping a rather large box on his desk. "What's this?"

"That's what the Kremlin wants to know."

Orlov's eyebrows rose as he stood, examining the box, an emblem of the Russian Navy emblazoned on each side. He flipped open the four sides of the lid, finding three items inside of varying sizes, all wrapped in towels. He picked up one and carried it over to a light table in the corner of his cluttered office, the life of a curator at the Ministry of Culture a solitary, unglamorous one, art and culture not belonging to Russia not a very high priority in his country.

He carefully unwrapped the item and gasped.

"Where did you find this?" He barely heard the answer as he carefully examined the ornate piece, a jade sculpted jewel in a shape best described as a comma. He stared at Krupin. "Sorry, could you repeat that?"

Krupin shook his head, smiling. "You academics. I *said*, it was confiscated from some Japanese nationals on one of the Kuril Islands. The Japs are raising quite the stink about it, so the Kremlin wants to know what we've got."

"Why? Why not just return them?" Orlov retrieved the second item from the box and brought it under the light, carefully unwrapping what turned out to be a bronze mirror.

"Well, it's odd, that."

Orlov looked up from the mirror, staring at Krupin. "What do you mean?"

"Well, the Japanese haven't actually asked for them."

"I thought you said they're raising a stink?"

"They are, but not about these items specifically."

Orlov leaned back, jamming a palm into his spine, his decision to start a workout routine this morning now regretted. "You're talking in circles, man."

Krupin shrugged. "I'm just a messenger here, but what I *do* know is that the Japanese have decided to enforce their territorial claims over the islands, and are demanding the return of any and all things taken from the islands."

"Odd."

"Exactly, which is why the Kremlin wants to know what's so important about these things that they'd be willing to risk war over them."

"War? Do they really think it will come to that? What's the president said?"

"So far, not much, except that trespassers were arrested, items stolen from Russian soil seized, and then the trespassers were released and escorted out of Russian territorial waters as a goodwill gesture in the hopes of fostering peaceful relations between our two great nations."

Orlov grunted. "So he bullshit them."

"What else did you expect?"

"Not much nowadays." Orlov held up a hand. "You didn't hear that."

Krupin grinned. "Hear what?" He nodded toward the table with the relics. "So, what are they?"

Orlov shrugged. "No idea, Japanese antiquities aren't really my area, but I'll find out. Is it okay if I bring in some outside help?"

Krupin made a face. "I wasn't told you *couldn't*, so…"

Orlov smiled. "So what Moscow doesn't know can't hurt them."

Krupin smiled for a moment then frowned. "Umm, I didn't hear that. What Igor doesn't know can't hurt him either." He pointed at the relics. "The Japanese know we have them, so I guess it's not that much of a secret." He sighed. "It's scary how everything old is new again in Mother Russia."

Orlov agreed, Krupin speaking the truth. As each day passed he felt less and less free, the stories his father and grandfather told of the past, days he could barely remember, could barely believe, now reflected in the sights he saw every day.

Russia was going to hell, a barking mad egomaniac at the tiller.

With his shirt off.

He lifted the mirror. "I'll let you know as soon as I find out something."

"Good."

Krupin left the room, but Orlov already knew the answer.

He just couldn't believe it could possibly be correct.

Though he did know someone who would.

Belmond Reid's Palace Resort, Island of Madeira, Portugal

"Man, this is the life."

Archaeology Professor James Acton sighed as a gentle, warm breeze swept over them, the rhythmic soothing sound of the Atlantic Ocean washing up on the coast of this island paradise a welcome white noise drowning out the sounds of families and singles at play on the sands and in the shallow waters.

He reached up and slightly twisted the umbrella jammed in the sand, blocking the sun from burning the bundle of English flesh lying beside him. To say his wife, Archaeology Professor Laura Palmer, burned easily, would be an understatement, yet she always seemed to manage somehow, whether it was here on the beach on spring break, or at a dig site in the middle of some unforgiving desert.

Sunblock.

Lots of it.

He, on the other hand, always seemed to easily manage a nice golden brown. Skin cancer might claim him one day, though when he thought back to his youth, lying on beaches with his parents lathering bronzing oil onto him, he figured the damage had already been done, and done young.

"Thanks, hon."

"No problem. Don't want you getting all sore for tonight. Got plans for you." He grinned at her.

She responded with a lazy, content look. "I'll just lie there if you don't mind. Just tell me when you're done."

He feigned a hurt expression. "Is that anyway to talk around our friends? They're liable to think we've already turned into a boring, married couple."

"Hey, when I was laid up in a wheel chair for a couple of years, all I did was lay there. Sandra had to do all the work."

"Gregory!"

Acton grinned at Laura then rolled his head to the other side, looking at his best friend, Gregory Milton and his wife Sandra. "But now you're an animal in the sack?"

"A beast."

"Unstoppable."

"Like a juggernaut."

"Wham, bam, thanks for the slam."

"Who's your daddy?"

"Smack the junk, tickle the—"

"James!"

Acton cringed at Laura's admonishment. "I think we went too far."

Milton shook his head. "*I* didn't, but *you* definitely did."

"Who's your daddy?"

It was Milton's turn to cringe as he looked at his wife giving him a none-too-pleased look. "Umm, new topic? I was thinking after the sun goes down a bit we would take a drive over to the ruins, walk around for a while. I realize it's not Greek ruins, but it should still be interesting."

Laura rolled into a seated position, facing them. "That sounds nice. I can only lie around for so long without going barmy."

Milton agreed. "It's really too bad we had to cancel Greece. I was so looking forward to that. It's on my bucket list, and now that Niskha's old enough to leave with her grandmother for a week, we were finally hoping to actually see some of the world."

Acton frowned. "Unfortunately a lot of your European bucket list will have to wait, perhaps forever."

"The refugees," muttered Milton, his head bobbing. "I wanted to do Bavaria one day, but Germany's essentially lost. I'm just glad I saw Paris before it was ruined."

"Yeah. But let's not call them refugees. The vast majority of them are just migrants. Hopefully Europe smartens up and realizes what's happening before it's too late."

"I think it already is," said Milton. "My parents go to Europe every year for a few weeks. They've been doing it since they retired, but now they've cancelled their plans for the first time in over a decade. It's just not safe anymore."

"Especially if you're a woman," said Laura, sticking her lips out as she searched for the end of a straw leading to a ridiculously feminine looking drink.

Acton grabbed his own identical one, draining it. "I would never let Laura go to Europe alone."

"*Let?*"

He cringed. "Poor choice of words. You know what I mean."

She winked at him. "I know. And you're right, I wouldn't want to go. With rapes and sexual assaults going through the roof throughout Europe, you'd be insane to travel alone as a woman. My heart breaks for those poor women who were born and raised in countries that were traditionally safe and now are so dangerous. I mean, what happened in Cologne was insane!"

"What was it, over a thousand women assaulted?"

"Something like that." Acton held up his drink and a cabana boy waved at him, rushing off to get another. "I watched a few videos of it and it was disturbing. RT News had a video showing this poor woman being groped and manhandled by dozens of men as she left the subway." His eyes dropped. "The sheer terror on her face was enough to make me want to go in there with an MP5 and thin the crowds a little." He shook his head. "If Europe isn't careful, that's exactly what's going to happen."

Milton rubbed some sunscreen on his wife's back. "You really think it could turn to civil war?"

Acton looked at his friend. "Think about it. If you lived peacefully in your hometown for your entire life, then suddenly thousands of people showed up with nothing in common with you, insisting you pay for their food and shelter and medical benefits, then some of them paid you back by robbing your stores, mugging you and raping and sexually harassing your wife and daughter, then laughed it up while your government did nothing to protect you, even denied that the very things you had seen with your own eyes had happened, don't you think you'd be tempted to take matters into your own hands?" He glanced at Laura. "I know if someone touched Laura I'd hunt them down and cut their heart out."

"Thank you, dear."

"Think nothing of it." He winked then turned back to Milton. "Then I'd have to decide whether to continue with the government truly responsible for letting it happen."

"Well, the far rightwing parties are certainly polling a lot higher since the migrants arrived."

"And that's the truly scary thing. When the people start to fight back, to enforce a way of life that their government won't, what happens then? Think about it. If you fight back, and the government orders the police or the military to intervene, and just *one* unit refuses those orders, instead standing down, what then? And what if those units instead decide to support their own people, rather than the migrants?" Acton shrugged. "A year ago I would have said the very idea of a European civil war was insane. Today? I'm not so sure."

Sandra looked at Laura. "Laura, honey, I think you might have chosen the right time to move to the US."

Laura nodded, sipping her drink then setting it aside. "As much as I'd like to say my husband is being paranoid, I just can't. I've been talking to a lot of friends back home in the UK and though it's not as bad as in France and Germany, they're terrified."

Acton's phone vibrated and he fished it out, his eyes narrowing at the number. "What country code is seven?"

Laura snatched the piña colada from the cabana boy then motioned toward her husband. "He'll be needing a new one as well." The boy grinned and hurried off, Laura raising her glass to toast her husband's good timing. "Russia, if I'm not mistaken."

"Huh." Acton swiped his thumb. "Hello?"

"Hello, Professor Acton, this is Arseny Orlov from the Russian Ministry of Culture. Do you remember me?"

"Arseny, of course I remember you. We met at the Antiquities Preservation Conference in Munich. What can I do for you?"

"Have you been paying attention to the news?"

Acton chuckled. "I'm on a beach in Portugal, trying to avoid the news, why?"

"Well, I suggest you check the news then call me back."

Acton's eyes narrowed. "Why not just tell me?"

There was a pause. "Professor Acton, Jim, please, just watch the news then call me back. You must understand the gravity of the situation before I ask the favor I must of you."

The call ended and Acton launched the browser on his phone.

"Who was that?" asked Laura.

"Dr. Arseny Orlov, Russian Ministry of Culture."

"What did he want?"

"He wants me to check the news then call him back."

Milton sat up, grabbing his iPad. "That sounds ominous."

Laura set aside her drink. "Did he say what it was about?"

Acton shook his head. "He said I had to 'understand the gravity of the situation' before he could ask me for a favor." The CNN headlines appeared on his phone. "Holy shit!"

"What is it?" asked Laura, crawling over so she could see.

Milton shoved his larger tablet toward them, the headline big enough for them all to see.

Japan and Russia on Brink of War?

South Kuril Islands, Russian Federation
Japanese name: Chishima Islands

"Sir, the Russian ship is not responding to our hails."

Captain Akira Yamada kept his expression emotionless, though inside he could feel the tension building. He was Japanese, the past seventy years dominated by a pacifist tradition adopted after the war. Only recently had they begun to participate in peacekeeping missions and other humanitarian activities outside their borders.

Never had they been in a possible shooting war.

Not since the great disgrace.

But his mission was clear.

Blockade the Chishima Islands, preventing any Russian ships from passing. It appeared that his government had chosen today to be the day they reestablished their sovereignty over the lands stolen from his people at the end of the war.

It's about time.

"Sir, the Russian ship is not breaking off!"

"Hold your position!" he snapped, detecting the panic in the man's voice. The Russian captain had decided to run the blockade, aiming his ship directly at his, it a game of chicken.

An idiotic game of chicken.

His ship was holding position with no way to avoid the collision. Chicken only worked if both parties were racing toward each other, the coward breaking off at the last minute to avoid the crash.

His was 8000 tons of ship, sitting dead in the water.

The Russian would have to break off.

There was no courage here. No honor. No age-old tradition of a joust.

This was arrogance, the Russian assuming, and asserting, his perceived superiority.

"Arm all weapons, prepare to fire." His order was calm, yet curt. He had no intention of firing, but his crew needed something to concentrate on, though he knew his crew was disciplined enough not to fire without orders.

The shame of a mistake was too great.

"Hail the Russian ship. Inform them that they will be fired upon if they do not break their approach."

"Yes, sir!"

"She's breaking to port, sir!"

"Reverse engines, hard to starboard!"

"Yes, sir!"

He felt the mighty beast under him struggle to move back, its massive bulk turning slightly to starboard, the prow of his ship swinging slowly away from the oncoming rush of Russian idiocy as it broke in the opposite direction.

Yet it was too late.

The Russian had misjudged his maneuverability.

"Brace for impact!"

An alarm sounded and he gripped the arms of his chair, his bridge crew grabbing handholds as the Russian frigate broadsided them, scraping along the front quarter with a screaming squelch of metal, sparks spraying across both decks, the ship letting out a moan of protest before it was all over. He leapt from his chair, rushing onto the weather deck with his binoculars, surveying the damage to the Russian vessel.

Paint. Scraped paint. Which meant his vessel was probably similarly damaged. He shifted his binoculars up and spotted his counterpart doing the same. The Russian lowered his binoculars, giving Yamada a clear view of his face.

Arrogance.

"Damage report!" he shouted over his shoulder before looking back at the Russian vessel as it continued to run along the line of Japanese vessels before turning away.

If someone doesn't smarten up, this is going to turn into a shooting war, fast.

Approaching Sheremetyevo International Airport, Moscow, Russian Federation

"Why do I get the nasty feeling coming here was a mistake?"

James Acton stared out the window of their private jet. They had left the Miltons in Portugal, fully expecting to fly in and out the same day, especially since their hastily arranged visas expired at midnight.

So the vacation could continue tomorrow.

In theory.

Though it never worked out that way.

Apparently, a Russian ship had just rammed a Japanese ship. More vessels from both navies were steaming into the area, and the US Seventh Fleet was also responding.

And so were the Chinese.

Leave it to them to take advantage of an opportunity.

At this point, the navies of Russia, Japan, China, the Philippines, the United States and Vietnam were on full alert, the incident originating north of Japan turning into a regional dispute over conflicting claims of islands and waters throughout the South China Sea and the East China Sea.

It was getting out of control.

He had been to Moscow before, and what he was seeing outside their plane was a level of security he had never experienced before. He couldn't possibly imagine the Russians actually concerned about a Japanese attack on Moscow, it clearly an intimidation tactic for arriving visitors and dignitaries, yet it was unsettling nonetheless.

"Are we sure we want to do this?" asked Laura, sitting across from him.

He looked at her, his lips pursed. "No. But we're here, we have the proper documentation, and Arseny did sound desperate. If he's right and he does have the Imperial Regalia, then confirming that might be enough to end this entire situation."

"I don't understand why the Japanese simply don't ask for them back. This entire pretense of asserting their historical sovereignty seems dangerous."

"Honor."

"Honor?"

"It's all about honor. It's incredibly important in their culture, I think so much so, that it's hard for people from our culture to understand."

"Sounds like a bunch of Klingons."

Acton grinned. "Honey, your first Star Trek reference!" He clasped his hands to his heart. "I think I love you more at this moment than I ever have."

She rose, the plane having come to a stop. "Don't make me regret watching twelve damned movies in two months."

"Babe, those were just to draw you in. When the new series starts, you'll want to have The Original Series, The Next Generation, Deep Space Nine, Voyager and Enterprise all under your belt. I'll spare you the animated series—"

"Bloody hell."

"—but if you insist, we can throw it in there."

Laura looked at the flight attendant. "Have my divorce attorney draw up papers for when we get back. Tell him my husband is an über dork."

The flight attendant stifled a laugh. "Yes, ma'am."

Acton winked at her. "Don't listen to her. She loves my dorkiness."

"Of course, sir."

They descended the stairs and with no luggage or personal belongings to deal with, were swiftly processed through customs, their visas indicating they were here as guests of the government expediting things. As they stepped through the doors, a young man stood near the exit holding a sign.

James Action.

"It couldn't possibly be for us."

Laura grinned at her husband. "You *are* a man of action."

"This is true, I am that. Should we risk it?"

"I think we must."

They walked over to the young man. "I'm Professor Acton."

"Oh, thank God you're here. We must hurry, things are getting worse by the moment."

The young man rushed out the doors, saying nothing more, not bothering to look behind him to confirm his clients were following.

Acton turned to Laura. "I guess we better follow him. I'm not sure he'll notice we're not in the car."

Laura giggled and they took off after him, the young man waiting beside a non-descript blue sedan, holding the rear door open. Laura climbed in first followed by Acton, the door slamming shut, the young man racing around to the driver's side and jumping in.

The engine roared to life.

And they were shoved into the back of their seats as he launched them into traffic.

"What's the hurry?" asked Acton in a veiled attempt at self-preservation as they both struggled to put their seatbelts on.

"The news. It's bad."

"What's happened?" asked Laura.

"Tass is reporting that a Japanese warship intentionally rammed one of our ships. Several of our soldiers were killed. The Kremlin has ordered the Eastern Military District on full alert and more ships are heading into the area. I fear my country might retaliate."

"I doubt that," said Acton. "The version of the news you're hearing is quite different from reality."

The young man peered in the rearview mirror. "Perhaps it is *your* news that is inaccurate."

Acton shrugged, it true he didn't necessarily trust his own news sources these days, though he'd trust them any day over Russia's. "You might be right."

"Why doesn't Russia just return the relics?" asked Laura.

"That's just it. According to my father, they haven't asked for them."

Acton leaned forward. "Wait, your father is Arseny?"

"Yes."

"Okay, sorry. I thought you were a government driver."

The man shook his head. "No, sorry, I should have introduced myself. I'm Vitaly." He shoved a hand between the seats. Acton hastily shook it, Laura doing the same, the hand returned to the wheel before an accident occurred.

"You said they hadn't asked for them," prompted Acton.

"No. My father thinks that if they admit what they're after then they have to admit they've been lying to their people for over seventy years. I guess they don't want to do that."

"Understandable," agreed Acton, it matching his own theory when he had heard what the boy's father had in his possession.

"They're insisting that the islands belong to them and that they want them back, along with anything removed from them."

"The Imperial Regalia."

Vitaly peered in his mirror at Laura. "Yes, this is at least what my father thinks."

"So it's all a smokescreen. The Japanese are rattling their sabers to get the regalia back, all so they don't have to admit they lost them in the first place." Acton shook his head. "Honor!"

Vitaly took a hard right. "Are these things really worth going to war over?"

Acton shrugged. "These aren't just relics. These are essentially holy relics to the Japanese, handed down for millennia, given to them by the gods, their possession confirming the divinity of their leaders for thousands of years. Are you Christian?"

Vitaly nodded.

"Imagine Russia was a deeply Christian country and possessed the bones of Jesus. Then imagine Japan stole them. Wouldn't you go to war to get them back?"

"Yes, I guess, though I must admit I'm not *that* religious." Vitaly shook his head. "But Japan against us? They can't possibly think they'll win!"

South Kuril Islands, Russian Federation
Japanese name: Chishima Islands

"Sir, Tokyo can't possibly think we'll win!"

Captain Yamada looked at his Executive Officer, Haruto Nakano, and motioned for him to sit in his cramped sea cabin. "Don't let the men hear you say that."

"Of course not, sir, I would never think of doing something so dishonorable."

"I know, I know." Yamada glanced at the orders from the Chief of the Maritime Staff then pushed them aside with a flick of a finger. "This explanation ignores history."

Nakano's eyes narrowed. "Sir?"

"The line from our government is that since these soldiers were killed after the surrender, it proves the Soviets occupied the islands illegally as they were in our possession at the end of the hostilities, and were not foreign territory to be taken back. They've decided to press this now of all times."

"But I thought pretty much everybody already knew the occupation was illegal? The Soviets declared war the day after we surrendered and illegally occupied all the islands, even challenging American overflights." Nakano shook his head. "This makes no sense! We're blockading the Russians because some soldiers were found on an island the world already accepts we own, claiming that it is proof that we own it?" Nakano pointed out the porthole. "And have you seen that thing? It's barely a kilometer across!"

"The size of the island is irrelevant, and the reason for this provocation has nothing to do with territorial rights."

"But the orders—"

"Are a story to tell the press and the public to keep them busy, while the real machinations occur behind the scenes."

"Forgive me, sir, but may I know what those are?"

Yamada regarded his Executive Officer. He was a good man. An honorable man. They had served together for years, and should the man fulfill his duties during this crisis, he was going to recommend he be given a ship of his own.

So he had to assume he could trust him.

"There's something few know about, that I didn't know about until just a few moments ago when I called my father to find out the truth." He flicked a wrist at the printout of their orders. "These were clearly ridiculous. Since when have our orders included a political explanation? Especially one so weak?"

Nakano remained wisely silent, listening instead to his commanding officer.

Definitely command material.

Keep your mouth shut when a senior officer decides to loosen his tongue, and you may get more information than if you interrupted him.

Yamada sighed, looking at Nakano. "The Russians have the Imperial Regalia."

Nakano gasped. "How? Did they steal them?"

Yamada shook his head. "No, they were found on Harukaru Island and confiscated by the Russians."

"What were they doing there?"

"They were hidden there near the end of the war and lost."

Nakano's head jerked back. "But that doesn't make sense. I remember watching the enthronement of His Majesty when I was a boy. The Imperial Regalia were presented as per tradition."

"Fakes."

Nakano's head tipped forward, bouncing slightly as his eyes opened wide. "Fakes?"

"Yes."

"But—" Nakano appeared at a loss for words. Yamada didn't blame him. He had been too, when his father had told him the truth. Few knew it, his father part of an inner circle in the bureaucracy that didn't change from one government to the next, he having served the people for over forty years.

He had been certain his father would know the truth.

He had just never expected the truth to be what it was.

Nakano finally gathered his thoughts. "The Russians have the Imperial Regalia, which was lost after the war, this fact hidden from the people since."

"Yes."

"Which means His Majesty was sworn in…" His eyebrows jumped, his eyes wide. "You don't mean?"

Yamada nodded. "You can see why this is a delicate matter."

Nakano eyes remained wide. "Yes!" He paused. "Do the Russians know what they have?"

Yamada shook his head. "We don't know. They must, but perhaps they don't believe it either."

"Surely they wouldn't keep them, would they?"

"Who knows with Russians? They are not honorable or principled like us. But one thing is certain, the people *cannot* know the truth."

"Why not? If they did, surely they would support the government's efforts to retrieve the Regalia."

"I have no doubt they would, then after we did retrieve them, they would promptly demand the resignation of the government, and the arrest of those involved in the conspiracy. It could topple not only the government, but the Imperial House itself."

"Then what do we do?"

Yamada rose, Nakano immediately leaping to his feet.

"We follow our orders, and hope that someone in Russia with honor and principles does the right thing."

Courtyard Moscow Paveletskaya Hotel, Moscow, Russian Federation

Arseny Orlov checked his watch. "Where are they?"

He continued pacing in front of the large windows, eyeing the road below, the news belching out of a flat screen television mounted to the wall.

News that wasn't good.

He looked at the table and the three relics so important to the Japanese they were willing to go to war with the massive military might of the Russian Federation.

They can't possibly think they'll win.

Yet they just might win in the court of international public opinion. Though the Russian press wouldn't report on it, the news was out there if one was willing to look, and the news wasn't favorable to the Russian position. A forgotten piece of history was being taught to the people of the world once again, and people were mad. The islands had been seized after the Japanese surrendered, and in violation of the Potsdam Declaration, the Russians didn't leave. Instead, within a year, his country had deported all 17,000 Japanese inhabitants then began to settle it with their own people. Even the American government had demanded Soviet withdrawal, a demand that went ignored, American planes sent in the immediate aftermath of the invasion to observe what was happening, intercepted and turned back by their Soviet "allies".

The Cold War had already begun, only days after World War II had ended.

And now that the world was being informed of the forgotten truth, talking heads and individual elected members of governments around the world were demanding the return of the islands.

These demands were also emboldening others, Vietnam and the Philippines sending their own navies into the South China Sea to assert their sovereignty over disputed islands ridiculously claimed by the Chinese.

It was a powder keg searching for a match, a match almost found earlier when two ships had collided. He didn't believe for a second it was the Japanese that had rammed his country's ship. That was a move of arrogance, of brashness, traits he didn't expect to see from modern Japanese.

And exactly what he'd expect from his people, of any era.

His phone rang and he checked the call display.

He ignored it.

It had been ringing with greater frequency for hours now, Krupin now aware that the relics he had delivered were no longer on government property.

His phone vibrated with a text.

Sorry friend warrant issued for your arrest.

Orlov sighed, his heartrate ratcheting up a few more notches as he stared out the window. He pulled at his shirt, it soaked with sweat, the cheap material matted against his chest and back. He stared in the mirror, the beet red visage that greeted him, startling, the fear in that unknown man's eyes bringing home just how terrified he was.

Why did you take them?

He sat on the edge of the bed, grabbing a pillow and using it to wipe his face dry, tossing the stained result aside. Why *did* he take them? He had to. He knew immediately what they were when Krupin had delivered them, and it would have been a simple matter to confirm them as genuine, though as the hours passed and he waited for the arrival of someone he could trust to verify what he already knew, the official news grew more dire, and the unofficial news even more so.

It was when Krupin had called for an update that he knew he had to act.

"Have you confirmed what they are yet?"

"I'm still working on it. Why the rush?"

"The Kremlin is anxious. I think they want to use them as leverage to settle some land disputes. Blackmail the Japanese into some concessions, I guess."

It hadn't surprised him at all. It was typical of the new Russia as shown with the taking of the Crimea, South Ossetia, and Eastern Ukraine. Not to mention the involvement in Syria. The Russian leadership didn't care what the world thought anymore since they had essentially been unopposed for eight years. "The Japanese are never going to admit these are the real thing. You realize that if they are, the current emperor is illegitimate."

He could almost hear the shrug. "So. They should toss that paper fixture like we did the Tsar."

"Not quite the same, I'm afraid. What's the Kremlin going to do if the Japanese won't stand down?"

Krupin's voice had lowered. "You didn't hear this from me, but I was just in a briefing where they said they're preparing to blow the Japanese fleet out of the water within the next twenty-four hours."

"But that would mean war!"

"A war we would easily win."

"Assuming the Americans stay out of it."

"They will."

"I wouldn't be so sure about that."

"They didn't get involved in the Ukraine or Georgia. They've stood by and let us do what we want in Syria. By the time they decide to do anything, it will be over."

"They're not talking occupation, are they?"

"Oh no, just blast their navy out of the water, demand formal surrender of the islands to us so this never comes up again, probably reparations, then we'll hand over their relics."

"Reparations. Is this about money?"

"Isn't it always? I heard that the boys in Foreign Affairs are coming up with a wish list of demands."

"This is insane."

"This is the new Russia, our pride and strength restored."

The conversation hadn't improved, and the moment it was over, he had called his son to pick him up, sneaking the relics out of the building, his security clearance at least affording him some privileges.

That's probably been revoked.

He had a plan, but it relied on a man he had met only once, and a woman he had never heard of.

A knock at the door had him nearly fainting.

He tossed a towel over the relics then grabbed the edge of the table and took a deep breath before tiptoeing to the door. He peered through the peephole and sighed in relief, pulling the door open and putting a finger to his lips. Everyone entered quietly and he closed the door before delivering traditional greetings to the two professors.

"I cannot thank you enough for coming!"

James Acton nodded. "You made it sound like we had no choice."

Orlov smiled, the next few minutes a blur as he showed the relics to the professors, his son joining them and guarding the door. And as he had feared, they confirmed them as most likely genuine, it taking a lab to be 100% certain.

Though he had heard enough to satisfy his initial assessment.

They were real.

And his government was going to use them to force a country that couldn't admit they had been lost, into paying an unforgivable price.

Laura looked at him. "Why won't your country simply return them?"

Orlov shrugged. "Politics, I fear, but whatever the reason, they must be stopped."

Acton frowned. "What's your plan?"

Orlov stared at them, taking a deep breath, this the moment of truth. "I want the two of you to smuggle them out of the country."

Tires screeched on the streets below.

Orlov rushed to the window, his suspicions confirmed. Police and other dark-suited men were pouring out of vehicles, rushing into the hotel below.

They had only minutes.

He pointed at his son. "Go get the car!" His son nodded and immediately left. Orlov turned to Acton. "They've found me—probably traced my phone. You need to leave. Now."

Acton peered out the window. "We've done nothing wrong."

"But I have, and you're with me. Remember, this isn't Russia anymore, this is the Soviet Union under a different name with a different flag. If you're found with these, God only knows when you'll be seen again."

He shoved the mirror into Acton's hands, the sword and jewel into Laura's.

"What are you doing, Arseny?" He could tell by Acton's tone he wasn't happy.

"You need to take these with you."

"What?"

"Get them out of the country and back to Japan. I won't let that egomaniac lead us into a war over some stolen islands. Getting these back to Japan will defuse the situation."

"Arseny, I don't really think we should be getting involved in this," protested Acton. "Christ, if we're caught with these things, they'll send us to Siberia. Or worse!"

Orlov placed both hands on Acton's shoulders. "My friend, I know I ask a lot of you. But you could save thousands if not millions of lives."

"We can't."

"You must!"

Orlov rushed for the door, Acton and Laura following him, continuing to protest, but it fell on deaf ears. He reached the stairwell door and glanced back at the clearly scared and angry professors. "Go! Now! They don't know who you are yet! You can still make it!"

Acton stood in shock as Orlov rushed through the stairwell door and disappeared. He looked at Laura. "What the hell just happened?"

She stared at the door as it slowly closed, the pneumatic closer doing its job as Orlov's hasty footfalls echoed down the hall. She held up the two relics forced upon her. "We can't be caught with these. Do we just leave them?"

Acton looked around. "Where, here?"

"In the hotel room?"

Acton tried the door. It was locked.

"We can't just leave them in the hall."

Shouts suddenly erupted from the stairwell just as the door clicked shut. "Shit! There's no time." He pointed at the small jade jewel. "Put that in your purse. Will the sword fit under your jacket?"

Laura shoved the jewel in her purse then stuck the short sword underneath her jacket. "Looks rather obvious."

Acton frowned then pulled open the jacket, tearing open the lining near the top. Laura smiled. "Smart thinking."

"Or desperate thinking. Let's go with smart." He slid the sword through the opening and it fell to the bottom of the long ankle length jacket. "Perfect."

She motioned toward the bronze mirror. "That's not fitting under a jacket."

Acton looked about and spotted a maid's cart nearby. He grabbed a garbage bag and handed it to Laura who quickly opened it up, he slipping the mirror inside, folding the plastic around it. "It'll have to do."

They hustled toward the elevator and he pressed the button, his eyes on the doors at the end of the hall, the shouts louder.

Acton glanced at his wife. "Ignore it."

"There's cameras." She nodded almost imperceptibly at a black dome on the ceiling only feet away.

He muttered a curse. "That means they've got our faces."

The doors opened and they boarded, trying to appear as calm as they could to the one passenger. Shuffling to the back, Acton pressed himself against the wall, trying to make the large garbage bag wrapped mirror appear as uninteresting as possible.

As they slowly made their way to the lobby, the elevator stopping several times to eventually pack it quite tightly, he could feel sweat trickling down his back as his heart slammed hard.

The elevator chimed, the doors opening, shouts immediately greeting them as everyone streamed into the lobby. Acton grabbed Laura's hand and he felt a tug, slowing him down slightly.

She's right. You're panicking!

He took a deep, slow breath, trying to gain control of the adrenaline fueling him as they continued toward the door, ignoring the police rushing around the lobby, their numbers still too small to control the large numbers of guests.

Something was shouted at them in Russian.

He ignored it and kept walking toward the doors.

The shout repeated behind them, a uniformed officer at the doors stepping in front of them, holding up a hand. Acton turned toward a plainclothes officer marching toward them.

He put on as innocent of a face as he could manage. "I'm sorry, I don't speak Russian. Did you want to speak to me?"

The man held out his hand. "Papers."

Acton smiled, reaching into his pocket and producing his passport with his visa, Laura doing the same. "Here you go. We're here as guests of your government, just for the day."

The man said nothing, inspecting the passports and visas then handing them back. "Go. And don't forget those expire at midnight."

"Thank you," said Acton, smiling and bowing slightly, the man already after the next suspect. The uniformed officer stepped out of their way and they pushed through the main doors and into the crisp afternoon air, the chaos of the lobby repeated outside as more vehicles with sirens arrived.

They said nothing as they turned right, making their way off the hotel property and to the sidewalk of the main street, their pace brisk though hopefully not suspicious.

A car skidded to a halt beside them, Acton cursing.

"Get in!"

Acton looked and breathed a sigh of relief.

It was Orlov's son, Vitaly.

En route to Sheremetyevo International Airport, Moscow, Russian Federation

"I'm afraid they got your father."

Acton held onto the passenger seat's headrest as Vitaly Orlov rushed through traffic, putting as much distance as he could between them and the hotel, retracing their route from the airport. It had been a split second decision to get into the car, one hastened by three more police cars wailing past them.

They needed to get to their plane.

"Thank you for picking us up, Vitaly, but you shouldn't be involved," said Laura. "They don't know we're involved, and they don't know you are either."

Vitaly grunted, checking his rearview mirror. "In today's Russia, you're guilty of the crimes your family commits. Especially something like this. They'll track him to you through your visas then they'll see me picking you up at the airport. There's cameras everywhere there. It's only a matter of time."

Laura turned to Acton. "Maybe he could come with us?"

"No!" Vitaly wagged a finger. "My father wanted you to get out of the country with the relics. Trying to sneak me onto your plane could just delay things. Besides, I won't leave my father behind." He spun in his seat, his eyes piercing. "Please, when you get out, ask questions about him. It may be the only thing that saves him."

Eyes on the road!

"You can count on it."

"Good!"

He returned his eyes to where they should be as Laura fished out her phone, quickly dialing. "Reggie, it's Laura. Get clearance to leave now. We're going to be there in about—"

Vitaly turned back toward them. "Twenty minutes." Acton jabbed a finger at the road ahead.

"—twenty minutes. We need to leave fast." She hung up. "Let's hope there's not a problem at the airport."

Acton pressed his lips together. "That plane is registered in our names. If they figure out who we are, they could trace it and force us to the ground."

Laura shrugged. "I don't see as we have much choice."

Acton frowned. "Neither do I."

Impiana Private Villas Kata Noi, Phuket, Thailand

CIA Special Agent Dylan Kane moaned, the expert ministrations of his masseuse slowly releasing the tension built up after two weeks outside Mogadishu, most of it spent in a beat up Toyota pickup truck with suspension shot for the better part of twenty years, and on dirt floors, his hosts not believing in chairs or beds.

Though the intel he had gathered had been worth it.

One less pirate cell terrorizing innocents, the drone strike he had directed after tracking their leader down, immensely satisfying.

And now he was enjoying his reward after a week stowed away on a cargo ship.

Downtime.

He would love to be back stateside, spending his time with the love of his life, Lee Fang, but it wasn't in the cards, his handler indicating he needed to stay in the region, ready to deploy at a moment's notice.

Which meant no alcohol that couldn't clear his system in less than three hours.

Which suited him just fine.

He still had the nightmares, they would probably never go away, but he no longer felt alone.

Fang had changed everything.

He'd sip his Glen Breton Ice, shipped in special for him, enjoy some fine dining—though uncharacteristically alone—and enjoy some pampering from expert hands.

He had a nasty habit of sleeping with his masseuses, so he had made a special request of the concierge that didn't involve breast size or willingness to have fun.

He asked for a grandma.

And they had delivered.

When the tiny lady had knocked on his door, her wrinkled visage grinning at him, he had smiled broadly.

Perfect!

Though he did have concerns she'd be able to deliver the vigorous massage he needed.

A few moments of warming up his skin followed by some deep tissue probes that he swore could have broken skin left him yelping and confident she was more than up to the task. As she continued her work, he let his entire body relax, his mind picturing the beautiful Fang, a flash of her on top of him, enjoying each other's bodies, causing Little Dylan to leap for a moment, wondering if he had been called to active duty.

"You turn over now."

Kane flushed. "Umm, better stick with the back."

"Ahh, you excited, huh? Grandma good but I no do that. I good woman."

Kane smiled. "I have no doubt. Just thinking of my girlfriend."

"Ahh, good looking man like you must have good looking woman."

"She's beautiful."

"She good to you?"

"The best."

"Then why you not marry her?"

Kane chuckled. "We just started dating." He pictured Fang in a wedding dress, and oddly enough, it didn't scare him."

"Don't let good woman get away. They hard to find."

"Don't I know it." His special issue watch pulsed with a small electrical current discretely indicating he had a secure message. He glanced over his shoulder at the little old lady. "I think I'm going to go call her. You've got me all loosened up now."

She nodded, stepping off the footstool she had been pushing around for the past hour, almost disappearing from sight. Kane swung off the table, wrapping a towel around himself, thankful things hadn't risen to full mast. He grabbed his wallet from the nightstand and pulled out a generous tip, the massage itself already billed to the room.

She bowed. "You treat her right."

Kane smiled. "I will."

The towel suddenly slipped loose, exposing her to all his glory. He spun around, shielding himself.

She smacked his ass then headed for the door, laughing. "Very good looking man. Very lucky girl."

Kane shook his head, smiling, then dropped on the bed when the door clicked shut behind her. He pressed the buttons on the watch in a coded sequence and a message scrolled across the display, it actually projected onto the glass of what appeared to be a perfectly normal Tag Heuer Monaco.

With about thirty grand in upgrades.

Urgent. Contact CL now.

His eyebrows rose. CL was his best friend from high school, Chris Leroux, now an Analyst Supervisor at the CIA. Kane had been the jock, Leroux the geek, and things hadn't really changed much. Leroux had tutored him through high school, helping him get into college, a college he left to join the military. Leroux's beautiful mind had been recruited into the CIA, neither knowing what the other did until a chance encounter in the cafeteria, a friendship reestablished.

And if Leroux was contacting him, and claiming it was urgent, it must indeed be.

He grabbed his phone, launching the secure encryption app then dialed. His friend answered almost immediately. "Hey, buddy, it's Dylan. What's up?"

"I thought you should know the Russians have just issued arrest warrants for Professor Acton and Professor Palmer."

Five minutes from Sheremetyevo International Airport, Moscow, Russian Federation

Acton's phone vibrated in his hand, startling him. His heart was already slamming hard as they raced toward the airport, their young driver just having told them they were about five minutes away. In the distance, planes could be seen landing and taking off, though a recent phone call from Laura to their pilot had gone unanswered.

Not a good sign.

Yet they had no choice but to press on.

The call display indicated a blocked number, but in a crisis, he had learned to always answer unless it might give away his position.

He answered.

"Hello?"

"Hey, doc, it's Dylan."

Acton breathed a sigh of relief at the sound of his former student's voice. Kane had come to him in a moment of crisis years ago as he debated whether to finish his post-secondary education or join the military to fight the terrorists who threatened the country he loved. Acton had been a sounding board for his thoughts, and in the end, supported Kane's decision to enlist.

Then never heard from him for years until the young man had shown up after a lecture, bursting into tears, spilling the pain and heartache of a mission gone bad, and a life filled with killing and lying, to the one person he felt he could trust with his secrets.

It had been a cathartic moment for both of them.

And Kane had saved their asses on multiple occasions since.

And if he was calling now, it meant their asses needed saving.

"Dylan, *please* tell me you've got good news. We're in the middle of something and we could really use some good news."

"Sorry, doc, no such luck. The Russians have just issued arrest warrants for you and your wife."

"Christ!" He glanced at Laura, the concern on her face clear as she squeezed his hand. "They've issued arrest warrants for us."

Vitaly jerked the wheel to the right, abruptly heading away from the airport.

Probably a wise move.

"Where are you now?" asked Kane.

"We *were* heading for the airport."

"Don't bother. You won't get ten feet. I want you to hang up, turn off every phone and electronic device you've got for exactly ten minutes. Then turn on *only* your phone. I'll call you with instructions. Understood?"

"Yes, got it. Thanks, Dylan."

"No problem. Talk to you in ten."

The call ended and Acton checked the time then leaned between the seats. "Find some place out of sight to park for about ten minutes, and turn off any phones or pagers."

Vitaly grunted, handing him a phone from the passenger seat. "I know a place."

Acton leaned back, turning off his phone, Laura already doing the same.

"What's going on?"

"The Russians have already issued arrest warrants for us despite not knowing we were involved until twenty minutes ago, so they're taking this seriously."

"How did Dylan find out?"

"He didn't say, but if he knows, then the CIA must know, which means this is big." He squeezed his wife's hand. "I think we're in deep shit."

She closed her eyes, squeezing back. "Why does this keep happening to us?"

"Because I'm an idiot. I should have just left the relics in the hallway."

Laura lifted his hand and clasped it to her chest. "You're not an idiot, you're a man who always does what's right. And getting these relics back to the Japanese and possibly preventing a war that could kill a lot of people is the right thing to do."

He smiled, leaning in and giving her a peck on the tip of her nose. "You married the wrong man."

She smiled, returning the peck. "Only if I wanted a boring life."

He grinned. "No risk of that, apparently."

Vitaly jerked the wheel to the right and they quickly found themselves in an aboveground parking structure.

Acton checked his watch.

"Now we wait."

Optima Apartments Avtozavodskaya, Moscow, Russian Federation

Viktor Zorkin sipped on his Russian Standard Vodka from a chilled tumbler. He sighed, the gentle numbing effect enough to take the edge off his septuagenarian bones that had seen far better days.

A jabbing pain shot from his knee up his thigh, as if to rebel against his self-medicating. He gasped, reaching for it, but with his nearly prone position on the couch, he gave up.

I should have died years ago.

Life as a KGB agent had been exciting, dangerous, glamorous even. Life as a retired servant of the old regime, one who showed no love of the new, wasn't so great.

Fortunately, he had money stashed away from his years spent spying on the West, though none of it was here. Here he lived on his government pension, using the extra money to buy a finer bottle of vodka or keep the heat a little higher, but he mostly saved it for a rainy day.

You don't have that many days left, rainy or otherwise, you old dog!

He frowned as he flipped through the channels, finally settling on Russian Idol out of morbid curiosity, reality television the embodiment of Western civilization's decline, its infliction on its former enemy a fitting last gasp of revenge.

My homeland is a disgrace.

At least when he served there was an ideology behind the actions that made sense at the time. Communism, Marxism, were better solutions than capitalism—at least that's how they felt back then. Now the ideology was lost, it merely gangsters and hooligans on ego trips running the show.

What kind of world leader prances around with his shirt off all the time?

He flipped the channel, a hockey game just starting.

And who honestly believes that their country's president scored seven goals against NHL players without it being rigged?

It was laughable, yet the proletariat ate it up, so used to being fed a steady diet of pro-Kremlin nonsense by a state-controlled media, they were complacent with the misconception they were being given the independent truth.

It was like the old days, only worse.

Now the people were naïve enough to think they had a free press, which gave them the false sense of security that the so-called free press would tell them the truth.

Not in Russia.

Not anymore.

He placed his glass on the cracked tile floor, tapping his Beretta sitting within reach in case some moron decided to try and rob the old man in apartment 603.

I wish they would.

At least then there'd be some action. The last time he had felt his heart pump for anything other than a difficult bowel movement was when he had helped his old nemesis Alex West with the suitcase bombs.

I should pay them a visit.

He kept in semi-regular contact with West, the rekindled relationship with his old flame and their daughter he hadn't known existed, apparently going quite well. It would be nice to see a familiar face, and the Black Forest in Germany was beautiful this time of year.

I wonder if they've been overrun as well.

That was one thing about living in Russia—you'd never have to worry about being overrun by refugees. Political correctness had no place here, and it could never be used to destroy a civilization. He felt bad for the

West. He had grown to respect it and even enjoy its trappings, but after the Cold War ended, things had begun to head south. He wasn't sure why. It could have been the lack of a unifying force that a common enemy brought, though he wasn't so sure.

And he frankly didn't care.

The world could go to hell as far as he was concerned.

He had served his country. Had served it well. He had been respected once, feared even, and now he had been abandoned by a "grateful" nation, his only means of survival the money he had stolen in the event his country one day betrayed him.

They never had, not in the sense he had assumed they would, yet here he lay, an old, decrepit man, alone in a rundown apartment in a rundown neighborhood, counting the days until blissful death removed him from the world's great equation.

Too bad I'm an atheist.

His phone vibrated on the tile and he reached down as Moscow Dynamo scored, causing at least an extra strong beat to slam in his chest. He fumbled around for a few seconds before finally gripping the phone.

"Da?"

"Go secure."

His eyebrows rose slightly and he entered a code on the phone as he struggled to an upright position. "Secure. Who is this?"

"This is Dylan Kane. Do you rem—"

"Of course I remember you, I'm old but not senile. You're the young American spy who helped me save the world."

"Better check that memory. I don't seem to recall it going down that way."

Zorkin chuckled. "You have your version, I have the Soviet version."

Kane laughed. "Listen, there's no time for chit-chat. I've got a problem and I need your help."

Zorkin's heart started to beat faster, the pain in his knee seeming to recede. "What is it?"

"Two friends of mine are wanted by your government. They're innocent, caught up apparently in this Japanese mess. Are you in Moscow?"

"Da."

"Can you help?"

"What do you need?"

"I need them taken safely out of the country."

Zorkin smiled.

Action!

"I will see what I can do. But remember, I'm an old man now with few contacts."

Kane laughed. "You may be old, but I've seen you in action, and a man like you never lets his contacts go cold."

Zorkin smiled. "This is true." He sighed. "Men like us should never grow old. It's too humiliating. You should retire while you can, young one, and settle down with that new girlfriend of yours."

He could hear the surprise. "How do you know about that?"

"I keep track of everyone who I consider important."

Kane chuckled. "I'm not sure how to take that."

"You shouldn't." Zorkin laughed. "I will begin to make arrangements. Have your friends contact me in exactly one hour."

Geroyev-Panfilovtsev Street, Moscow, Russian Federation

Acton stared at his watch, ten minutes rapidly approaching. Vitaly had tucked them away into a discrete corner of a parking garage and they had been waiting with bated breath since, no one saying anything.

It was nerve-racking.

"Thirty seconds."

He turned his phone on, watching the interminably slow boot sequence, his foot tapping impatiently.

I should have started it with a minute to go.

It was ready.

It vibrated with a call and he quickly swiped his finger across the display. "Hello?"

"It's me. Pen and paper?"

Acton breathed a sigh of relief at the sound of Kane's voice, holding out his hand, Laura placing a pen in it, then a small notepad on his knee, holding it for him. "Go ahead."

"Okay. He answers to Viktor. He's an old friend. Literally. *Old.* Here's his number." Acton jotted it down. "You will call him precisely fifty-seven minutes from now. He will have instructions for you."

Acton checked his watch, jotting down the time. "Are we supposed to just sit here?"

"No. As soon as you hang up, I want you to wipe then destroy your phones. You still have those apps installed I gave you?"

Acton nodded, Kane having insisted, once he gave them his secret contact number, they download an application on their devices that would wipe them clean should it become necessary. "Yes."

"Good. Wipe them, destroy them, then go buy new ones. Burners. Do you have my number memorized?"

"Yes."

"Good. Text me your new number when you get it and your first initial. Do the same with Laura's. Understood?"

"Yes." Acton paused. "Dylan, just how deep are we in?"

"I'm not going to sugarcoat it, doc, but deep. And we don't have time to talk, they could trace your phone. Wipe and destroy them as soon as you hang up, abandon that vehicle because it can be traced, get new phones and hole up somewhere out of sight. Call Viktor in fifty-five minutes precisely. Got it?"

"Yes."

"Okay, good luck, doc."

Acton turned off the phone and took in a deep breath, closing his eyes.

Deep. Why is it always deep?

Abbotts Park Apartments, Fayetteville, North Carolina

"The worst part is the lying."

Command Sergeant Major Burt "Big Dog" Dawson nodded at his friend, Sergeant Leon "Atlas" James as he took another sip of his bottle of North Carolina's own The Guilty Party brew from Gibb's Hundred, the bottom looking like another. Atlas spotted the problem and grabbed a fresh one from the cooler beside him, tossing it to Dawson.

He snatched it from the air, twisting the cap off and placing the bottle on the balcony floor. He snapped the cap at Atlas whose lightning fast reflexes caught it, immediately firing it back at him. Dawson snatched it and pretended to pop it in his mouth, chewing.

"Good one."

He fake spat it over the railing. "I've been hanging around Niner too much."

"Any amount of time with that man is too much."

Dawson chuckled, knowing full-well Atlas didn't mean a word of it. Atlas and Niner were best of friends, their sometimes none-too-gentle ribbing of each other proof, if any was ever needed. Dawson looked at his friend. "Maggie is the first relationship I've been in where I would have felt the need to tell her what I do, but I got lucky."

"Damned lucky. Who dates the Colonel's secretary?"

Dawson raised a finger. "Personal Assistant."

"Huh, you finally figured it out, eh?"

"If you're going to marry a girl, you should at least know what she does for a living." He leaned over, picking up his fresh brew. "And speaking of marriage"—he sniffed the air, his nostrils dragging in some of the damned fine aroma coming through the open balcony door—"do you see that in your future?"

Atlas' head bobbed, though a frown formed. "That's the problem. I do. We've been dating for a while now, and she's starting to ask a lot of questions. I hate lying to her, and I get the sense she knows I'm lying. I'm afraid it could derail the whole thing."

Dawson nodded. They were Delta Force, special operators in America's most elite of fighting units. Officially 1st Special Forces Operational Detachment—Delta, they didn't exist, their missions classified, few privileged enough to know what they did.

To their casual acquaintances—and some not too casual—they worked in logistics, making sure the soldiers deployed to the hellholes of the world were well supplied.

Somebody shouted from below, a splash indicating a new addition to the pool. Both Dawson and Atlas leaned over in their chairs, checking out the scenery below.

You're practically a married man.

He glanced at Atlas who shrugged.

"Look but don't touch?"

Dawson raised his beer. "Hear! Hear!" He took a swig then glanced into the apartment, laughter from the love of his life and Atlas' carrying outside as the two women worked in the kitchen. Vanessa was training to be a chef, her experimentation on them almost always a success. He felt for his friend. Maggie knew what he did because of her job, so went into the relationship fully aware of what she was getting into. He couldn't tell her where he was going or what he was doing when deployed, but at least she knew why.

With Atlas and the other guys in the Unit that had other halves that hadn't been read-in, they'd have to lie. And with the amount of times they were deployed at the last minute, it could grow frustrating very quickly for their loved ones.

"So marriage. When?"

Atlas shrugged. "She wants to finish her education first and get a job. She swore to her mother she wouldn't get married until she had a skill and some experience in case something went wrong and she ended up on her own having to fend for herself."

"Smart girl."

"She gets it from her mother."

"What's she like?"

"A handful. Doesn't like that I'm a soldier."

Dawson took another swig. "Why?"

"Vanessa's father was Army, killed in a training accident, and I guess they had a hard time of it afterward. She doesn't want the same to happen to her daughter."

Dawson nodded. "Understandable. Good thing she'll never know what you really do for a living."

"And what *does* he really do for a living?"

Dawson gave Atlas a "busted" look then turned toward Vanessa as she stepped out onto the balcony, Maggie behind her.

"He pushes useless paper around a desk. A man's liable to go nuts if he does it long enough, and certainly won't earn the respect of any future mother-in-law."

Vanessa dropped into Atlas' lap and gave him a gentle peck on the lips, patting his massive chest, his nickname earned when someone saw him exercising with a medicine ball, Atlas Shrugged coming to mind. "I think my man's future lies outside the Army."

Atlas' eyebrows rose and Dawson exchanged a quick glance with Maggie as he sensed an uncomfortable moment about to start.

"Umm, baby, the Army is my life. I won't be leaving it until it asks me to leave."

She patted him on the chest again. "Well, we can talk about that later."

Atlas leaned away from her, staring into her eyes. "There's nothing to talk about. You know what I do. You know I love my job."

"But that's just it! I *don't* know what you do!"

Uh oh, here it comes.

"What do you mean? I'm in logistics, you know that."

Vanessa leapt to her feet, her hands on her hips. "Bullshit. I looked it up on the Internet. There's no way a logistics guy goes away as often as you do."

"I go for training, go out on exercise. Sometimes I'm needed in the field. You know that."

She wagged a finger at him. "I'm no fool, Leon James. I know what goes on at Fort Bragg. You're Delta, aren't you!"

Dawson rose, glancing around at the other balconies, some occupied, most not. "I think we should take this conversation inside."

Maggie stepped inside first, Dawson following as Atlas gently urged his still protesting girlfriend off the balcony. He quickly slid the door shut.

"That's it, isn't it? You're Delta!"

Atlas closed the window then turned to Vanessa. "Delta? Those guys are awesome and I'd kill to be one of them, but all you've got is a hardworking clerk for a boyfriend. I'm sorry."

Vanessa's shoulders sagged, her head dropping as her shoulders heaved a few times. She stared up at him. "If you can't tell me the truth then what kind of future do we have?"

Dawson stepped into the kitchen, Maggie following. She stirred a couple of different pots, using a spatula to shove something around in a frying pan before glancing at him.

"I didn't realize how lucky I was until just now."

Dawson nodded. "Yeah, me too."

"Do you think it's serious?"

"Atlas seems to think so. They're talking marriage eventually."

Maggie pursed her lips. "Maybe she should be read-in?"

"That's for the Colonel to decide."

"Don't you think you should call him?"

Dawson frowned, checking his watch as the one-sided shouting match grew. "He'd be home by now."

Maggie shook her head. "No, he was still there when I left, and besides, his sister-in-law is visiting, so, you know."

Dawson grinned. If there was one woman who could keep Colonel Clancy away from his own home, it was his sister-in-law, the two apparently like oil and water. He pulled his phone out of his pocket and dialed.

Clancy answered on the second ring.

"Hello, sir, it's Sergeant Major Dawson. We've got a little situation with Atlas' girlfriend. I think she might need to be read-in."

Clancy grunted. "How long has it been going on?"

"Over a year."

"And it's serious?"

"Very. Talk of marriage. But if she doesn't find out the truth, I think that's dead. She knows he's lying and she's accusing him of being in the Unit."

"Permission granted."

"Thank you, sir."

"Don't thank me yet. If she blabs, you get to shoot her."

Dawson chuckled. "I'll make it look like an accident."

"Be sure you do."

Clancy ended the call and Dawson smiled at Maggie, stepping back into the heat of the ongoing battle. Atlas looked at him and Dawson nodded, the big man closing his eyes for a moment as he breathed a sigh of relief.

"Okay, baby, it's time you learned the truth."

Dawson stepped back into the kitchen as his phone vibrated in his pocket.

Shit! Hope it's not the Colonel changing his mind!

He answered. "Hello?"

"Hey, Jarhead, it's Dylan."

Dawson smiled as he recognized the voice of his former comrade-in-arms, Dylan Kane, part of his Bravo Team before leaving to join the CIA. "Jesus, I thought the toilet had backed up but it was just you wafting back into my life."

A yelp of joy from Vanessa in the other room was apparently overheard. "What was that?"

"Just Atlas' girlfriend discovering why he's been lying to her since they first met."

"Ahh, getting read-in. Never had to do that myself."

"Me neither." He winked at Maggie who was beaming at the sounds of relief in the next room. "I assume you're not calling to swap recipes. What do you need?"

"What makes you think I need something?"

"Because you never call just to say 'hi'."

"This is true. I'm a horrible friend."

"Admitting it is the first step."

Kane chuckled. "Okay, here's the scoop. The Russians have just issued arrest warrants for the professors."

Dawson became all business, James Acton and Laura Palmer two of the few civilians he actually considered friends, their history together over the past few years interesting to say the least. It had started with the shameful act of trying to kill them due to false-intel indicating they were terrorists, then a series of unfortunate events in which Bravo Team had helped them out, and on more than one occasion, the professors returning the favor.

His team owed them their lives on more than one occasion.

And not a man in the Unit would stop at nothing to help.

"What did they do this time?"

"Looks like they're mixed up in that Japanese mess."

Dawson's eyes narrowed. "How the hell did they manage that?"

"Not sure yet, but the warrants are real. We might need your help."

"I'm not sure what I can do if they're in Mother Russia. There's no way the Colonel will authorize anything—on the books or off."

"Don't worry about that. I'll get them out of Russia. I need *you* to secure them once they're out."

"I'll see what I can do."

"Thanks, buddy."

Dawson ended the call as Atlas and Vanessa rounded the corner, tears wiped clean, smiles on their faces.

Vanessa nodded toward Dawson. "Are you?"

He smiled. "I could tell you, but then I'd have to kill you."

Her jaw dropped and everyone laughed, she joining in after a few moments. She looked at Maggie administering to the food. "How's it look?"

"Good to me, but you're the expert."

Vanessa gave Atlas a quick kiss and stepped over to the stove as Dawson and his muscled friend returned to the living room.

"Thanks for that."

Dawson smiled. "Thank the Colonel."

"Oh, I will."

"Just make sure she understands she can't tell anyone, not her mother, best friend, priest or cat."

"I have, but I'll explain why after you guys leave."

"This is your first read-in, isn't it?"

Atlas nodded. "And hopefully the last."

"Amen to that."

"Let's eat!" called Vanessa from the kitchen.

"Give me a minute!" Dawson fished his phone out. "I've got a call to make."

Bakuninskaya Street Parking Garage, Moscow, Russian Federation

Viktor Zorkin eyeballed the photographs one last time. An American professor, a British professor—rather attractive—and a fellow Russian with pimples. Nothing about them appeared to stick out, which would help in their escape, though according to their files, neither visitor spoke Russian.

And that could be a problem.

Any challenge would be met with an English response, and that would immediately flag them for further scrutiny, the entire country on the lookout for two English-speaking foreigners.

A head poked around the corner, Zorkin immediately recognizing the man as Professor Acton. Zorkin stepped out of the van he had borrowed from a contact as his three lost souls rounded the corner on foot.

"Professor Acton?"

The man nodded. "Yes. Are you Viktor?"

"Yes."

"Who sent you?"

Zorkin smiled, this Acton no fool. "Dylan Kane, a brash young CIA agent who I understand is a former student of yours who told you a secret once in your classroom."

Acton smiled, a loudly exhaled breath signaling his acceptance. "Only someone who knew Dylan would know that."

Zorkin slid open the rear door. "Quickly. Everyone inside, there's no time to waste."

Pimples climbed in first, holding out a hand for Laura Palmer. Acton helped her from behind and looked at Zorkin. "Is it bad?"

Zorkin nodded. "It's bad, but I've seen worse." He motioned to the door. "And the longer this takes, the tighter the noose around Moscow. Now get in."

Acton climbed in and Zorkin yanked the door shut, jumping into the van and turning the key, the engine struggling to life. Acton leaned forward as Zorkin pulled out of the parking spot. "Can you get us out?"

"Maybe. Maybe not. If this were America, I would say no problem. But here, where your rights can be violated? Possibly problematic."

"Who are you?"

"I am Viktor."

"That's not what I meant."

Zorkin chuckled as they pulled onto the road. "I know what you meant. Let us just say that my war was a cold war, back when there was mutual respect. Today, all honor has been lost in my old profession."

"How do you know Dylan?"

"Best we don't discuss that."

"Okay. Where are we going?"

Zorkin made a left. "To a place I know. We will be there in fifteen minutes, then you will prepare for a most uncomfortable journey." He jerked a thumb over his shoulder. "Now sit back, out of sight, before someone sees you."

Operations Center 3, CIA Headquarters, Langley, Virginia

"Have you got them?"

CIA Analyst Supervisor Chris Leroux glanced toward the door of the operations center, his boss, National Clandestine Service Chief Leif Morrison, entering. Leroux motioned toward the wall-to-wall curved display at the front of the room. "Agent Kane gave us their new number and we've been able to track it."

"Good." Morrison glanced about the room at Leroux's trusted team. "I know I don't need to say this, but keep this to yourselves." Nods from the team indicated they understood. Morrison stared at the screen, taking up a position beside Leroux. "The White House wants to know the moment we know where they're heading. If Agent Kane's contact can get them out, we want people there to meet them."

Leroux nodded. "Are the Russians aware we know they're after them?"

Morrison shook his head. "Not officially, but you can be certain they do."

"Do we know why they're after them?"

Morrison grunted. "Not yet."

Sonya Tong, one of Leroux's best analysts, and a young woman who had an inappropriate crush on her supervisor, held up a hand. "I might have something on that."

Leroux and Morrison both turned toward her. "What?" they asked in unison.

Tong flushed slightly then pointed at the display, her fingers flying over the keyboard. Russian visas appeared. "Their visas were rushed, pushed through in hours by someone with a lot of pull or a lot of push behind them."

Leroux stepped toward the screen, quickly reading the visas, noting their expiry date of later today. "Do we know who?"

"This man." An image appeared, various documents flashing by. "The visa applications were made by Arseny Orlov from the Ministry of Culture."

"What do we know about him?"

"He's a curator located in Moscow. A few foreign trips to conferences, nothing of note."

Randy Child, the whiz-kid addition to Leroux's team, interrupted. "He's just been arrested." He pointed at the screen, footage appearing from LiveLeak, a frame frozen, facial recognition points mapped on it as well as the file photo Tong had brought up, the computer indicating a match.

"Where was this taken?" asked Leroux.

"Courtyard Moscow Hotel a couple of hours ago. Just a few minutes before the arrest warrants were issued for the professors."

Leroux turned to Tong. "Do the Actons know him?"

"I'm running a background check now, but they're both in similar fields of study, so it's definitely possible."

Leroux pursed his lips as he stared at the data on the displays. "Let's summarize. A curator from the Russian Ministry of Culture gets two last minute visas for the professors, visas that are only good for one day. They enter the country hours later, then minutes after their arrival this same man is arrested at a hotel and arrest warrants are issued for our professors."

"Got something!"

Leroux turned toward Child. "What?"

"I crosschecked that curator's name. His son is also wanted. The warrant was issued in the same dispatch as the professors."

Leroux drew a deep breath, processing the new intel. "Okay, so it's definitely connected."

Morrison agreed. "Now we need to know why the hell they went to Moscow in the middle of an international crisis."

Leroux grunted. "If I know them, that's precisely *why* they went there."

Morrison glanced at him. "Explain."

"Something happened in the Kuril Islands that's pissed off the Japanese. There's no way they would take action like this unprovoked."

"Agreed. They're demanding the return of anything taken there. Does that famous gut of yours have any theories?"

Leroux nodded. "The fact they're demanding the return of *anything* taken I think is the key to this entire thing. Something was found. Sovereign rights have nothing to do with this, that's just a smokescreen. The problem is figuring out what could possibly have been found that Japan would be willing to provoke a war with Russia, a war they couldn't possibly expect to win."

"Military secrets?" suggested Tong.

"Naked photos of Tokyo Rose?"

Leroux glanced at Child, the youngest of their team—and the one with the least developed filter. "No, I think this is something different. If the Russians found something then it must be important. And the Japanese know they found it, otherwise none of this would be happening. If it was important enough for this reaction today then it would have been last year or ten years ago. This was discovered very recently. And it was obviously recognized by the Russians as important."

"And important things get sent to Moscow," said Morrison.

Leroux smiled. "Exactly. And I don't believe in coincidence. I'm guessing that whatever it was, it was sent to Moscow and given to this

Orlov guy to identify. And if that's the case then it's some sort of relic, which would explain why he would call the professors in."

"Don't they have archaeologists in Moscow?" asked Child.

"Yes. But his actions would suggest he doesn't trust them for some reason."

"A man of conscience," muttered Morrison, gazing at the man's file photo.

"Exactly. If he knew what he had been asked to identify was the key to preventing a war, and he didn't trust his country to do the right thing, which would be to return it, then he just might call in outside help."

"Acton and Palmer." Morrison shook his head. "Thank God we've gone digital. Their files would take up a room by now." He looked at Leroux. "Okay, let's assume you're right. Why would the Russians want to arrest the Actons if they've already arrested Orlov? It just ratchets up tensions with us once we officially find out."

Leroux frowned. "I can only think of one reason."

Tong gasped. "They have the relic!"

*1st Special Forces Operational Detachment—Delta HQ, Fort Bragg, North Carolina
A.k.a. "The Unit"*

"Hi, sir, you're working late."

Colonel Thomas Clancy looked up from his laptop, motioning for Dawson to enter. "No rest for the wicked."

Dawson stepped inside, closing the door. "Your sister-in-law still awake?"

Clancy chuckled. "Good one. I'll do you the kindness of not telling her you said that. You don't want to get on her wrong side."

"I get the sense you made that mistake."

"Twenty years ago. I've been paying for it ever since." Clancy pointed at a chair and Dawson sat, noticing the half-full ashtray with a freshly lit cigar burning.

"I thought you quit."

"I did. But that battle-axe has me so on edge, I decided to reward myself for not disappearing her."

Dawson grinned. "I'm sure she'd forgive you if she knew the alternative."

Clancy grunted. "Oh, don't be so sure about that." He pushed a file across the desk toward Dawson. "After *you* called, *I* got a call." Dawson took the file, flipping it open. "You're officially on standby to deploy. Team of six. We're sending you to Italy so you're in theater, then we'll hopefully get an idea where you're going to be needed."

"What do we know?"

Clancy frowned. "Not much, except that the Russians are horny to get their hands on the professors. Langley is standing by to give you a briefing."

Dawson closed the file, it merely dossiers on the professors he was already quite familiar with. "So this is official?"

"Yup. Our friends have once again got themselves into the thick of things, and this time there's not much we can do about it but watch."

Nikolskaya Street, Moscow, Russian Federation

"Keep quiet and keep your heads down until we're clear," hissed Zorkin through clenched teeth.

Acton held Laura's hand as he consciously sealed his mouth, his entire body tense. The drive hadn't been long, but every wail of a siren, every halt of the van, sent another surge of adrenaline pumping through his veins.

And a sudden jerk to the right didn't help, the light from outside gone, the van pulling into darkness. Two men emerged from the black, rushing past the van, the sound of a garage door slamming behind them causing his heart to skip a beat.

It won't be a bullet that kills me. It'll be my damned heart exploding.

Zorkin turned off the engine and glanced back at them as they were flooded with light. "We're clear. Everybody out, but keep quiet."

Someone opened the side door of the van and Acton stepped out, helping Laura and Vitaly down as Zorkin talked to the others in Russian, Vitaly getting redder by the moment as he listened.

"What are they saying?" asked Acton in a whisper.

"Checkpoints are being set up around the city. He says we're not going to be able to get through without being challenged."

Zorkin stepped toward them, nodding at Vitaly. "He's told you?"

"About the checkpoints and being challenged, yes. What are we going to do?"

Zorkin smiled. "We're going to have to go old school, as you Americans might say."

"And that will work why?"

Zorkin jerked a thumb at the world on the other side of the garage door. "These young punks have lost the touch. They're not suspicious enough. Give it time and our supreme leader will have us back to the old ways soon enough, but for now, over two decades of being soft should work for us."

Vitaly raised a finger. "Umm, any w-word on my father?"

"Just that he's been arrested and being held at Lubyanka."

Vitaly stifled a cry, Laura reaching out and taking his arm. She turned to Zorkin. "Will they hurt him?"

Zorkin looked at Vitaly, the young man's eyes red with tears, but said nothing.

That's a yes.

Acton motioned toward the Imperial Regalia still sitting in the van. "What if we give them the relics?"

Laura nodded. "Yes, surely they'd let him go then?"

Zorkin shook his head. "No, we can't be sure of that. They may just take you into custody and torture you. Dylan asked me to get you out, and that's what I'm going to do."

Acton felt his chest tighten slightly with anger. "Don't we have a say in it?"

Zorkin stared at him. "Only if it agrees with what I say."

Acton held his gaze for a moment then shook his head, exasperated. "I can see why Dylan trusts you. You're just like him."

"I'm about fifty years older. I'd like to think he's just like me."

Acton smiled. "Good point." He motioned at the garage they found themselves in. "So, what's this old school method you were mentioning?"

Zorkin pointed at a beat up curtainsider truck, its cloth back emblazoned with faded Cyrillic letters and a phone number. "Meet your luxury ride."

The Unit, Fort Bragg, North Carolina

"Here's the scoop. Our professors are in the thick of it once again."

Sergeant Carl "Niner" Sung shook his head. "Okay, who'd they piss off this time?"

Dawson clicked a link on his laptop then jerked a thumb over his shoulder, the display highlighting the Russian Federation. "The Russians."

Sergeant Will "Spock" Lightman cocked an eyebrow. "Christ, they're punching above their weight this time."

Sergeant Gerry "Jimmy Olsen" Hudson leaned forward, jabbing a finger at the map. "You're telling me that Washington has authorized us to go inside Russian territory?"

Dawson shook his head. "No, and I don't anticipate they will. But Dylan—"

"Oh shit, he's involved?" Niner looked at the others. "Now I *know* we're in trouble."

Atlas' impossibly deep voice rumbled in agreement. "Never trust the CIA to have your back."

"True dat," replied Niner.

"Don't be appropriating my culture," said Atlas.

Niner's eyes opened wide, staring at Atlas with a WTF expression on his face. "What the hell are you talking about?"

"It's the latest buzz word. Apparently you're not allowed to enjoy creole food, and I'm not allowed to enjoy Chinese food."

"I'm Korean."

"Same shit, different flies."

116

"Now *that's* insulting. When I shove my stainless steel Korean chopsticks up your ass, you'll realize just how different they are from those pussy wooden things the Chinese use."

Atlas sighed. "Again with my ass."

Dawson shook his head. "Done?"

"Yessim." Niner whipped an easily caught pen at Atlas.

"Anyway…Dylan has his contacts working on a way to get them out of Moscow, and hopefully out of Mother Russia. Washington wants us ready to get them to safety once they cross whatever border they're going to cross."

Sergeant Ronny "Jagger" Leibowitz leaned forward, his pronounced lips pursed. "Why is Washington so horny to protect them? What's the difference this time? Usually we're having to sneak one by them."

"Langley thinks that the professors may be the key to stopping what's looking like a potential armed conflict between Russia and Japan."

Spock's eyebrow rose. "So what you're saying is that if we don't save the Actons, sushi prices are going up?"

Dawson nodded. "Yup. Say your goodbyes and get yourselves squared away. We're wheels up in sixty mikes."

Operations Center 3, CIA Headquarters, Langley, Virginia

"They're on the move."

Leroux turned to Child. "Do we have a visual?"

Child's fingers flew over the keyboard. "Hacking the traffic cameras now."

Leroux watched the map of Moscow, a red dot representing Acton's phone, tracing out a slow route from where it had sat motionless for the last half hour. "Any projections as to where they might be heading?"

Tong shook her head. "Not yet. There's just too many main arteries in that area that lead everywhere. We'll get a better idea when they get on one of them."

"Where are those feeds?" asked Leroux, not bothering to look at Child.

"I'm having trouble getting in. Looks like they've put up—" He paused for a moment then a camera feed suddenly appeared, a busy street shown. "Got it."

"Do we know what vehicle they're in?"

Child shook his head. "No, but we'll be able to narrow it down as we keep track."

Leroux stepped closer. "They won't be in a car." He pointed at the steady stream of vehicles. "They'll need to be kept out of sight since the entire city is searching for them. They'll be in something that can hide them."

"A van or a truck?" suggested Tong.

Leroux shook his head, the camera angle changing as Child tried to keep the view in synch with the movements of the cellphone. "Not a van. They won't be hiding in the back. If it were me trying to smuggle them out, I'd be in something like…" He smiled, pointing at a covered truck. "That."

They watched the truck in question take the on-ramp onto what appeared to be a major highway. Child updated the view.

"What direction is that?"

"South," replied Tong. "They still can go east or west off this, but I think we can probably rule north out."

Leroux nodded. "East as well, at least for the long haul. There's no way they're going to try and drive to the Pacific coast."

Tong giggled.

Child leaned back in his chair. "I think you're right, sir, the cellphone tracking is in synch with that truck. Everything else is accelerating far faster."

"Good. Do we have any checkpoints coming up?"

Child frowned, updating the map.

"They're about to hit one now."

M2 Highway Checkpoint, Moscow, Russian Federation

I swear something is trying to jimmy my ass.

Acton shifted again, trying to get comfortable, though it was proving to be an impossible task. They hadn't been in their "getaway" vehicle for more than ten minutes and his body was already aching. It had been a hasty exit from the garage, the relics and three passengers stowed under the wood floorboards of the truck, a load of boxes piled atop them.

They hit a bump and Laura moaned.

If we have to stay like this much longer, I'm going to go postal.

Which was probably why Zorkin had been extremely vague about how long they'd be stuck in their cramped conditions, breathing in diesel fumes, the roar of the engine and the whine of the tires on the asphalt drowning out his ability to think, let alone talk.

Though every moment of movement meant they were that much closer to getting out of the cordoned off Moscow.

One thing Zorkin had been clear on was that should they stop, no matter what they heard, they were to remain silent. Even if the vehicle was impounded, they should remain quiet and await rescue.

Rescued by whom, was the question he didn't bother asking.

He just assumed it would be the elderly gentlemen at the garage.

Zorkin was definitely ex-KGB and the others probably were too, though he couldn't be certain. He just wondered how well they could trust these men who now held their lives in their hands. If just one of them got word of a hefty reward, something he had a feeling would be soon offered—if not already—this journey might be cut incredibly short.

The truck began to slow, the squealing brakes so ear-piercing it caused him to wince in pain. The engine began to idle, the distinctive shouts of officials barking orders, heard.

Checkpoint!

Zorkin frowned. "I've got a schedule to keep. You've delayed me enough with this damned roadblock!"

The officer wasn't impressed with the crotchety old man routine, instead pointing to the side of the road where several other vehicles were being searched. "Over to the side, now!"

Zorkin shook his head, putting the truck in gear. "Da, da, it's more like Chechnya here every day."

As the truck jerked forward, the officer jumped on the running board, reaching inside and grabbing the wheel, Zorkin hammering on the brakes. "I served in Chechnya. You don't want me treating you like we did them."

Zorkin forced a slightly scared, slightly apologetic look on his face. "Of course not, I meant no disrespect."

"Uh huh." The man stepped down and pointed at an empty spot. "Pull over there and turn off your engine."

Zorkin complied, stepping out to watch as a security detail quickly poked their heads inside every nook and cranny they could find, telescoping mirrors used to check underneath.

The rear gate lowered with a bang.

"What are you transporting?"

"DVD players."

"To where?"

"Volgograd."

The officer stared at him for a moment. "Aren't you a little old for such a long haul?"

The sad old person face made an appearance. "Son, when you're my age, you'll realize how useless a government pension is when inflation is running at fifteen percent."

The young man nodded, his expression softening slightly. "This is true. I send as much as I can to my parents, but it's never enough." He lowered his voice. "I now deliver for Pizza Hut in the evenings. Can you believe it?"

Zorkin chuckled. "My friend, you do what you have to do to survive." He regarded him with a genuine look of respect. "You're a good boy, working hard to help your parents. I'm sure they appreciate it."

The young officer said nothing, the shared moment over as one of his men opened several of the boxes in the back. "Check the floor," he said, pointing at the wood slats. The security officer stomped a few times.

"Sounds hollow."

The officer turned to Zorkin who had to admit his heart was racing a little bit with the excitement.

You're out of practice. This wouldn't faze you at all thirty years ago.

"What's under there?"

Zorkin shrugged. "The truck? I just drive it, I didn't build it."

"We'll have to empty your cargo and inspect what's under there."

Zorkin shrugged again. "Go ahead. It's not like I'm transporting vegetables. DVD players don't rot if you keep them waiting." The officer was about to signal his men to empty the truck when Zorkin continued. "But it will mean I'll be late so I probably won't keep my job."

The officer stared at Zorkin, chewing his cheek, then jerked a thumb over his shoulder. "Get going old man, before I change my mind."

Zorkin smiled, patting him on the arm. "You're a good boy, your parents raised you well."

Operations Center 3, CIA Headquarters, Langley, Virginia

"Record everything. I want visual proof the Russians have them if they're captured. It may be the only thing that saves their lives." He pointed at the screen. "Can we get a shot of the driver?"

Child nodded, the camera angle changing as they watched an old man leaning out the truck window, handing over identification papers. Facial recognition points quickly mapped and a search began on the massive intelligence databases stored in the Langley server farm.

An ID appeared, surprisingly quick.

"Viktor Zorkin, former KGB. That's definitely them."

He watched, unconsciously holding his breath as the old man pulled the truck to the side, a search begun.

Tong gasped as someone climbed in the back of the truck. "Would they be behind the boxes?"

Leroux shook his head. "I doubt it, too obvious. My guess is they're underneath the truck."

Child cursed. "That can't be comfortable."

Leroux had to agree. The vehicle appeared old, Cold War era, and if he had to hazard a guess, designed with this exact purpose in mind. He wouldn't be surprised if Zorkin himself had used it in the past when he was still active, though why he would want to smuggle people within the Soviet Union escaped him.

Double agents?

He nodded to himself.

Possible.

He breathed a sigh of relief as Zorkin climbed back in the truck, it jerking away, the security team already turning their attention to the next vehicle singled out. He pointed at the screen. "Okay, where are they headed?" He stepped toward the map. "If we assume they're heading south, we can probably rule out Finland, the Baltics and Belarus."

"The Ukraine?" suggested Child. "Pretty risky though."

Leroux shook his head. "No, I can't see Kane taking them through that mess, though it would be a crazy-ass move, so maybe."

"East?"

"No, like we already said, too long. Time is of the essence here. Zorkin is going to try and get them off his hands as fast as possible, and judging from the look of that truck, it's not up to travelling thousands of miles."

Tong highlighted several countries on the map. "He'd try to get to a friendly country, though, right? Besides the Baltics, there's none bordering the Russians."

"There's not a lot of friendly countries in the area." Child pointed at the map. "What's left? Georgia, Azerbaijan and Kazakhstan."

"Don't forget the Black Sea," said Leroux. "Get them on a boat, zip them across to Turkey." Leroux shook his head, dismissing his own idea. "With what's been going on there, especially with the Russian takeover of the Crimea, they're monitoring those waters like nobody's business." He sighed. "Delta should be in the air by now. Let's keep monitoring and see where they end up. Hopefully in a few hours we'll be able to give them at least a general idea of where they need to be."

Prosecutor-General's Office, Bolshaya Dmitrovka, Moscow, Russian Federation

"We need to find them. Fast!"

Agent Alexey Dymovsky gripped the phone tightly, the feeling of excitement from the adrenaline rushing through his veins one almost forgotten. "Yes, sir, absolutely, sir."

"Use whatever means necessary. I want them in custody, now!"

"Yes, sir!"

The receiver slammed down at the other end, the call over. Dymovsky rose, straightening his tie, checking himself with a small mirror he kept in the top desk drawer. It had been a long time since the brass had called him, and from what he had just been told, there was only one reason he had been called.

His bosses wanted a scapegoat should something go wrong.

Since the failure to recover the lost American nuke, their so-called Brass Monkey, he had been sidelined. He wasn't officially blamed. That would mean something on the record, and nothing of that incident had been recorded.

It kept his record clean, but his career idled.

Until now.

Find and arrest two visiting professors and a Russian national who had stolen the property of the Russian people.

What that property was, he had no idea, but whatever it was, he knew already from the massive cordon descending around Moscow and the Federation itself, that it was of the utmost importance to the Kremlin.

And he would take the opportunity to succeed brilliantly and reclaim what was once a promising career.

Satisfied with what he saw in the mirror, he left his office and marched toward the command center, the door opened for him by a young officer who snapped to attention.

"Report!"

The coordinator stared at him, slightly surprised at who had been sent to take over, it well known in the building that he was to be shunned. She responded quickly, there no reason for her to doubt Dymovsky was now in charge.

"Sir, we're monitoring all routes heading out of the city, including rail and air. Nothing yet, but we'll catch them."

Dymovsky took up his place in the center of the room, shaking his head. "No, forget monitoring the checkpoints. If we can spot them, so can our men on the ground. Besides, they won't be stupid enough to leave in plain sight. They'll be hidden in a vehicle somewhere."

"Then what should we look for?"

"We need to figure out where they went after they left the hotel. Do we have the footage yet?"

"Yes, sir," said a young woman to his left. "And I think I found them. Watch." She motioned toward the screen at the front of the room, footage showing a man and woman leaving the hotel, hand-in-hand. The image froze and facial recognition points were mapped, showing a match to their subjects.

"That's them alright. Good work. Where did they go from there?"

The footage continued and a car pulled up, the two subjects climbing in almost immediately. As the car pulled out, the driver turned for a shoulder check, the camera getting a good shot of his face. The image froze, the face plotted, and the subject identified.

The son.

"Excellent. Follow that car. I want to know where they went."

Outside Tambov, Russian Federation

Acton grunted as the truck bounced, shoving his body into the wood slats only inches above him. He felt Laura's hand squeeze his, it the only form of communication they had managed for hours, it simply too loud on the highway.

The good thing, however, was the fact they had been travelling at full speed for some time without anyone stopping them.

They were out of Moscow.

And heading God only knew where.

God and Zorkin.

The truck slowed then made a gentle turn, the entire sensation changing, even the smell.

Dirt road?

The whine of the engines and tires lowered to the point where he could actually attempt a conversation. He stared over at where Laura was, the pitch-blackness leaving her barely a shadow against a shadow. "Sounds like we're on a dirt road."

"Maybe we're there already?"

"Maybe. But where's there? We haven't been driving long enough to get out of Russia."

Laura moaned. "I don't care where we are. I just have to get out of here. Every muscle in my body is screaming."

Acton smiled at his wife, squeezing her hand as the truck came to a halt, the engine turning off. Laura let go of his hand as everyone held their tongue. The driver door opened and they heard muffled voices before a double-slap on the wheel well indicated the all-clear. Acton breathed a sigh of relief as the rear gate was opened, the sounds of boxes overhead being removed signaling the end of their imprisonment.

The floorboards overhead lifted and a flashlight shone in his face.

"Quickly," said Zorkin. "We must get you inside before you're seen."

Acton struggled up, every inch of his body protesting, but the urgency in Zorkin's voice had him pushing through the pain. The young hand of Vitaly pulled him to his feet, they both helping Laura. Jumping to the ground, an old woman, probably in her seventies, ushered them inside what appeared to be an old farmhouse, the door quickly closed behind them.

Zorkin took off his hat. "May I present Boris and Darya. Old friends of mine. They used to be part of the underground railroad that smuggled spies in and out of Russia. I caught them in 1983 but decided to let them continue."

"Why?" asked Laura, shaking the elderly couple's hands.

"It let him know who was coming and going," replied Acton.

Zorkin grinned. "You think like a spy."

Acton shook their hands. "So you were double-agents."

The look of shame on both their faces was obvious, and Zorkin immediately leapt to their defense. "Not by choice, I assure you. It was cooperation or the gulag." Zorkin sighed. "Those were different times." He motioned at their surroundings. "We will stay here to rest, wash, eat. We will be leaving first thing in the morning."

"Should we be waiting that long?" asked Laura. "I mean, do we really have any time to waste?"

Zorkin smiled reassuringly. "The truck will have been recorded leaving Moscow. If they are at all suspicious, they will expect it to arrive at a certain time. If I drive without resting, they will think something is wrong. Then there's the fact that I need sleep, too! We've been driving almost six hours."

"Ugh, has it been that long?" Acton frowned then sniffed, his stomach suddenly taking over. "What's that? It smells delicious!"

Darya gave a toothy smile. "Zharkoe."

Acton shook his head. "Never heard of it, but I can't wait to try it."

Darya pointed at a set of stairs. "Wash first. You look like the pigs." Acton looked at her, puzzled. She pointed behind him and he turned to see himself in a mirror.

And muttered a curse.

He was covered head to toe in a black film. He glanced over at Laura who seemed almost spotless. "What the hell?"

She shrugged. "I'm a lady."

"Uh huh."

"You also sat over the tire. Pretty much everything was kicked up on you."

Acton stared back at himself in the mirror.

"Now I know how a mud flap feels."

Prosecutor-General's Office, Bolshaya Dmitrovka, Moscow, Russian Federation

"Sir, we've got something."

Dymovsky glanced up from his laptop. "What is it?"

The coordinator pointed at the screen, footage playing of a parking structure. "We traced them to Geroyev-Panfilovtsev Street where they entered a parking garage then abandoned their vehicle." The footage advanced to show the three suspects leaving the building, facial recognition positively identifying them.

Dymovsky grunted. If they were abandoning their vehicle, they obviously feared it could be tracked, but they also had to have an alternative. He couldn't believe they would be trying to hide within Moscow. They had to know with all the cameras in the city they would be traced, so they must have arranged alternate transportation. "Send units to impound the car. Tell them I'll be attending myself."

"Yes, sir." The coordinator pointed at another tech who executed the order.

Dymovsky rose. "Do we know where they went?"

"Not yet, sir, we're still tracking them. It's a slow process."

Dymovsky nodded. "Notify me the moment you have a destination."

"Yes, sir."

Dymovsky strode out of the room on autopilot as he made his way to his government issue Chevrolet Lacetti. It had been a long time since he had his own car, the forgotten perks flowing in over the past few hours as the official notification of his high-profile assignment trickled through the bureaucracy.

Life was good again.

If only for the moment. If he failed, he would be blamed, and in today's Russia, that could mean imprisonment.

I have to leave this godforsaken place.

But it was his home. He loved his country, he loved its people, but he hated its government. Things had seemed bright after the collapse of communism, but in a country that respected strength, it mistakenly embraced a leader who projected it, and now they were paying the price. The rumors were that their diminutive leader had siphoned off over $70 billion dollars over his tenure, with much of that coming from the Winter Olympics in Sochi, the most expensive Olympics in history.

Of course, the government dismissed the claims as nonsense.

Yet if they were, how could their judo-chopping leader afford to build himself a billion dollar mansion on the edge of the Black Sea?

And with corruption at the top—such blatant corruption—Dymovsky had to be careful. He didn't know why these three people were wanted, all he knew was that they were. And if he valued his life, he would do whatever it took to catch them.

He just hoped that if he did, he wouldn't regret it.

Please let them be genuine criminals, not so-called enemies of the state.

Though he feared it was the latter. He had pulled their files, and from what he could tell, these two professors had a propensity for getting into trouble. Reports had Acton in Mecca during the Brass Monkey incident, though he appeared to be some sort of advisor, and they were both present at the suicide bombings at the Vatican.

Along with at least a dozen other significant international incidents.

These aren't innocent people.

The question was whether they were acting for the greater good, which too often nowadays meant contrary to the interests of the Russian government.

He grunted out a laugh. It was almost fitting that all these years later it would be *their* capture that might get his career back on track. Yet at what cost? Russia wasn't the Russia he loved anymore. Justice was arbitrary, subject to the whims of the leadership, the country quickly receding into the old, corrupt ways, and judging from what he had read, these professors probably *were* innocent.

At least innocent in the eyes of any lawful country.

Though if his government got their hands on them first, it wouldn't matter.

He sighed. He knew what he had to do. Getting his career back on track at the expense of innocent people was not what he wanted. It went against every fiber of his being.

I have to get to them first.

If he found them first then he could determine what was truly going on then act accordingly. It could mean the end of his career, perhaps his life, yet at least he'd die knowing he had done the right thing.

Life is never easy.

It didn't take him long to reach the parking structure where the foreign professors and their local abettor had abandoned their vehicle, lights and sirens working wonders, especially at this hour when the streets were mostly empty. Reports from dispatch indicated they had found the car on the third level. He wound his way up, finding several marked units, the area cordoned off by half a dozen uniformed officers.

He parked nearby then stepped out, flashing his ID at his first challenger. "Report."

"We've found nothing in the car of importance, but we did find these in a garbage bin." He led Dymovsky over to the hood of one of the cruisers, three smashed cellphones on display, two quite expensive. Dymovsky's head bobbed in appreciation. There'd be no way to track them now by their cellphones, which was going to make things much more difficult. He motioned toward the devices. "Bag them and get them to the lab. Let's see if we can get anything off of them." Dymovsky sighed, leaning on the cruiser as he watched the men work on the car. "How do you escape Russia if you're a wanted criminal?"

"You need help?"

Dymovsky glanced over at the young officer, smiling slightly, the question meant for the ether of his subconscious rather than those around him. "Yes. But how do you coordinate help if you're a foreigner?"

The officer shrugged. "You ask for it?"

Dymovsky chuckled. "Yes, I suppose you do." He shoved himself off the hood of the car, his jaw dropping, his eyes widening as he had a sudden thought. "And you'll need a new cellphone to do it!"

Operations Center 3, CIA Headquarters, Langley, Virginia

"Is that the parking garage they went to?"

Child nodded. "Yes, sir. It looks like the Russians have found it."

Leroux pointed at an officer stepping outside, handing something over to a newly arrived unit, entry to the garage now blocked from the street level. "Zoom in on that."

Child's fingers flew over the keyboard, the image zooming in, coalescing around the object in question. "Evidence bags?"

Leroux stepped closer. "Enhance it." The image pixelated as the advanced algorithms took elements from multiple frames and morphed them together to produce a single, crisper image. His eyes narrowed. "Cellphones?"

"Looks like it."

Leroux cursed.

Tong looked at him. "What's wrong? We knew they destroyed them so they couldn't be traced."

"Yes, but now *they* know."

"So?"

"So, if I were the lead investigator, I'd be trying to find out if they bought a new phone."

Child groaned. "They should have hidden the destroyed phones."

Leroux agreed. "Exactly. Now that they know they're looking for a cellphone purchase, probably in the immediate vicinity, they might be able to figure out the numbers."

Child cursed. "We need to warn them."

Leroux shook his head. "If we do, and they trace the phone, they'll be able to trace any prior activity. If they're able to trace it somehow back to us, they'll know we're involved."

"What do we do?"

Leroux stared at the map showing the current location of the professors, a pulsing red blip that hadn't moved for hours. "We wait and see if the professors can beat the clock."

Prosecutor-General's Office, Bolshaya Dmitrovka, Moscow, Russian Federation

Dymovsky jerked up from the couch in his office, glancing about to see what had woken him. Another knock at the door answered the question.

"Come in."

The door opened and his newly assigned junior partner, Abram Filippov, poked his head in. "Sorry to wake you, sir, but we've found where the van went."

Dymovsky immediately leapt to his feet, adrenaline fueling his sudden alertness. Dozens of agents scouring video feeds had caught the three suspects walking into another parking garage almost two hours after they had abandoned the car, a van leaving minutes later, it the only vehicle to leave for another half hour, and it having only arrived a few minutes before them.

He was certain they were inside.

They still didn't know where they had gone in between, the search still on, he convinced new cellphones had been purchased.

All in good time.

He grabbed his mirror from his top drawer and checked himself, running a hand over his day's growth.

No time.

He stepped out of his office, Filippov on his heels. "Talk."

"We were able to trace the route of the van. It pulled into what appears to be a garage on Nikolskaya Street."

"Another parking garage?"

"No, an auto shop. I've sent teams to surround it."

Dymovsky nodded with satisfaction as they burst through the doors and out into the crisp night. "Don't have them enter until we arrive."

"I've already ordered them to wait, sir."

Dymovsky smiled slightly, glancing over at the young man as they climbed into their car. "Good work."

This kid might just work out.

Operations Center 3, CIA Headquarters, Langley, Virginia

"They're getting closer, sir. They've found where they switched vehicles."

Leroux yawned, cursing. He'd kill for a Red Bull right now, but it had been some time since he'd kicked his addiction to the caffeine infused energy drinks, and he had made a promise to his girlfriend that he'd never touch them again.

And she had promised his lips wouldn't touch any part of her body if he went back on his word.

And her body was worth sacrificing air for, let alone Red Bull.

He had just texted her that he wouldn't be home tonight, the events in Moscow, unfolding seven hours ahead, suggesting he might not see the outside of this room for another twenty-four hours, day just about to break on the other side of the world.

Though that could all change if the professors were caught.

He stared at the pulsing dot, it still not having moved. He shook his head. "What the hell are they doing?" he muttered.

"Sleeping?" suggested Tong, she looking like she could use some rest herself. The morning shift was about to arrive, but Tong and Child had already insisted on staying if he were staying, and there was no way he could leave in the middle of a rapidly developing op.

Quick catnaps in the sleep room would have to suffice.

"Definitely." Leroux sat in his chair.

A burst of frustration erupted from Child as he threw his hands toward the screen. "Don't they realize they're being tracked?"

"Maybe they don't," said Tong. "This guy Agent Kane sent to help them is pretty old school."

Leroux looked over at her. "So?"

"Well, maybe he's a little *too* old school. As in, it wouldn't occur to him that he could be tracked through traffic cameras and cellphone traces."

Leroux smiled, shaking his head slightly. "Men like that never let their skills get rusty, just their bones." He looked over at the image of Viktor Zorkin, his eyes narrowing. "He knows perfectly well what's going on."

"Well then he's just an idiot."

Leroux turned to Child. "I doubt that. My gut's telling me he wants to be tracked." He pursed his lips, turning back to the image of the former spy, staring at the man's eyes. "The question is, why?"

Nikolskaya Street, Moscow, Russian Federation

"Proceed."

Security teams rushed forward, silently, both ends of the street blocked off to keep civilian interference at a minimum. As his team covered him, one of the operators placed an explosive charge on the entrance to the left of the large garage door. He rushed back to safety, raising a hand to signal the imminent detonation, looking to Dymovsky for the go-ahead.

Dymovsky nodded and a small explosion tore through the early morning calm as his lighter flicked, a cigarette dangling from his lips, lit. The team rushed inside, shouts heard but no gunfire, the all-clear sounded in less than two minutes. He took a long drag, exhaling the life shortening deliciousness.

Filippov looked at him. "Those will kill you."

Dymovsky grunted. "Hopefully before the job does."

A disheveled, bloodied man was led out, his silver hair and wrinkled skin betraying his advanced age. Dymovsky tossed his cigarette onto the ground, striding quickly toward the man. He flicked his wrist toward the door. "Take him back inside."

The man was half-dragged, half-pushed inside as Dymovsky followed them into the dusty garage, it clearly having seen better days, though its condition suggested it was from the Soviet era, so perhaps it had *never* seen good days. He pointed at a chair, his men shoving the suspect into it. Dymovsky slowly rounded the well-organized garage, it old and decrepit though clearly operated with pride. The shell of an old Lada sat in the corner, an apparent labor of love underway.

Then there was the large rectangle where the dust seemed to have been blocked by something.

Something large.

He finished his circuit in front of the man. "Your name?"

The man said nothing, simply staring at the ground, blood from a broken nose dripping onto his overalls, 'Andrie' sewn proudly onto a patch over his heart.

"Old man, don't test me. You know we'll find out soon enough."

"Andrie."

"Your last name?"

"Volkov."

"Good, that wasn't so hard, was it?" He knelt down in front of the man. "Two professors were here earlier. An American male and a British female. James Acton and Laura Palmer, along with Vitaly Orlov, a Russian citizen." This elicited no reaction. "They are wanted by your government for crimes against the state. Do you deny they were here?" Still nothing. Dymovsky stood. "I'll take your lack of a reply as confirmation they were. Someone opened the door for them. I'm assuming that was you. Who was driving the van?"

No answer.

"We'll find out, old man, with or without your help." He shoved the man's head back so he could look into his eyes. He was met with a blank stare. "You know what will happen to you if we have to find out without your help?"

The man stared at him as if he didn't care, as if anything they could do to him was nothing compared to the life he had already endured.

"Sir!"

"What?" snapped Dymovsky at his underling, his stare fixated on the suspect.

"You need to see this!"

He was about to dismiss his junior partner, but the excitement in the man's voice suggested he truly did need to see whatever his partner had discovered. Dymovsky pointed at the old man. "Take him to headquarters. We'll soften him up a bit, see if he'll talk then." He stepped outside, the morning light barely breaking on the horizon. "What is it?"

Filippov pointed down the street. "What do you see?"

Dymovsky looked, seeing nothing at first, then a smile broke out on his face as he spotted what his underling had discovered.

A private security camera, angled so that it would catch anyone walking in front of the store's door.

And anyone approaching the garage door that stood beside him.

Outside Tambov, Russian Federation

Acton groaned then bolted awake as something kicked him in the ass.

"Hey, what the hell?"

"Up you lazy American. Don't make me believe the propaganda about your people."

Acton threw his pillow at Zorkin, the old man easily catching it, his reflexes still good.

Laura moaned. "I'm British."

Zorkin tossed the pillow back at Acton. "Bah! You *don't* want to know what they said about *you*!"

Zorkin left and Acton leaned over to give his wife a kiss, instead crying out in pain, his back spasming. He dropped back down, driving a handful of knuckles into the small of his back. "I can't believe how sore I am."

Laura rolled him over and straddled him from behind, working her thumbs and heels of her hands into his back, he moaning in pain and pleasure. "God only knows how many more hours—or days—we're going to have to spend underneath that truck."

"Ugh, don't remind me." He reached back with one hand and gently swatted her away. "That's good, let me see if I can stand up." She jumped off him, apparently none the worse for wear, the few years of youth she had over him apparently working wonders.

"Come on, old man," she laughed, dragging him to his feet. "Look!" She pointed at two stacks of neatly folded clothes. She picked up the pile of women's clothes, holding up a pair of slacks. "They're even in our sizes."

Darya walked into the room carrying a tub of hot water, Acton grabbing the pillow and covering what was now Laura's exclusive domain. She pointed at the pillow then the water. "You wash." She tossed her head back and roared in laughter as she waddled out of the room, Laura grinning. She closed the door, Acton tossing the pillow aside. A bar of soap floated in the water, several clean towels already sitting beside the piles of clothes.

Acton began a quick bird bath, Laura joining him. "I feel like I'm at a dig."

Laura laughed. "I thought we were supposed to be pampering ourselves this week."

"I guess not."

Laura gasped, her eyes wide as she turned to her husband. "Oh my God, Greg and Sandra must be worried sick about us by now!"

Acton continued to wash, working out some road grit from the nether regions he had missed last night. "We did say we might be a couple of days and not to expect a call because of the hush-hush nature of things."

"True."

Acton grinned. "He's been feeling pretty good lately, maybe they won't even notice we're gone."

Laura eyed down below. "He *has* been acting a little frisky lately…"

Acton turned his midsection away from her slightly. "Don't get any ideas. There's no locks on these doors and we're in a hurry." He sniffed. "Oh God, is that meat candy I smell?"

Laura drew a breath through her nose. "If your American bastardization of a perfectly good language my people invented is meant to suggest bacon, then yes, I believe it is."

Acton gave her a toothy grin. "Sex is out. Bacon is in."

She laughed and they quickly finished washing and getting dressed, Zorkin giving them a displeased look from the table, Vitaly giving a friendly wave as he ate. "You two took your time." He dropped his head slightly and gave them a look. "You two didn't sneak in a little, you know, private time?"

Laura flushed and Acton chuckled as they sat at the table, a generous breakfast slid in front of them. "Jealous?"

Zorkin laughed. "I outlived my little guy. He died an ignominious death years ago."

Laura stifled a giggle, Acton shaking his head. "They've got pills for that now," he mumbled through a mouthful of bacon and eggs.

"Bah!" Zorkin swatted the air. "You need someone to share it with, and an old dried up spy doesn't have much to offer a good woman." He raised a finger to cut Acton off from the obvious retort. "And I don't go for bad women."

Laura leaned over and patted him on the leg. "You're a good man."

Zorkin grinned at her. "Careful, we don't want to test my claim."

She laughed and gave his leg a squeeze before tucking into her breakfast, their plates cleaned within minutes.

"When do we leave?" asked Acton, shoveling in a second helping.

"Now."

Acton glanced out the window, barely a sliver of sunlight in the east. "Jesus, even the early birds aren't threatening any worms."

Zorkin grunted, standing up, signaling the end of the meal. Acton grabbed the bacon off his plate with his fingers, Laura giving him a look. He gave her a "whatcha gonna do" shrug.

"Trust me, the more distance we travel before the sun comes out, the better off you'll be. It's going to be scorching hot in your hiding place." Zorkin pointed at a box of water bottles as Acton shoved the last piece of bacon in his mouth, glancing about for a paper towel.

Darya whipped a tea towel at him.

"Thank you," he mumbled, his mouth full. He swallowed, wiping his mouth and hands. "At least this time we won't go thirsty."

"Or hungry?" prompted Laura. The old lady lifted three bags that looked heavy, handing one to each of them. Laura gave her a hug and kiss on each cheek. "Thank you so much, you've been such a dear."

"You welcome, you welcome," said the woman, her husband exchanging handshakes.

Zorkin opened the door. "Enough of the love in. Let's move before they find us."

Nikolskaya Street, Moscow, Russian Federation

"There!"

Dymovsky pointed at the tiny monitor, the variety store's owner standing in the corner, biting his nails as Filippov operated the computer. A van pulled up on the screen, coming to a halt in front of the garage door before it opened, then disappeared inside, the door immediately slamming shut.

"Back it up and see if you can get a clear image of the driver."

Filippov reversed the video and froze it, a shot of the driver doing a shoulder check giving them a perfect view.

Dymovsky smiled. "Get that to headquarters. I want to know who he is."

Filippov shook his head. "No need, sir. I already know who he is."

Dymovsky's eyes narrowed. "You do?"

"Yes, sir. That's Viktor Zorkin. I'd recognize him anywhere. He's a legend!"

"In what?"

"The KGB, sir. I read a profile on him. He was one of our greatest spies during the Cold War. He retired a Hero of the Soviet Union."

Dymovsky grunted. "It would appear he's switched sides." His phone vibrated in his pocket and he grabbed it. "Da?"

"Sir, this is Polzin at HQ. We've found them!"

"Just a moment." Dymovsky stepped back, pointing at the screen. "Get that to HQ anyway, I want it on the record. And see what kind of vehicle they left in. Something big was in that garage." Filippov nodded as Dymovsky stepped outside. "Go ahead."

"You were right, sir. They *did* buy new phones."

Dymovsky smiled.

I love it when I'm right.

"We've got footage showing them going into a repair shop then leaving a few minutes later with a bag. We traced the shop owner and were able to confirm the type of prepaid phones purchased. We contacted the company and they provided a list of all the activations made after the purchase time."

You have to love not needing pesky things like warrants.

"How many?"

"Hundreds within an hour, but only three were made all at the same time, all pinging off cellphone towers within the store's area, and the only ones still all together."

Dymovsky smiled. "Where are they?"

"Just outside Tambov. About six hours south of Moscow."

Got you!

"Get me a chopper."

Operations Center 3, CIA Headquarters, Langley, Virginia

"Sir, we've got a problem."

Leroux jerked awake, his head bobbing up from its momentary perch on his chest. He looked at Tong who appeared aghast at having woken him. "What?"

"Someone just pinged all three cellphones."

Leroux leapt from his chair, pointing at the screen, Tong immediately streaming the data to the large displays. "Origin?"

"Moscow."

"All three?"

"Yes, sir. One after the other."

Leroux cursed. "They've found them." He stared at the still stationary dots, all one atop the other. "Why aren't they moving!"

"It's a safe bet the Russians are on their way." Child's eyebrows rose. "Maybe they left them there?"

Leroux shook his head. "No, if they did we would have been contacted with their new contact information. They know they need to be tracked in order for us to help them. They just don't realize they're also being tracked by the wrong people."

"Sir!"

Leroux looked at Tong then where she was pointing.

The blips were moving.

"Christ, that means they still have them." Child slammed his fist on his console. "We have to warn them."

"Agreed." Leroux turned to Child who cut him off, his fingers flying over the keyboard.

"Don't worry, I've already been working on it. I'll bounce the call over several dozen relays. They'll never be able to trace it, at least not until it's too late."

Leroux smiled. "Do it."

Outside Tambov, Russian Federation

Acton shifted his hips slightly to the left, beginning to wonder if he shouldn't have tried lying on his stomach instead. At least this time he had a pillow under his head and a thick blanket underneath, protecting him from much of the road grime.

The several bottles of water and generous helping of snacks within hand's reach were also going to make this trip far better than last night's ordeal. The sun was barely up, enough to give them some light, though if Zorkin was right, by this afternoon he'd be cursing what he now appreciated.

Fourteen hours to the border.

"I have a new appreciation of what it meant to be a spy in the old days."

Laura squeezed his hand. "Try and get some sleep. That's what I'm going to do."

"Hon, if you can sleep in here, you've got a waaay more comfortable spot than I do."

"It's not so bad once you get used to it."

"There's no—" Acton's burner phone vibrated in his pocket. "What the hell?"

"What is it?"

"My phone." He fished it out, fumbling with it in the cramped space, almost dropping it before he got it on his chest then flipped open. "Hello?"

"Professor, destroy all your phones immediately. They've traced your current location."

The call ended and Acton stared at the phone for a moment before slamming a fist on the side of the truck. It jerked to a halt, they not even having cleared the dirt road leading to the farm.

"What is it?" asked Laura as Zorkin's door opened.

"What's wrong?" asked the old man. "Don't tell me you have to go to the bathroom!"

"I just got a call from someone. They said they've traced us to this location, and we need to destroy our phones."

"Quickly! Quickly!" shouted Zorkin. "Remove the batteries and give them to me!" The rear gate opened and the truck shifted as Zorkin climbed in, the sound of him struggling over the boxes mixed with occasional curses going unnoticed as Acton tore apart the phone, the others beginning to do the same.

A board just over his head, near the cab of the truck, suddenly lifted. Zorkin's hand reached in. "Give it to me." Acton handed him the phone through the small opening, Laura passing hers then Vitaly's. Snapping sounds overhead indicated Zorkin's preferred method of disabling the devices. "Wait here."

The board was replaced, Zorkin climbing out the back, the sounds of him running down the lane, shouting something in Russian, quickly fading to nothing.

"What do you think they'll do with them?" asked Laura, the concern in her voice for the elderly couple obvious.

"I'm afraid to even think about it, but it won't be good."

South of Moscow, Russian Federation

"The signals have gone dead, sir."

Dymovsky glanced at Filippov as he turned the laptop to face him. "When?"

"Just now, sir. They started to move, another tower picked them up then the signals went dead."

Dymovsky frowned. "They must have figured out we were tracking them."

Filippov's eyes narrowed. "That doesn't make sense. How could they know that? I mean, how could they know that *now*. If they were concerned about it, they would have got rid of those phones long ago."

Dymovsky agreed, his junior partner correct. It did make no sense. "They must have detected our pinging their phones."

"Two archaeologists? There's no way they could figure that out."

Dymovsky pulled out his phone, dialing headquarters. "This is Dymovsky. Has the mechanic talked yet?"

"No, sir. I was just about to call you. The interrogator is requesting permission to escalate."

A vision of the old man, beaten to a pulp, flashed before his eyes.

Use whatever means necessary.

Moscow would condone it, of that he had no doubt.

Though his soul wouldn't.

"Negative. We know everything he knows already. They were at his garage, brought there by Zorkin, and they left in a delivery truck that is now outside Tambov. We'll pick up the trail there." He hung up, turning to

153

Filippov. "What concerns me more is how they knew to destroy their new phones. They must have help."

"They have Zorkin."

Dymovsky nodded. "Yes, but he should know better. Why would he leave those phones on?"

"He's old, sir. He probably just screwed up."

Dymovsky peered out the window of the chopper. "Possibly. But I doubt it."

Westbound E-38 Highway, Russian Federation

The whine of the engine was almost overwhelming, conversation no longer possible. It was clear that Zorkin was pushing the vehicle to its limits as they tried to put as much distance between them and the farm as they could. Zorkin had said nothing upon his return except to keep quiet, their journey immediately resumed.

I hope the old couple get away.

He frowned. But where would they go? He and Laura had the CIA's best helping them. Who would help an old Russian couple? From the looks of things they had little to no money, the daylight revealing what was at best a subsistence farm.

If something happens to them, it's our fault.

His stomach suddenly churned, his mouth filling with bile.

He said a silent prayer.

The truck abruptly ground to a near halt before jerking hard to the right, sending Acton slamming against the side of his mobile coffin. He cursed, slightly miffed that Zorkin wasn't taking things a little more gently.

Maybe I should drive for a while so he can see what it's like under here.

They came to a stop, the engine shutting off and the door opening. "Everybody out!" shouted Zorkin, the sound of the rear gate dropping moments later then boxes being moved overhead adding to the confusion.

"What's going on?" asked Acton, the first board pried out of the way, Zorkin's red face revealed.

"We're switching vehicles."

He reached down and pulled Acton upright before climbing down to the ground, leaving Acton to move the rest of the boxes, Laura and Vitaly soon joining Zorkin behind the truck. Acton looked about, it a barren piece of road, not a vehicle or sign of civilization in sight beyond the asphalt.

"I don't see anyone," said Laura.

"They'll be here."

Acton held a hand up to shield his eyes, staring down the road, seeing nothing. "Should we be exposed like this? I thought they knew our faces?"

"They do, but they know this truck by now." Zorkin suddenly pulled a gun from his belt and pistol-whipped Vitaly, the young man dropping to the ground in a heap, crying out in pain as his hand darted to a bloody tear in his cheek. Laura cried out, rushing to the young man's aid as Acton stepped forward and expertly disarmed Zorkin with a move taught him by Laura's former SAS security team.

He kicked the weapon aside and gripped their supposed friend by the shirt.

Zorkin smiled. "Very good. Textbook. But thirty years ago I would have stabbed you with this." Acton followed the man's eyes down to see a knife pressed against his ribs." Acton eased his grip. "Why the hell did you hit him!"

"To save his life."

Acton had to admit that wasn't the answer he was expecting. "Huh?"

Zorkin gently pushed Acton's hands away then knelt beside the young man, tears in Orlov's son's eyes. Laura glared at Zorkin, though said nothing. Zorkin pushed Vitaly's head to the side, examining the wound. "Good. It looks real."

"Because it is real, you bloody lunatic!"

Zorkin chuckled at Laura's outburst, but kept his eyes on the boy. "Listen, this is your story. You picked up the professors at the airport because your father told you to. Then you saw them outside the hotel and asked them if they still wanted a ride, not knowing what was going on because your father had sent you to get the car to take them back to the airport. They instead told you to take them to the parking garage. You did so because you didn't know anything was wrong." Acton began to relax as the yarn to save the boy was laid out. "You then showed them where to buy new phones, then you were picked up by me. I forced you into my van at gunpoint. We went to the garage then to the farmhouse. I told you that if you said anything I'd shoot you and your family. We arrived here, I ordered you out then I pistol-whipped you. You woke up, found the keys to the truck in your hand, and headed back to Moscow to turn yourself in."

Zorkin pulled Vitaly to his feet, the boy's eyes still watering, the sniffling subsiding as the fear of the moment slowly dissipated. "I-I'm going back to Moscow?"

Zorkin nodded. "Yes. Your part here is finished. You need to get back and turn yourself in at the Prosecutor-General's Office. They're probably the ones trying to track us." He raised a finger. "But I want you to obey the speed limits! Don't attract any unnecessary attention. The longer it takes for you to get there, the better. Don't do anything suspicious like drive too slow. Just be natural. But, if you're pulled over or encounter a checkpoint, you tell them your story."

"And what do I tell them?"

"Exactly what I just told you to tell them."

"And if they ask where you're going?"

"You don't know."

"I don't know."

"Exactly. So you'll be telling them the truth."

Acton handed a handkerchief to Vitaly. "Press this against the wound. You need to stop the bleeding then clean yourself up. You'll stick out like a sore thumb if you have to pull over for gas or anything."

Vitaly pressed the handkerchief against the wound, wincing. He looked back at Zorkin. "But I *do* know."

Acton froze, exchanging a quick glance with Laura.

"What do you mean?" asked Zorkin.

Vitaly motioned toward a sign just ahead indicating the highway number and direction. "We're heading west, toward the Ukraine I guess."

Zorkin leaned in, raising a finger. "You *can't* tell them that. Under *any* circumstances."

Vitaly's eyes bulged with fear. "I-I won't."

"Good." Zorkin handed him some cash. "For gas and food along the way." He shook Vitaly's hand. "Good luck, young man."

Acton shook Vitaly's trembling hand, Laura giving him a hug.

You're going to need it.

Outside Tambov, Russian Federation

Dymovsky watched out the window of the helicopter as the door to the humble farmhouse opened, an elderly couple stepping out onto their porch, no hint of fear evident, despite the advance team already searching the property. They shielded their eyes from the dust, Dymovsky watching a milking pail bounce across the property, slamming into the side of their weathered abode.

The door slid open and he stepped down, crouching under the blades as he walked toward them, Filippov slightly behind him, the pilot powering down. Dymovsky pulled out his ID, showing it to the old couple.

"I am Agent Dymovsky from the Prosecutor-General's Office. I believe you know why I'm here."

The old woman glanced at her husband, a slight hint of concern momentarily visible. It was gone before she looked back. She motioned toward the door. "Please come in. I just put tea on."

Dymovsky paused for a moment then nodded. He was exhausted, and a cup of tea might be just what he needed. And if it put them more at ease, it might loosen their tongues.

Filippov seemed shocked at the offer's acceptance, though wisely said nothing.

The old lady motioned toward two chairs in the kitchen.

"Thank you." Dymovsky sat, Filippov at his side. He sniffed, the smell of fresh biscuits filling the air, the golden brown bits of heaven sitting in a basket, nestled in a red and white checkered tea towel.

His empty stomach growled.

The old lady turned into the hostess he had no doubt she regularly was. "You look hungry." She grabbed the basket and put it in front of them followed by a block of butter and two knives. "Eat."

Dymovsky smiled, grabbing a biscuit as his tea was poured. "Thank you. I haven't had anything since yesterday."

Filippov overcame his reluctance and he eagerly slathered butter on his own, it instantly melting, soaking into the steaming biscuit. Dymovsky smothered his own then took a bite, the warm creation melting in his mouth.

He moaned.

"This, ma'am, is the best biscuit I think I've ever tasted." He took another bite, savoring it, a slow chew allowing him to enjoy all the sensations this woman's hand had created. "I'll deny this if you ever repeat it, but I think this is better than my mom used to make."

The old woman was blushing at the compliments, her husband saying nothing, instead sitting expressionless across from them, his tea untouched. "Please, I'm sure your mother's are delicious."

"They are," smiled Dymovsky, tapping the table. "But yours are *here*." He finished his last bite then wiped his mouth with the back of his hand, downing his tea. "Incredible," he said as he put his cup down. "Now, down to business. Viktor Zorkin was here earlier with an American professor and his British wife, along with a Russian citizen named Vitaly Orlov. Don't bother denying it, we know it to be true."

The old man finally spoke. "It is."

Dymovsky managed to hide his surprise at the easy admission. "You let them stay?"

"Of course. Viktor is an old friend. He was travelling through the area with friends and needed a place to stay." The man finally took a sip of his tea. "Wouldn't you invite a friend in need to stay the night?"

"He was in need?"

"Of a place to rest. He was delivering something and picked up the others on the way here."

"He picked them up."

"Yes, that's what he said. Where they were going was on his way."

"Did he say where?"

The old man made a face. "Donets'k, I think."

Dymovsky glanced at Filippov. "That's near the Ukrainian border." He looked back at the old man. "Why would they be going there?"

The old man shrugged. "You'd have to ask them that."

"I intend to." Dymovsky rose. "You'll be taken to Moscow for questioning as soon as a transport unit arrives."

This elicited the first emotion out of the man. "But who will take care of the animals?"

"Animals?"

"This is a farm! Our eldest son was killed in Afghanistan, our youngest in Chechnya. We're all that's left."

Dymovsky frowned, peering out the window at the barn. "Call a neighbor, tell them to tend your farm while you're away."

"H-how long will we be gone?" asked the wife.

Dymovsky regarded her, truly feeling for them. "I wish I could tell you."

Perhaps forever.

E-38 Highway, Russian Federation

"Someone's coming!"

Laura gripped her husband's hand tightly as two cars raced toward them, the first they had seen since Vitaly had left with the truck a few minutes before. She was tired and sore, her entire body aching, though she wouldn't let James know, he too much of a worrier when it came to her.

They were both in misery.

And he didn't need to share in hers.

As the cars rushed toward them, Zorkin didn't seem concerned, though it was clear from the grip her husband was returning, he was. And so was she. Three people, standing on the side of the road in the middle of nowhere, matching the descriptions of wanted criminals, had to be a major red flag to any law enforcement that might happen by.

And still, Zorkin seemed unconcerned.

I just want to get home. Forget the beach, forget the sun, take me home to Maryland.

She smiled slightly at the thought.

Home. Maryland.

If someone had asked her five years ago if she thought she'd be calling Maryland, home, she'd have called them daft. London was her home. Always had been, always would be.

Then James entered her life.

In a whirlwind of guns, knives, fists and explosions.

And her life had never been the same.

Her scar throbbed for a moment and she ran her free hand over it, tracing the outline under her shirt with her finger.

Not all the changes were good.

They had been talking starting a family when she had been shot, the damage inflicted by the bullet eliminating any hope of a future child.

At least their own biological child.

Her chest tightened.

The cars began to slow and Zorkin showed his first sign of potential concern as he reached behind his back and gripped his weapon.

I wish there were enough to go around.

She was an excellent shot, James an exceptional one. Her money and their brief history had forced her to hire a security team for their dig sites. The head of the detail was ex-British Special Air Service, an incredibly dedicated former soldier who she felt completely safe with when James wasn't with her. He and his men had agreed to train them in all manners of combat. Initially it had just been self-defense, but as their encounters became more violent, it was clear they needed to know how to shoot and kill.

And they were good at it.

Not as good as their detail, definitely not as good as the razor sharp Delta operators they had come to know, though still quite capable in a firefight.

Zorkin pulled his gun out slightly.

Another firefight?

The two cars drove past them, the occupants staring at them, Laura's heart in her throat, James' hand gripping hers a little tighter.

Then they pulled U-turns, coming to a stop in front of them.

She suddenly felt the urge to pee.

The lone occupant of the first car stepped out, saying nothing, instead simply getting in the back of the second car, his left idling.

Wheels chirped and the second car raced away.

Nothing said.

Nothing exchanged.

Except a dusty vehicle that looked deliciously comfortable.

A four-door sedan.

"Who were they?" she asked.

Zorkin shrugged. "I don't know. But more importantly, they don't know who we are."

James' eyes narrowed. "Then how'd they know we'd be here."

Zorkin gave him a bemused look. "You've never watched a spy movie before? This is how things are done."

James grunted. "What, conveniently?"

Zorkin laughed, reaching inside and popping the trunk. "No, well-coordinated and compartmentalized."

They stepped over to the trunk and James whistled. "What the hell is that?"

Zorkin grinned. "Our newest partner."

South Kuril Islands, Russian Federation
Japanese name: Chishima Islands

"Sir, another vessel is approaching from the east."

Captain Yamada rose, stepping over to the port side of the bridge and raising his binoculars. Their damage from the previous collision was as expected—minor. Scraped paint, a torn anchor housing, nothing more.

Nothing that would take them out of the fight.

Should that be what was to come.

He sometimes wondered what it must have been like to serve in the navy of the Empire. When the war started, it was the most powerful fleet in the world, Japan the fifth most populous country and the economic powerhouse of Asia.

Now it was a shadow of its former self.

He understood why. What his country had done was shameful, an ego driven bloodlust that had the mighty empire trying to save Asians from themselves, from their adoption of Western ways.

They had hoped to become the counterbalance to the growing influence of American, British and Russian meddling in the region, China and the Philippines two prime examples of what could go wrong—one a puppet empire, the other under the thumb of the Americans.

At least they were benevolent.

Though superior.

The new Japanese way was to be apologetic, inferior, self-deprecating, and he wasn't a fan of it. Manners and civility had always been hallmarks of his country, but the shame it felt, seventy years later, was uncalled for. There was a bit of an awakening, what with the military finally engaging

165

beyond its territory in peacekeeping operations, yet with an ever-belligerent China, not to mention the crazed lunacy of North Korea, Japan had to expand its military so that it could truly defend itself. The United States had promised to defend it against any and all enemies, but could they truly be counted on anymore? The ongoing disasters in the Middle East, the ever-increasing aggression by China in the South China Sea, unchallenged Russian aggression in the Ukraine—all of these showed that America was no longer willing to be the world's policeman.

Which was fine by him. It shouldn't have to be.

But let us defend ourselves!

Their constitution, adopted after the war under the guidance of the American occupiers, restricted their military in so many ways, they would be able to put up a token defense at best should something happen.

Like today.

They had a dozen ships setting up the blockade, separating the North and South Kuril Islands, as the Russians called them. Islands that were traditionally Japanese, once with over 17,000 citizens living on them.

Now they were a constant insult, Russian forces stationed far too close to Japan, on land they had stolen in the dying moments of his nation's folly.

The sad part was that now, the dozen ships here today, were nearly a quarter of the Japanese once mighty navy. The Russians only had half a dozen to counter them, sitting three nautical miles to the north, though more were on the way, and many more would be joining them.

They wouldn't be winning this if it came to a firefight.

"It's American, sir! The USS Shiloh. Part of Carrier Strike Group Five." His XO smiled. "Their captain wants to speak to you."

Yamada suppressed his emotions, instead crisply taking the comm. "This is Captain Yamada of the JDS Atago. Identify yourself and your intentions, over."

An American drawl responded. "This is Captain Shephard of the USS Shiloh. We are under orders to act as mediators in this situation, over."

Yamada frowned. "There is nothing to mediate, Captain. This is Japanese territory and we intend to defend it, over."

"Captain Yamada, are you prepared to die for it? Sir, I'm not sure if you're aware of this, but every ship in the Russian Pacific Fleet is heading in your direction, including their submarine fleet. You *will not* win this fight." There was a pause. "At least not without help."

"Your help?"

"If you'll have it."

Yamada drew a deep breath. "I'll have to confer with my superiors."

"You do that. In the meantime, we're just going to park ourselves riiight over here."

Yamada smiled slightly as he watched the USS Shiloh slow, taking up a position between the two navies.

Broadside.

His XO grunted. "He's got balls, I'll give him that."

E-391 Southbound, Russian Federation

"You're heading south."

Zorkin nodded. "Yes."

Acton's eyes narrowed. "But I thought we were heading west?"

"No, that's what you were meant to think."

"Huh?"

"Young Vitaly thinks we are heading west. So do our hosts from last night. Right now everyone honestly believes we are heading west, and the vehicle we were in is actually heading north, back to Moscow."

"Huh." Acton nodded slightly. "It was all a ruse to mislead them if they were interrogated."

"Exactly."

"Clever. Except that the people who delivered this car know we're not heading west."

Zorkin shook his head. "No, all they know is they delivered a car. They have no idea where we're going. We should be safe until the next checkpoint, and fortunately there are none before the border, unless something special has been set up."

"And wouldn't there be?"

"Not if everyone thinks we're heading west."

"And if you're wrong and there is a checkpoint?" asked Laura, leaning forward between the seats, Zorkin insisting Acton sit up front, it appearing more natural to anyone who might cross their paths.

Zorkin glanced at her in the rearview mirror. "Then, my dear, we avoid it."

Acton waved the tablet showing footage from their new partner, a small drone with transmission capability. Footage from its camera was streaming to the tablet showing the road ahead. "Who's flying this thing?"

"It's automatic. Tied to the device. I've set it to keep one kilometer ahead of us, so just keep your eyes on that screen and the moment you see something, you let me know so we can stop."

Acton grinned. "This is so cool! I had no idea this type of spy tech existed. Where'd they get it?"

"Probably the same place I'd get it."

"Where's that?"

"eBay."

Narita International Airport, Tokyo, Japan

"Don't tell them what we're looking for unless it becomes absolutely necessary."

Sasaki bowed slightly in acknowledgement of his final instructions from Minister of Foreign Affairs Yamazaki. "Understood." He paused. "How far are we willing to go?"

Yamazaki lowered his voice. "The Prime Minister has ordered troops and vessels into the area. Troops are landing on the unoccupied islands as we speak. At the moment we're avoiding direct contact with Russian installations."

Sasaki's eyes widened slightly. "He's escalating the situation while sending me to Moscow to de-escalate it?"

"He's strengthening your hand. And your job is not to de-escalate, it's to retrieve the Imperial Regalia, no matter what. You must convince them that we are prepared to fight to have our property returned, and they need to realize that the cost may be too high, as the Imperial Regalia are of no importance to them."

Sasaki frowned. "I fear the cost may be too high for us, as well."

"That is not for us to debate. We have our instructions. You must succeed, otherwise there *will* be war."

"Will we return the islands if they return our property?"

Yamazaki frowned, leaning closer so only Sasaki could hear. "I have been told, no, however I sensed hesitation when I was briefed. *Intentional* hesitation. Should that be what you must promise, then do so. I'll make it work. Somehow."

Operations Center 3, CIA Headquarters, Langley, Virginia

"Sir, we've got a message from Special Agent Kane."

Leroux breathed a sigh of relief. Nearly ten hours had passed since they had heard anything, the phones the professors had used no longer transmitting, and the only progress—if it could be called that—was satellite footage showing a brief helicopter visit to the farmhouse the professors had stayed at overnight.

And nothing since.

They hadn't been able to find the truck on any routes heading south or west, east and north having been ruled out. The only good thing was there were no reports of them having been captured, so they were still out there, somewhere, fleeing for their lives.

And at this moment, there was absolutely nothing they could do to help them.

Though hopefully Kane was about to change all that.

He rose, walking over to Child's console. "What is it?"

Child's eyebrows rose slightly. "It's just an IP address."

"Bring it up."

Child's fingers tapped at the keyboard, a video feed appearing on his console. "Huh, what's this?"

Leroux pointed at the main screen. "Put it up." An overhead shot of a road cutting through a fairly unremarkable landscape appeared. "What the hell am I looking at?"

"Drone footage?" suggested Tong. "It would be about the right height."

"Get me a location on this."

Child worked his magic, the map of Russia showing the last known location of the professors—the farmhouse—updating to show a new red dot. "Southern Russia. It must be them."

Leroux watched the footage for a few moments. "Can anyone see them?"

A chorus of negatives.

"Okay, they're heading south from their last known location, and they're significantly south. That means we can now rule out the Ukraine."

"Whoever's flying that thing has a pretty steady hand," commented Child. "I mean, look at that. It's flying nearly perfectly straight and level."

Leroux smiled. "It's tethered."

"Cool!" Tong blushed, dropping her chin slightly. "They must have it set to travel ahead of them so they can see any roadblocks."

Leroux smiled. "Smart."

Child grunted with appreciation. "Huh, I guess you *can* teach an old dog new tricks."

Northbound M-6 Highway, Russian Federation

Vitaly's first instinct was to slam the brakes on and turn around, but that would be useless.

You can't outrun a radio.

Besides, it would go against Zorkin's instructions. He had managed to travel all morning and afternoon without encountering a checkpoint or any other unwanted attention. He could honestly say he had had no opportunity to ask for help from the authorities.

Until now.

He slowly came to a halt behind a long line of vehicles, his mind reeling with what to do. He closed his eyes, trying to calm his slamming heart, the blood rushing in his ears as sweat rolled down his back.

What should I do?

He opened his eyes, staring at the checkpoint ahead.

You do what you were told!

He blanked, closing his eyes once again.

What was I told?

He sucked in a long, slow breath.

Turn yourself in.

He sighed, opening his eyes slightly, the line of vehicles still not having moved.

Okay, how do I do that?

His thumbs tapped on the steering wheel.

You don't sit in a truck and patiently wait. Move!

He turned the truck off and jumped out, rushing toward the checkpoint ahead, waving his arms in the air. "Help me! Help me!"

Officers spun toward him, heads leaned out car windows, and guns aimed at him.

He stopped.

Several guards charged toward him, shouting at him to get on the ground. He complied, just as he imagined an innocent person would. As he was cuffed, he turned his head and made eye contact with the man who seemed to be in charge. "Please, you've got to help me. I was kidnapped and held at gunpoint!"

"Sir, it's him!" One of the officers standing nearby waved a piece of paper, Vitaly's driving license photo briefly visible as the page twisted in the wind.

The man in charge stepped forward as Vitaly was hauled to his feet. "Vitaly Orlov, you are under arrest."

"But I'm innocent!" he cried. "I did nothing wrong!" This wasn't the way it was supposed to happen. He was supposed to tell them the story and everything would be okay.

But nobody had said what to do if he never got a chance to actually *tell* his story.

Panic began to set in, his heart slamming even harder, his vision beginning to blur as his breathing grew more rapid.

I have to get out of here!

He wrenched at the iron grips holding his arms and was rewarded for his efforts.

With a rifle butt to the face.

Security Station, Kashira, Russian Federation

"Who did this?"

Dymovsky shook his head as he entered the interrogation room, his suspect bloody and whimpering, it clear he had taken a beating.

"He says the man who abducted him did it."

Dymovsky stepped toward the young man, tilting his swollen face back to get a better view. "These wounds are fresh." He turned the man's face to the left. "And that looks like the butt of an AK-74." He glared at the commander of the checkpoint. "Now how am I supposed to know the truth when the first thing out of your mouth is a lie?" He held up a finger, cutting off the forthcoming reply. "I'm done with you. Leave and get me your second-in-command."

The man flushed, anger raging across his face, though he didn't dare talk back to someone from the Prosecutor-General's Office.

It could be a career ender.

The man stormed out of the room, getting the last word in with a slam of the door.

Dymovsky didn't care.

He sat at the table, across from young Vitaly and retrieved a handkerchief from his pocket, sliding it across to the young man. "I'm sorry for what they did to you." The boy said nothing, the handkerchief left untouched. "Now, why don't you tell me what really happened. And I promise you, if you tell me the truth, no one will lay a finger on you again."

Vitaly looked up at him, trembling, still saying nothing.

Dymovsky leaned forward, his voice gentle. "You have my word."

A cathartic sob erupted then a story spilled, so fantastic, so full of bullshit, it had to be the truth. Sort of. He had no doubt the story had been fed to him by Zorkin, any former member of the KGB a master at deception, and he had no doubt the young man had rehearsed his story for hours while driving here.

But despite being well told, it was bullshit.

It's the eyes.

You could always tell from the eyes. At least with the amateurs, which this kid clearly was. He thought he was helping his father, so he could be forgiven for what he had done.

Though Moscow likely wouldn't.

Dymovsky kept his voice gentle. "Listen, son, you and I both know that almost everything you just told me was a lie. If you insist on continuing with the lie, it's your choice, but I must warn you, Moscow won't be as forgiving as I am. You were with the professors and Mr. Zorkin. This we know. You've even admitted to it. Let's ignore whether or not you were there voluntarily. You then separated. Again, let's ignore whether or not that was done voluntarily." He leaned forward, staring into the young man's eyes. "All I want to know is where they were headed."

Vitaly's breathing grew more rapid, his eyes darting to the left, then staring at the door—anywhere but his interrogator.

"Tell me and this is all over."

Vitaly gasped. "I-I don't know."

Dymovsky smiled. "I can hear it in your voice." He took the untouched handkerchief and pushed it against one of the open gashes on the boy's face.

Vitaly winced, tears filling his eyes.

"Son, if you react to that little bit of pain, you won't survive the hell Moscow will put you through. Now tell me. Your friends will never know it was you. And besides, I already know the answer, you'll just be confirming it."

This elicited a response, Vitaly's eyes darting toward him for a moment. "H-how?"

"You remember Boris and Darya, your hosts from last night?"

"A-are they okay?"

Dymovsky smiled. This was a good boy, mixed up in something bigger than he could have possibly imagined. "Yes, of course they are. We're not Chechens. In fact, I enjoyed delicious homemade biscuits with them this morning. And a cup of tea." Dymovsky winked at him. "She's a good cook, isn't she?"

Vitaly shook out a nod, a hint of a smile appearing for a flicker of a moment.

"Now, think of it this way. *They* betrayed you. Zorkin and the professors left *you* to be captured. Left *you* to be tortured. What do you owe them? Nothing. Help me and I can help your father."

The boy's eyes widened slightly, his head lifting at the mention of his father.

There's the key.

"Th-they were heading west. On the E-38."

Dymovsky smiled.

"There, was that so hard?"

Approaching Italian Airspace

"I think I'm getting spoiled."

Dawson glanced over at Niner, the rattle of the C130J Hercules causing everyone to shout. There had been a delay in getting off the ground and they were just now finally reaching Italy, the last update from Langley suggesting they were still not confident enough to project a final destination.

"Why's that?" asked Atlas.

"After travelling on Palmer's private jet, this thing is just damned criminal."

Spock agreed. "Cruel and unusual."

"Yeah, I mean, with the amount of money our government has invested in us, the least they could do is cushion our delicate behinds."

Atlas leaned back, closing his eyes. "Maybe if you weren't so obsessed with skin care products, that ass of yours wouldn't be so soft."

"Hey, I'll have you know that taking care of one's skin and performing a little manscaping now and then is a perfectly acceptable use of a real man's time." Niner pointed at Atlas' crotch. "And that friggin' forest could use some attention."

"I knew you were looking."

"Hey, don't judge me. You checked me out for the same reason."

Spock cocked an eyebrow. "Umm, and why was that?"

"To test the stereotype. Happy to say I feel more confident in knowing it's not true."

Atlas grunted. "Don't worry, it was in your case."

A round of "oohs" followed.

Niner laughed. "It's not the length of the sword, it's the fury of the attack."

Atlas' head lolled to the side, winking at Dawson. "I think a challenged man came up with that one."

Dawson chuckled. "So, things better with Vanessa?"

Atlas nodded. "I think so. At least I didn't get all the usual complaining this time when I told her I had to leave."

"That's good. Do you think she can keep it to herself?"

Atlas sighed. "God, I hope so. I'd hate to have to kill her." A round of laughter erupted. "In all seriousness, I told her to call Maggie or one of the other wives if she was having trouble."

Spock leaned forward. "I remember when I told Joanne. Man, she was shocked, but relieved. She knew I had been lying about something. She told me that she'd thought I was cheating on her or something, or just wasn't committed to the relationship. I think it came as a relief that *all* I had been hiding was being in the Unit."

Niner gave an exaggerated sigh, staring up at the fuselage. "Ahh, yes, I wonder what it will be like when I let Olivia Wilde know that the man she desperately loves is a superhero."

Atlas grunted. "Isn't she like two feet taller than you?"

Niner whipped an apple from his box lunch at him. Atlas caught it and took a bite. "Thanks. I'm a little peckish."

Dawson's comm beeped in his ear and he held up a finger, cutting off the conversation. "This is Zero-One, go ahead Control."

"Zero-One, it looks like they're heading south. Redirect to Turkey, Diyarbakir Airbase."

"Roger that."

Dawson rose to tell the pilot. "Looks like we're heading for Turkey, boys."

Maggie Harris Residence, Lake in the Pines Apartments, Fayetteville, North Carolina

"I'll never forget the day Will told me," said Spock's wife Joanne. "I think he was convinced I thought he was cheating on me. Really, I just knew there was some part of him that he was keeping hidden from me and I wanted in. Once I realized what was actually going on, I really felt he was committed to the relationship."

Heads bobbed among the women gathered. Shirley, wife of Dawson's closest friend Master Sergeant Mike "Red" Belme, leaned toward Vanessa. "You know, that's the most important thing to take from all this."

Vanessa put her glass of wine down. "What do you mean?"

"If he felt he could tell you the truth then that means he's committed to the relationship." She flicked a wrist at her. "Girl, you've got him locked up!"

Squeals.

Vanessa smiled awkwardly. "I guess so. I never thought of it that way." She reached for her glass then stopped, leaning back. "I knew he was lying to me and I just wanted to know the truth." An exasperated burst of air punctuated her words. "I *hate* being lied to. I don't know why, I guess maybe it goes back to my mother lying to me for so long about what happened to my daddy. When she finally told me the truth, that he was never coming home because he was dead"—she paused, forcing in a breath as she struggled for control—"it tore me up. I couldn't trust her. It took me years before I'd ever believe her about anything." She shook her head. "I just don't want it to be like that with the man I might marry." She threw her hands up. "Like right now! Where are they?"

Joanne leaned forward. "You *never* ask that question."

Shirley put her glass down. "And you can *never* tell your friends or family, no matter how proud you are of what he does, or how scared you are."

"That's right," agreed Maggie. "If you're ever having trouble, you call one of us."

Shirley nodded. "We're our own support network. When the men are off saving the world, it's our job to make sure things are sane when they get back, and that includes ourselves."

Maggie agreed. "You don't think I get terrified every time BD goes out on a mission?"

Joanne motioned to Maggie. "And it's worse for her! Half the time she actually *knows* where they're going."

Vanessa's eyes narrowed. "Why?"

"I'm the Colonel's personal assistant. I tend to overhear a lot of things."

"It must be nice though, not having to wonder."

Maggie shook her head. "No way. Half the time they're off training or just providing extra security to some dignitary. Routine stuff. I'd rather be able to sit here thinking that's where he is rather than knowing he's in some hellhole where everybody, even the so called innocent people around him, want him dead."

"So you know where they are now?"

"Nope." Maggie raised her glass of chardonnay. "It's my day off! I'm blissfully ignorant, just like the rest of you."

"Welcome to the club!" cheered Shirley, glasses raised, those closest to each other clinking them together.

All but Vanessa.

Maggie leaned over, placing a hand on the young girl's arm. "What's wrong?"

Tears poured down Vanessa's cheeks, her shoulders heaving, her arms trembling. "I-I don't know. I can't stop shaking." She looked up at Maggie. "I think I'm terrified!"

Shirley rose, sitting on the edge of Vanessa's chair, wrapping an arm over her shoulders. "It's okay, dear. I was the same way. I was scared of being the wife of someone who could die tomorrow in some country I'd never heard of, knowing I'd never really be told the truth about what happened. I'd be left to raise our children alone, to fend for myself." She gave Vanessa a squeeze. "But I got through it, and now I have Bryson who I wouldn't trade for the world, and a husband who I'm immensely proud of, who saves lives for a living and keeps the world safe for me and our son. I feel blessed every day I'm married to him, and even more so when he pulls up in the driveway after being away."

She smiled at the others, knowing nods around the room. "My heart still races when I get a sneak text from him and I know he's safe enough to be able to do it. And if he didn't come home tomorrow, I'd know he died doing what he loved, with friends he loved doing it with. And remember, you now have us. And not just us. If you marry a military man, you marry the military. The entire armed forces is your family. We help each other out, we stick together. It's nothing like the life you had before. People are here to help you, are *happy* to help you, because we've all been through it, and we're all still going through it." She smiled at Vanessa. "You're going to be okay."

Vanessa shook her head, wiping her tears away with the back of her hand. "I-I just don't think I can do it. T-tell him I'm sorry."

She leapt to her feet and bolted from the apartment, leaving the room in stunned silence.

Maggie sighed.

Poor Atlas.

R-297 Highway, Russian Federation

A vehicle passed them, a young girl pressed against the glass waving. Laura smiled and waved back, absentmindedly running a finger over the scar on her stomach, it permanent evidence of how close she had come to death, and how she could never have a child like that to hold.

They had discussed adoption, though after a lengthy discussion in which they were both mostly in agreement, they had dismissed it—they couldn't risk a child's life, not with people like the Assembly possibly after them. Their careers as well didn't lend themselves to parenthood. And neither, at this point, were willing to give them up, there simply too much good they could do to advance mankind's knowledge.

It was selfish, perhaps, but it was reality.

With her money, yes, they could afford nannies, but if you weren't going to raise the adopted child, why bother? She could use the money to help kids where they truly needed it, in Africa and Asia and other Third World areas. They already funneled millions every year to these countries through charities she supported, the returns on her investments obscene.

She had no interest in following in the footsteps of some of the über rich who were pledging to divest themselves of most of their wealth. She didn't buy it. There was no way these people were going to give up everything and live like paupers the rest of their lives. They could make these pledges because they knew they were far more diversified than the public knew. Giving up 99% of your stock in one company might appear noble, but what about the dozens of other companies?

She doubted these billionaires would be willing to give up their mansions, yachts and private jets when push came to shove. And she wasn't about to be made to feel guilty for having money. Her brother had worked extremely hard to get to where he was before he died, and though she hadn't earned it, he had wanted her to have it. She used it to make her life a little easier, though more of it went to help others, and with the reins held by her, she knew where it was going, and that she wasn't being robbed.

She didn't trust the big banks or Wall Street to manage her money, not after the financial crisis that had Western governments bailing out banks just to have them turn around and bonus out millions to their executives that had created the problem in the first place.

Instead, she, now with James, managed everything. Could she do more? Perhaps, but then she wouldn't know that it was truly going to those in need. Far too often charities had massive administrative expenses, too much of the money going to those supposedly managing the groups. Some even paid over half their money raised to companies that were professional fundraisers.

It was disgusting.

People thought they were donating their hard earned money to a worthy cause, when the reality was, in some cases, less than 10% was actually reaching those in need.

She refused to be a part of that.

She would help those less fortunate, trying to lift the Third World up through direct investments in health and education programs. She could never understand why Western governments talked so much about helping these poor people, when in the next breath they'd take in hundreds of thousands of the best and brightest as immigrants.

Don't these desperate Third World countries need their best and brightest? Isn't taking them into our own countries simply perpetuating the cycle of poverty and desperation?

It was all so frustrating to her.

Save them all *by letting them progress!*

If you always took the best laying hens out of the henhouse, why would you be surprised that in the end you had an unproductive group of chickens?

"Stop!"

Zorkin slammed on the brakes, pulling over to the side of the road at James' warning, a truck blasting past them with its horn blaring in protest.

Zorkin glanced over at the tablet. "What is it?"

"Road block ahead."

Laura leaned forward to look. "What now?"

Zorkin did a shoulder check and pulled a U-turn. "We get off this road and find another way."

"Will there be another way?" asked James. "What if they have this entire border shut down?"

Zorkin shrugged. "Then we'll go off-road."

Acton gave him a look. "In this?"

"No."

"Then what?"

Another shrug. "I'll think of something."

"Well, you better think fast."

The sound of gunfire behind them had Laura twisting in her seat.

"Look!"

She turned around to see her husband holding up the tablet, soldiers at the bottom of the image pointing weapons in the air, small bursts of brightness erupting from their muzzles. "They've spotted the drone!"

Zorkin pulled over, grabbing the drone and tapping at the display, it abruptly changing direction, heading east, if Laura wasn't mistaken.

Suddenly the image jerked and the ground rapidly approached, the image of a shrub filling the screen.

Then nothing.

James cursed. "There goes our eyes."

Zorkin handed the tablet back then hammered on the gas. "Find us an alternate road heading west."

James brought up the map application. "So now we *are* heading west?"

"We don't have a choice at the moment. As we speak, Moscow will be getting informed of what just happened, and someone will want to investigate, so this entire region is going to be flooded with security personnel in a matter of hours."

"So we're screwed."

"Da. We're screwed."

South Kuril Islands, Russian Federation
Japanese name: Chishima Islands

"Turn, you arrogant bastards, turn!"

Captain Yamada watched in horror and rage as a Russian frigate tried to storm the blockade, attempting to thread between two American ships that had placed themselves between the two adversaries.

"Turn!"

He could hear the collision alarms on the USS Shiloh, Captain Shephard standing his ground, refusing to move, instead his engines in reverse as he closed the gap with the other American vessel.

If it were a movie, he'd be tossing his sardine rice crackers back without looking away.

The Russian ship suddenly tipped hard to starboard as their Captain ordered his ship hard to port, less than a hundred meters coming between the two vessels, a distance that might appear huge on foot, but far too close when dealing with 10,000 ton ships that didn't turn on dimes, the wash causing the American vessel to noticeably rise then drop, waves cresting over the decks as the oceans calmed, the Russian vessel steaming along the invisible border now under dispute, the USS Shiloh ordering full ahead as it matched the Russian's speed should they try to break around them.

They didn't.

The Russian turned away in a gentle arc, leaving to rejoin its fellow vessels.

"Sir, the Russians are broadcasting in English."

"Let's hear it."

"—States vessels. You are requested to disengage and leave Russian territory. We have no quarrel with you. We will be opening fire on the Japanese aggressors, and do not wish harm to come to you accidentally. Again, please withdraw."

Yamada frowned. Would they dare fire with the Americans in the way? It would certainly be possible, naval warfare more of a ballistic affair above the water, the Russians easily able to fire over the Americans without harming them.

Though things tended to go wrong in a firefight.

Even at sea.

"This is United States Navy vessel USS Shiloh. Negative on your kind request. Our country does not recognize your claims to these waters, and are conducting naval exercises with our Japanese allies. You are welcome to join us should you want to." There was a pause. *"Would you like to play the good guys, or the bad guys? Over."*

Yamada stifled a chuckle.

"Missile launch! Missile launch!"

Yamada leapt from his chair, the distinct white plume of a missile rushing into the sky from one of the Russian ships unmistakable. "Activate counter measures!"

His men leapt to action, warning alarms blaring as the missile streaked over the American vessels, racing toward his ship. The thunder of the Phalanx Close In Weapons System belching rounds at 3600 feet per second filled the bridge, a wall of lead tearing apart the missile only thirty meters from them, the blast wave rocking the entire vessel, one of the windows splintering.

"Prepare to return fire!"

"Sir! The Russian captain is signaling it was a misfire!"

Bullshit.

Yamada peered through his binoculars at the Russian vessels. "Have they launched anything else?"

"Negative, sir!"

Yamada lowered his binoculars. "Inform the Russian captain that if we detect another misfire, we will blow them out of the water."

Security Station, Kashira, Russian Federation

"A drone?"

Dymovsky pressed the phone tighter against his ear, not sure he had heard the officer correctly.

"Yes, sir, a drone."

"Any markings? Is it military?"

"Negative, sir. It appears to be civilian. Small, nothing fancy."

"And it was just hovering near your checkpoint."

"Yes, sir. When we spotted it we shot it down."

Dymovsky raised his eyebrows slightly, a small drone in the air a difficult shot. Most likely a lucky shot. "Good shooting, Lieutenant. Have it sent to Moscow immediately for analysis. Use a helicopter, we need it fast."

"Yes, sir."

"Was there any unusual traffic at the time?"

"No, sir, nothing out of the ordinary. We've held all vehicles trying to pass and are searching them thoroughly. If they try to come through here, we'll catch them. The criminals will *not* pass through this checkpoint."

"Very good, Lieutenant. I will make sure Moscow knows of the excellent job you are doing."

"Yes, sir! Thank you, sir!"

Dymovsky could almost hear the heels click.

He ended the call, staring out the window of the checkpoint, Vitaly Orlov having been sent on to Moscow as he waited for a lead.

And he just got it.

It had to be them.

And if it was, then they were headed south, *not* west as he had been told. He didn't believe for a second that he had been lied to. It wasn't in the character of his prisoners, especially the young man who had taken such a beating. *He* was definitely telling the truth. Or at least what he *thought* was the truth. Zorkin had tricked those helping him.

And it had nearly succeeded.

He rose, pointing at Filippov.

"Redirect all our efforts south. Now!"

Operations Center 3, CIA Headquarters, Langley, Virginia

Leroux frowned, the feed lost. "Do we have eyes on that area?"

Child shook his head. "ETA three minutes for the next bird to be in range."

"Show me."

The map of Russia he had been staring at for the better part of a day zoomed out slightly, a green cone rapidly moving toward the area showing the coverage of the spy satellite about to pass over the region.

Leroux walked toward the map. "Show me all the routes they could take from their last known location, assuming they turned away from the checkpoint. There's no way they're staying on that road."

"Give me a second," replied Tong, expertly working her station. Routes began to appear, snaking out from the last known location.

Too many routes.

"Eliminate anything that doesn't eventually head south."

"Wouldn't they try a different direction?" asked Child. "I mean, they can't go south now. There's no way this wasn't reported to Moscow."

Leroux shook his head. "Zorkin definitely knew he'd be running into a checkpoint. He's planned for this."

"They could still make for the Black Sea. That's not too far."

"No, too well patrolled. He's definitely heading south. That leaves Abkhazia, Georgia or Azerbaijan. Care to take a guess as to which one?"

Child leaned forward. "Abkhazia is pro-Russian and gives them access to the Black Sea only. If they're staying off the water then they'd have to go through Georgia anyway to get to Turkey."

Tong pointed at the map. "Azerbaijan is farther from their current location, and it only gives them access to the Caspian Sea, which is less helpful than the Black Sea, Georgia again, Armenia, which again is just taking them around Georgia, and Iran, which they're definitely not heading for."

"So where do we think they're going?"

A round of Georgia's filled the room.

Leroux smiled. "Exactly what I was thinking. There's no reason at this point for Zorkin to change his plan. He's arranged something. There was no way he was going to just drive across the border—any border—using the main highway. And besides"—he pointed at the map—"they can reach Georgia in about an hour if they can find a route."

"Updating that now, sir." Tong motioned toward the screen, the non-southern routes slowly disappearing.

"Show me routes that would have matched up if they had kept going south on their original route. We have to assume he was going to turn off at some point, just not at *this* point."

Tong hammered at her keyboard, more routes disappearing.

Then there was nothing.

"Huh." He turned back to Tong. "Is that an error?"

Tong shook her head. "No, sir, there's nothing leading to the border, just a few small roads that essentially end in the middle of nowhere."

"Then they're going off-road. And he would have planned for that." He pointed at the display. "Let's get a look at the terrain a little closer. See if there's anything Google missed."

Child grinned at the joke, knowing full-well they were using military maps, far more accurate in these areas than anything Google might produce. "Pretty mountainous."

Leroux agreed. "Yup. If they're planning on going through the mountains then that means local guides."

Child cursed. "Isn't that dude like seventy-five or something? How's he going to hike through the mountains?"

Leroux shrugged. "No idea. And remember, Professor Palmer was shot only a few months ago and underwent major surgery. I'm not sure how well she can travel either."

"But Zorkin would know that, wouldn't he? He'd try to arrange something that would address both those situations?"

Leroux sat down, the satellite coming online. "He'd know about himself, but may not know about Professor Palmer." He jumped up, pointing at the top of the screen. "What's that?"

"There's a chopper inbound toward that checkpoint," replied Tong.

Leroux looked at the checkpoint, a long line of vehicles backed up, the Russians obviously searching for the owner of the drone. "Search pattern?"

"Negative. Looks like it's heading directly for the checkpoint."

"Could be picking up the drone to take it to Moscow," suggested Child.

"Sir, you've got to see this." Tong hit several keys, the satellite image changing.

"What am I looking at?"

"This is Budyonnovsk Air Base. It looks like they're launching everything they've got."

Leroux muttered a curse as he watched several helicopters lifting off, more powering up. He shook his head. "There's no way they're getting away from this. Not without help." He snapped his fingers. "Get me Delta."

Ten miles from Georgian Border, Russian Federation

Acton grunted. "Something tells me this wasn't part of your plan, otherwise you'd have had an SUV delivered." His jaw rattled as Zorkin navigated along what might be at best a goat path.

"It was supposed to be a Jeep, but what was I supposed to do? Refuse the vehicle? It wasn't like Avis was dropping off a rental."

Acton slammed on his imaginary brake with his foot as a particularly large pothole suddenly appeared. "Just be thankful they didn't bring you a Jag."

"It would have broken down before they delivered it," giggled Laura.

Zorkin chuckled. "If they did make it, the electrical system would have been fried the moment the drone took a picture of it."

"We would have been able to cruise right through the border, though," said Acton as he gripped the dash. "There's no way they would have believed we'd be stupid enough to try and escape in one." The car jerked hard to the right as a tire caught in a rut. "Do we have to go so fast? We're going to break an axle or burst a tire."

"I know, I know, but this entire area is going to be flooded with aircraft shortly, all looking for us. We need to get to the border as fast as we can."

Acton stared at the map on the tablet. "At this rate we're at least half an hour away. There's no way we're making it in time."

Zorkin shook his head, pointing at the foothills ahead. "We only need to reach those hills."

"Why?" asked Laura. "What's there?"

Acton waved the tablet. "It's not the border."

Zorkin swerved to the left. "No, but it *is* where we get rid of this damned car."

Acton exchanged a surprised look with Laura. "And then what? Walk?"

Zorkin grinned. "Look at me. What do you think?"

Diyarbakir Airbase, Turkey

"Do we have clearance for the op in Georgia?"

"Negative, Zero-One, but we do have permission for a flyover."

Dawson grunted at Langley's response. "So a HALO entry. Do you have coordinates yet?"

"Negative. We'll send them as soon as we have them."

Dawson shook his head, the lack of intel frustrating, though he understood it. This was an almost blind op. They had no way to communicate with the professors, with only occasional visuals. At this point, it was a "best guess" game.

But a High Altitude Low Opening jump to a best guess set of coordinates was never a good idea.

"Do we at least know if we're heading into the Russian controlled area? South Ossetia?"

"Negative. All indications are that they will be crossing the border between Abkhazia and South Ossetia."

Dawson rolled his eyes. "Well, that's one piece of good news, at least, though I doubt we can expect the Russians to respect the Georgian border."

"I wouldn't count on it. I'll update you as soon as I have more. Control out."

Dawson pulled off his comm, Niner already pulling up a map of the area on his tablet. "A HALO jump into those mountains? Are they nuts?" He pointed to the much smoother foothills the professors were currently in. "We could do a HAHO jump just at the border, get them, hoof them out and get a helo extraction three feet inside the border. Hell, let's just take a helo and get them!"

Dawson shook his head. "If we crossed the Russian border, it would be considered an act of war, and our navy is now involved in the Japanese conflict, so we can't risk any provocation."

"But why not a helo extraction at the border?" asked Atlas, his rumbling voice so deep Dawson almost swore there were Jurassic Park style ripples in his glass of water.

"No can do. The Georgians are apparently sick and tired of having their airspace violated by their not-so-friendly neighbors, and have decided that pushing back against us is the safest way to try and regain some hair on their cropped balls."

Spock cocked an eyebrow. "Colorful."

Dawson grinned. "Thank you."

"So HALO is the only way, fine. I assume the Georgians don't know about that part."

"No, they don't."

Niner tossed the tablet onto the table. "And what if they shadow our plane? Won't they get suspicious when five lithe and one bulbous"—he jerked a thumb at Atlas—"forms fall out the back like aeroturds?"

"That's a risk we're going to have to take," replied Dawson. "I doubt they'd do anything, even if they spotted us. There's no way they're going to start shooting at what they know are American soldiers. They'll be pissed, but they're not going to start shooting."

"You hope," said Jimmy.

Dawson shrugged. "Yup. That's about all we've got at this point."

Niner exhaled loudly. "It's not the Georgians that worry me. It's that damned terrain we're landing on. Those are mountains. Unless we can find some sort of plateau to land on, we could be looking at some significant injuries, then we're not only trying to get the doc and his lady out, we're hauling one or more of our own as well." He looked at Atlas. "If you break an ankle, I'm leaving you for the wolves."

Atlas eyeballed him. "And if it's you, I'll just put you right up here"—he patted his shoulder—"so the little girl you are can get a nice view."

Niner jabbed a finger at him. "You're jumping first."

"Why?"

"Because I want something big and soft to land on."

Atlas flexed his right arm, a ridiculous bicep bulging. He gave it a kiss. "You might want to reconsider. This is harder than those mountains."

Jagger leaned over and gave it a squeeze before looking at Niner. "Yup. I'd definitely reconsider."

The Kremlin, Moscow, Russian Federation

Sasaki forced a smile for the cameras as he shook hands with his Russian counterpart, the strobe-like effect nearly blinding. The journey had been intimidating as expected, their plane escorted by fighter jets the moment they entered Russian airspace, his pilot complaining they were too close, the response always to move even closer for a few moments before banking away rapidly.

They were playing games.

And of course it didn't end in the skies. The moment the plane came to a stop on the tarmac security personnel surrounded it, their weapons trained on the plane, not the other way around, despite Russian assurances they were there for the protection of their "honored" guests.

At least they had let the limousine provided by the Japanese embassy travel unscathed, the Russians respecting the sanctuary provided by diplomatic plates.

"I think that is enough," said the Russian Deputy Foreign Minister Ivan Maksimov. He held out a hand, directing Sasaki to a side door. Sasaki gave one last smile to the cameras then strode through the door, his delegation and the Russians following, the door shut, the mayhem outside immediately silenced.

"I thought we had agreed this meeting would be held in the strictest of confidence."

Maksimov shrugged, taking a seat at the center of one side of the conference table. "There must have been a leak. I'm quite certain it wasn't from our side."

The very idea was ridiculous. If there had been a leak, who let the photographers inside? He decided it was best to forget what had just transpired and realize that these negotiations were going to be even more difficult than expected, it clear the Russians were angry and as a result, up to their usual childish antics.

Maksimov held his hands out to his sides, playing the magnanimous host. "Now, how may we help the Japanese people today?"

Sasaki kept his expression neutral though his heart was pounding with anger. "You know why we are here. We want our property back."

Maksimov's eyes narrowed slightly. "And what property is that?"

And the games continue.

"Anything removed from our sovereign territory."

"If you are referring to the Kuril Islands, that is *Russian* territory, and you are currently illegally occupying it. In order for any negotiations to begin, you must remove any personnel you have stationed there, and remove your naval blockade."

Sasaki took long, slow breaths during the bombastic display, controlling his desire to drop kick the man into the next room.

His wrist spasmed.

He ignored it, instead smiling slightly. "While we respect the Russian position, the international community does not recognize your claim to the *Chishima* Islands. We have not disputed it aggressively in the hopes that a negotiated settlement could be reached, however after seventy years, it is clear that this will never be possible."

Maksimov's face held the bemused smile of someone watching a child deliver a book report he didn't understand. "Something has changed, I think. We find bodies of your soldiers from the Great Patriotic War, *return* those bodies with full military honors, and days later you invade our territory." He leaned forward, his eyes piercing. "What is it that has you so concerned?" He sat back in his chair. "*Something* has changed."

Sasaki glanced at his aide, Etsuko, who nodded slightly. He trusted her, she an excellent, capable assistant, her levelheadedness always appreciated, though neither had before tried to negotiate their country out of a war.

It was time.

"You took something from those islands."

Maksimov steepled his fingers. "What did we take?"

Sasaki felt his chest tighten, his cheeks flush. "Do you deny you took something?"

Maksimov smiled slightly. "I deny nothing. I merely ask what it is you think we took."

Sasaki sighed, closing his eyes for a moment, the shame of having to admit the great dishonor to a man of no honor, almost overwhelming. "The Imperial Regalia."

"And what is that?"

"They are our most ancient and precious relics."

Maksimov laughed, looking at the others in his delegation who joined in. "Relics? Trinkets? That is what this is about!"

Sasaki kept calm. Outwardly. "These are not just *trinkets*. His Majesty the Emperor must be in possession of them to hold power."

Maksimov chuckled. "You should have done with your emperor what we did with our Tsar. Your lives would be much simpler."

Sasaki contained his rage at the offensive insult, it unprecedented in all his years of dealing with foreign governments. Etsuko sucked in a loud breath of anger through her nose, her eyes flaring.

"So you think we have this, what did you call it, Imperial Regalia?"

"Yes."

"Why?"

"The bodies you found were of soldiers sent in the final days of the war to hide the relics from the Americans. They were never heard from again. Your discovery shows they obviously reached the islands and were killed by your troops when you illegally occupied them after the surrender."

"An interesting theory."

"It is not a theory. Citizens of my country found the relics on Harukaru Island, what you call Kharkar Island, and I was present at their discovery. Your people confiscated them."

"This is the first I am hearing of this. I'll be sure to have it looked into. In the meantime, we must insist you withdraw."

Sasaki squared his shoulders. "Sir, we have no intention of withdrawing until the Imperial Regalia are returned."

Maksimov said nothing, staring at Sasaki as if sizing up a piece of meat. He finally spoke. "I wonder what your people would think if they knew your emperor held the throne illegitimately."

Sasaki held his breath for a moment. "They wouldn't believe you."

"Perhaps. Though these are different times. I think they *would* believe it. At the very least they'd demand to see proof he is in possession of these Regalia, or whatever they are called."

Sasaki ignored what was, unfortunately, probably an accurate supposition. "I have still not heard any denial that you have them in your possession."

"As I said, I will investigate the matter."

"I suggest you hurry, otherwise brave men and women will be dying, all for something that means nothing to you."

Maksimov smiled from half his mouth. "*We* will not be dying for some trinkets. *We* will be dying for land that belongs to the Russian people."

Sasaki played his final card. "If it is land you want, then it is land you will get. *When* you return the Imperial Regalia. But *not* before."

Approaching Georgian Border, Russian Federation

"Status report."

Dymovsky frowned. The deputy minister that had assigned him to the case, the man who held his entire future in his hands, sounded pissed. He still hadn't been able to piece together what was truly going on here, though he had an idea. The professors were both archaeologists, Orlov was a curator, and his son had mentioned something about a set of relics his father had brought the professors in to see.

Relics that appeared Asian.

And now a delegation had arrived from Japan, no doubt searching for a way to avoid war, a war that made no sense.

Could this all be over some ancient relics?

It made no sense to him, it made no sense that a country as weak as Japan would dare threaten war over some archaeological discovery.

"Sir, a drone was spotted and shot down near the Georgian border. I'm heading there now."

"I thought they were heading west, toward the Ukraine?"

"We were misled, sir."

Deputy Minister Maksimov cursed. "I knew I shouldn't have given you the job. Your incompetence in the Brass Monkey incident nearly caused a war. The billions we had to pay the Americans to compensate India for the false admission of a nuclear test are billions we could have spent on our citizens, but thanks to you, those billions are gone. And now we face war with a pissy little country with a joke of an armed forces, where no matter what we do we'll look like the bad guys, all because you can't find two academics who stole some worthless trinkets!"

Dymovsky smiled, rage usually a great way to let secrets slip. "I'll report as soon as I have something."

He hung up, closing his eyes as the helicopter thundered south. Now he knew what this was all about, though not why. The Japanese wanted some relics that the professors now had. Orlov had obviously taken them when he shouldn't have and given them to Acton and Palmer, and they were now trying to get them out of the country.

To what purpose?

Their dossiers suggested they were good people, and agents of no one. In fact, Palmer's worth was immense, they obviously not motivated by money.

If he had to hazard a guess, he'd have to say they were planning on returning them to the Japanese, and the only reason they'd do that is because Orlov had asked them to.

He didn't trust his own government.

And Dymovsky didn't blame him.

Perhaps I should just let them escape.

It was an option, but his life and that of his family were now at stake. And what if that wasn't their end game, what if they had some other intention?

Or what if someone else stopped them, the relics disappearing?

They were headed most likely for Georgia, not exactly known for law and order, at least not in its northern regions. Anything could happen. Any*one* could happen.

Then war would be inevitable.

Japan was no competition, not in the least. But the Americans were already involved, clearly taking sides though claiming neutrality. And according to a briefing he had received from headquarters, the Chinese were already taking advantage of the distraction, expanding their claims in the South China Sea, sending more ships and troops into the area, stepping up air patrols, reports they were rapidly expanding one of their artificial islands just breaking news a few hours ago. Vietnam and the Philippines were already protesting, sending in their own limited navies.

This could spin out of control quickly, leading to a conflict that could cost thousands, perhaps millions of lives, and destabilize the entire region.

All because some relics that meant nothing to Russia and apparently everything to a nation that had become pacifist after decades of uncontrolled aggression.

He had to retrieve them.

Then decide what to do with them.

Five miles from Georgian border, Russian Federation

Acton climbed out of the car then opened the rear door for Laura, the child locks enabled. Zorkin popped the trunk and pulled out camouflage netting, Acton impressed at the planning. He helped the aging spy drape the car with it, it soon blended nicely with the rocky, barren scenery surrounding them.

"Now what?"

Zorkin pointed to the hills. "Now we walk."

"Are you kidding me?" Acton looked at Laura then down at where her scar was. There was no way she'd be able to make it any significant distance.

"Would you rather stay?"

Acton frowned, deciding to challenge Zorkin's so far well thought out plan with the man's own limitations. "No, but, umm, you're…"

"Old?"

"You said it."

"I am." He pointed toward the foothills and a growing patch of dust. "See that?"

Acton's eyes narrowed as he tried to figure out what it was in the fading light. "What is it?"

"Our ride."

Acton breathed a sigh of relief, extending his hand, Laura taking it. "You could have just told us that."

Zorkin shrugged. "Where would be the fun in that?"

Acton grunted. "I hope whoever is meeting us has something more appropriate than a sedan."

Zorkin smiled. "Let's hope."

Operations Center 3, CIA Headquarters, Langley, Virginia

"I've found the car!"

Leroux turned to Tong who motioned toward the screen, an infrared image showing what was clearly a vehicle under some netting, its engine still glowing red.

And no indication of anyone inside.

"Any sign of them?"

"Negative."

"And the Russians?"

"We're showing dozens of aircraft and helicopters heading for the area. They're going to spot that vehicle soon."

Leroux frowned as the image zoomed out showing the various Russian assets being inserted into the area. "Focus south of the vehicle. They can't have gone far now that they're on foot."

"Got 'em!" Child pointed at the screen, another image appearing showing three heat signatures moving south.

"Let's hope whoever they're supposed to meet is close. How far from the border?"

"Less than five miles," replied Child. "But the Russians aren't going to care about that."

Leroux was about to open his mouth when Tong interrupted.

"Sir, I've got at least a dozen large heat signatures heading toward them from the south."

"Show me."

Leroux stepped toward the display as the new satellite images resolved.

"What the hell is that?"

Four Miles from Georgian border, Russian Federation

Acton stopped, raising his hands slightly as he placed himself between Laura and the new arrivals.

A dozen men on horseback, three spare horses obviously for them.

More suitable than a sedan, I guess.

Though hardly capable of outrunning the Russian Army.

Words exchanged between the leader and Zorkin, a large wad of cash handed over, all in Euros. The men appeared to be criminals of some sort, their AK-47s and bushy beards along with a full set of teeth shared among them, suggested that trusting these men would be a mistake.

At least he now had a nice Beretta tucked into his belt courtesy the sedan's well-stocked trunk.

Zorkin turned to them. "You know how to ride?"

Acton nodded, Laura swinging onto the back of her horse, he quickly following. Zorkin struggled slightly, the new arrivals laughing, probably cracking jokes at the man's age.

He was tempted to jump to the man's defense, but there was no point. These men probably wouldn't understand him, and Zorkin would likely be embarrassed that someone felt he needed defending.

Zorkin had more than proven himself.

He had rescued them, got them out of Moscow, most likely saved Vitaly's life, and now had them within sight of the border and safety.

Just get across the border then worry about how trustworthy these new people are.

"Let's go!" ordered Zorkin, everyone urging their steeds forward, they soon at a full gallop toward the mountains, it clear everyone agreed time was of the essence. Acton glanced behind him and frowned, the cloud of dust they were kicking up significant.

And likely visible for miles.

His heart caught in his throat as he stared up at the sky, contrails streaking across it.

We're not going to make it.

He felt the heavy weight of the relics in his bag, almost like an albatross dragging them all down. One bomb would be all it would take to end this. The Russians could drop it right on them, killing them all, ending the pursuit in seconds.

Though that would destroy the relics, and he had to believe that was in the best interests of no one.

As they charged toward the border, the relics slapping against his side, part of him wanted to just leave them behind and tell the Russians where they were, though experience told him that if they were to give up the only piece of leverage they had, they'd be dead for sure, or if allowed to live, the war that was brewing might not be stopped.

Zorkin had been translating news reports over the radio as they approached Georgia, uncensored broadcasts making it over the border providing a little more truth as to what had been happening in the less than two days they had been gone. Apparently shots had been fired, the Russians claiming they had fired a retaliatory shot at the Japanese for an unprovoked attack, the Japanese and Americans claiming only one shot had been fired, it by the Russians, any other shots belonging to the Japanese who had shot the missile down.

And now the Chinese were on high alert and the North Koreans were shaking their fists at everyone, putting the South Koreans on edge. The entire region was about to erupt, and these three ancient relics they now possessed seemed to be the key to defusing it all.

And he wasn't about to trust the Russians to hand them over.

Five miles from Georgian border, Russian Federation

Dymovsky stepped down from the chopper as it bounced to a rough landing, every moment now critical. Soldiers swarmed the area, one waving him toward a large rock outcropping, the rear of a car visible, camouflage netting lying on the ground beside it, fluttering in the brisk, cool wind coming off the mountains to the south.

"Anything?"

The lieutenant in charge shook his head. "No, sir. Nothing inside except left over food and water and a case in the trunk that looks like it probably held the drone we shot down."

"Fingerprints?"

"We're waiting for a forensics team, but I think there's little doubt it's the criminals you've been looking for."

Dymovsky nodded, there indeed little doubt. He surveyed the area. "Any sign of another vehicle?"

"Negative."

Dymovsky frowned, his eyes narrowing. He walked south of the scene, scanning the ground for footprints, tread marks, anything, but the hard ground gave up nothing.

Except three sets of footprints on a soft patch of ground. He ran for a couple of minutes, Filippov and some of the soldiers rushing after him, before he stopped at the final clue.

A large pile of shit.

He smiled then scanned the horizon, spotting nothing. He spun around, heading back to the chopper. "They're on horseback!"

"Sir?"

He pointed at the pile of manure. "They're obviously heading for the border. Somebody must have met them."

"Probably Georgian bandits," suggested Filippov.

"Probably. And bandits can't be trusted." He spun, staring at the mountains. "Put the word out that there is a reward to anyone who turns them over to us."

Filippov grinned. "Yes, sir!"

South Kuril Islands, Russian Federation
Japanese name: Chishima Islands

"Sir, reinforcements have been ordered to the Senkaku Islands."

Captain Yamada nodded, the report unimportant with respect to the present situation, except that they may soon be battling two foes on two different fronts.

He wondered how eager the Americans would be to join in the fight against the Chinese. More American ships had arrived, including the entirety of Carrier Strike Group 5, sitting within sight to the east, the aircraft carrier USS Ronald Reagan impressive, it a massive ship that had him envious of its captain.

We were once that powerful.

There were now a dozen Russian vessels opposing them, spread across the sea to the north, their challenges at the moment having stopped, perhaps the politicians having a go at things. He still couldn't believe his government was willing to use the islands they had given up on seven decades ago as a pretense for war, islands that were no longer home to a single Japanese citizen, the Soviets having deported them all within the first year of the occupation.

Privy to the real reason, he had a luxury none of the other captains had, and he understood the thinking in Tokyo over the show of force, though he had to question them pressing on with this charade after the near disaster just hours ago.

The lives of the men and women under his command were at risk because of lies and deceptions instigated over seventy years ago, and perpetuated by men in power all these years later terrified to reveal the

214

truth. He had no doubt some of them were fearful of the effect it could have on His Majesty, though more likely most were only concerned about themselves and the shame it would bring.

When the truth is revealed, the news will be filled with ritual suicides.

At least if they truly believed in what they were doing.

Those that didn't would most likely resign, lose their positions and power, yet continue their pampered lives.

But he and his crew could die here today, while those safely ensconced in Tokyo tried to save face.

Yet he had his orders.

And they were specific.

Blockade the islands, fire if fired upon.

Unprecedented orders.

"Sir, we've got a significant number of aircraft on our radar."

Wonderful.

"Which direction?"

"Coming from the northwest."

"Russian."

"Yes, sir, most likely, sir."

"And the US fleet?"

"The USS Ronald Reagan is launching intercept aircraft."

Yamada sighed.

What had been a slow, methodical game of chess on the seas, had just become a high-speed, high-adrenaline ice hockey match in the clouds.

We've just crossed the point of no return.

"What are their orders?"

Yamada rose from his seat, staring at the radar showing the two air forces racing toward each other, sweat dripping down his back now. This was escalating quickly, and with air power now involved, it could go bad within seconds, triggering an all-out response by everyone, whether they were in the air or not.

And his ships were no match in a sustained battle with the Russians who now outnumbered them. The only thing that would save them would be their training, their honor, and the Americans.

Something he wasn't sure he could count on should it turn into a shooting war, he not certain how far their ally's rules of engagement would allow them to go.

They certainly hadn't made any attempt to intercept the so-called misfire earlier, and if the Russians were to be smart about it, they wouldn't target the American vessels, only the Japanese.

Forcing the Americans to pick sides.

But in the air, it was an entirely different ball game. If a single pilot on either side fired, just a single round, it could unleash a flurry of missiles that within seconds would leave pilots and airframes hurtling toward the ocean, any decision the Americans had been hoping to put off, made for them.

None of the prospects were appealing.

"We're not on their frequency, Captain. I'm trying to hail the American commander but have been told he's unavailable."

Yamada nodded.

Probably busy wondering if he's about to start World War III.

He stepped out onto the weather deck and raised his binoculars, staring up at the sky, it now night, the only light from the stars and a full moon.

More than enough to see the contrails streaking toward each other, tiny blotches of black at their heads, each representing a life that may about to be lost.

Whoever fires first will go down in history as the person who started what could be the war to end all wars.

He thought of a quote he had read once from Albert Einstein.

I know not with what weapons World War III will be fought, but World War IV will be fought with sticks and stones.

He shuddered at the thought.

Had mankind come so far only for it all to end over a politician's unforgivable order to a navy never designed to be more than a maritime defense force?

His XO walked up beside him. "Sir, reports indicate more Russian ships are heading this way, and…"

Yamada lowered his binoculars and looked at his XO, the fear on the man's face obvious. "What is it?"

"Sir, one of our vessels has just taken fire from a Chinese vessel in the Senkaku Islands."

Yamada closed his eyes and sighed.

And so it begins.

Caucasus Mountains, Georgia
Seven miles inside the border

Acton shivered, his feet blocks of ice. They had been given thick fur wraps that were helping, but his feet were freezing inside his casual shoes, shoes worn for a meeting in a hotel room with a fellow lover of antiquities, not for fleeing from Russian authorities across the mountains of northern Georgia.

His teeth chattered.

Thankfully, the horses didn't seem to mind. They had been travelling for almost half an hour, the going slow along the trail carved through the mountains over probably hundreds if not thousands of years, but he was happy. They had crossed the border and there was no sign of pursuit. And as every minute passed, with every foot of terrain covered, they were deeper into friendly territory.

Though if he remembered his Georgian geography correctly, they were nowhere near any form of civilization, which meant potentially days of travel on horseback before they could truly be saved.

And that meant days more for the world to erupt in chaos, while the keys to peace lay trapped in the mountains of a country most people didn't know existed.

We should have got a satellite phone!

Operations Center 3, CIA Headquarters, Langley, Virginia

"I've found them, sir. They're seven miles inside Georgian territory, but there's two choppers heading directly to where they abandoned their vehicle."

Leroux frowned, staring at the images from the newly arriving satellite. "What kind?"

"Mi-24 gunships." Child cursed. "Looks like they aim to take them out."

Leroux shook his head. "Where's Delta?"

A map appeared showing the helicopters, the professors, and the C130J carrying the Delta team at 30,000 feet.

"Christ. ETA?"

"They're about to jump, sir. Should be less than five minutes until they're on the ground."

Leroux shook his head then pointed at Child. "Contact Zero-One, let them know what they're getting into." He stared at the screen. "And get me the Director!"

Over Georgian Airspace
30,000 feet

Dawson tugged at Atlas' gear, confirming everything was in good order, then slapped on the man's helmet, thumbs up exchanged.

"Everybody good to go?"

A round of affirmatives came in over the helmet's comm system. The jump light was still red but the cargo ramp had been lowered, wind whipping around the cabin, two crewmembers manning either side of the exit.

"Yo, Atlas, don't forget what I said."

Atlas glanced at Niner. "What's that?"

The bass is good on these new helmets.

"You go first so I can land on you."

"Little man, if you land on me, I'll split you like a wishbone."

"Don't make promises you won't keep."

Atlas looked at Dawson, confused for a moment. His jaw dropped. 'Dude!"

The light went green and Niner grinned, walking backward then stepping off the rear of the plane, blowing a kiss as he disappeared from sight.

Atlas shook his head, turning to Dawson. "We've gotta get that boy a girlfriend, soon."

"Not my department."

Caucasus Mountains, Georgia
Ten miles inside the border

Acton turned in his saddle at the clap of helicopter blades echoing through the rapidly rising mountains. He couldn't see them, the twists and turns blocking any line of sight, but they were there, there no doubt of that.

His heart raced, his ice cold feet momentarily forgotten.

The Russians clearly weren't respecting the Georgian border, and with the walloping the Georgians took only a few years ago, he doubted they would mount any challenge to the incursion.

They were at the Russian's mercy.

Yet they did have one thing working for them.

He could see no place for them to land.

"Let's move!" shouted Zorkin. "Faster!"

Acton urged his mount forward when he heard the distinctive sound of ringing. One of their escorts pulled a phone out, bending up the distinctively thick antenna of a satellite phone.

Are you kidding me? Why haven't we used that!

The conversation was one sided, mere grunts from this end, the occasional word uttered that Acton couldn't understand, though the glances at them were clear.

Something was wrong.

"Get down," whispered Zorkin, he clearly getting the same feeling Acton was.

Acton dismounted, casually, placing the horse between himself and their escorts, Laura doing the same behind him, walls of flesh their only protection from the men surrounding them.

Zorkin slowly backed toward a large rock outcropping to their right, it almost a divot in the mountainside. "Get ready."

And the conversation was over, the phone shoved back in the pocket, and something shouted, weapons abruptly raised.

Zorkin's Beretta was out almost instantly, three rounds squeezed off, the three men in the rear dropped in seconds before he dove behind a large rock near the edge of the path, rolling to a halt only inches from the steep ledge. Acton shoved Laura into the alcove, drawing his own weapon, squeezing off several rounds at the group in front of them, hitting at least one, the man crying out before falling off the path and into the valley below.

Gunfire rang out, the chatter of AK-47s echoing through the pass, shards of rock splintering off all around them. Acton glanced over at Zorkin, one hand on his hip, the man in pain.

"Are you hit?"

He shook his head. "I think I broke my goddamned hip!"

Acton fought a smile, the man clearly more embarrassed than concerned.

Though he should be concerned.

He wasn't going to be any use to them if they had to move.

"What's going on?"

Zorkin fired two rounds blindly. "Apparently there's a five million ruble reward for our capture."

Acton frowned. "Lovely. I figured we'd be worth at least ten."

"Funny. I thought it was all for me."

"Ha ha."

"Any suggestions?"

Zorkin nodded. "Yeah. Don't get shot."

Operations Center 3, CIA Headquarters, Langley, Virginia

"Something's going on."

Leroux agreed, that much obvious from the satellite feed. The horses were bolting, leaving their until now difficult to make out riders in plain view. He pointed toward three unmoving heat signatures. "Please tell me that's not them."

There was silence as everyone examined the footage, he praying that all of this hadn't been for naught.

He pointed. "There. There's two heat signatures, almost out of sight, like they're tucked under the rock."

"They're hiding!" Tong pointed. "And the other one, behind that rock, the one that looks like he's lying down. I think he's firing at the others."

"They've turned on each other," said Leroux, watching the action play out in front of them, helpless to do anything. "But why?"

"I might have an answer to that," replied Child. "I've been monitoring all the traffic in the area like you told me to and got a hit mentioning the professors. Moscow has announced a five million ruble reward for their capture."

Leroux whistled. "Christ, in that part of the world it might as well be a billion. That's life changing money there." He paused, turning toward Child. "Any mention of what they get if they're dead?"

"Two million."

Leroux shook his head. "Still life changing money."

Child agreed. "And it looks like they've decided to go the easy route."

Leroux watched the footage on the large screen. "Knowing the professors, I wouldn't count on it being easy." He turned to Tong. "Get me Delta."

Inside Georgian Airspace

"Sir, we've just crossed into Georgian territory."

Dymovsky leaned forward, peering through the cockpit window, adjusting the microphone in front of his mouth so he could reply to the pilot. "Any indication the Georgians have detected us?"

The pilot shook his head, glancing back at him. "Negative. We're low and in the mountains, so we should be okay unless we're spotted from the ground. As long as we find them soon."

Dymovsky nodded, leaning back in his seat. And that was the key. Finding them. He was sure there were several ways through the mountains, and they knew none of them.

Though they had time.

More of their forces were on the way, but for now Moscow had only authorized two choppers to violate the border, probably not wanting to tip anyone off as to the location of the relics.

It didn't matter.

They would find them, in time.

And then he'd have a decision to make.

Kill them.

Arrest them.

Or let them go.

With whatever it was both his and the Japanese governments wanted so desperately.

USAF Major Chariya "Apocalypta" Em jumped into her cockpit, her F-15C Eagle's engines immediately beginning to power up as she started a rapid pre-flight check. She gave a thumbs up to her crew chief as the canopy closed around her, then turned to check her wingman, Captain Rosie "Riveter" Bugnet, a thumbs up received while the mighty mega-million dollar jet began rolling toward the taxiway on a priority clearance.

This was the real thing.

And she couldn't wait.

Her heart slammed with excitement, there a hint of fear, but that just kept you smart. As long as you didn't let it take over, it helped fuel your reflexes, the surge of adrenaline keeping you sharp.

But it could exhaust you if you kept it up too long.

And she'd need every fiber of her being at 100% when she reached the combat zone, where she had no idea what she might be facing beyond two Russian gunships with apparently hostile intentions.

In Georgia.

Where? She didn't care. Why? She didn't care. She had a mission. Protect those being targeted by the Russian forces violating Georgian airspace and territory.

And that last word had her a little curious.

Territory.

That suggested to her there might be a ground component as well.

She shoved her throttle forward and her F-15C blasted down the runway, reaching almost two hundred miles per hour in seconds, the thrill of lifting off the ground something she'd never tire of.

God I love the Air Force!

She checked her display, confirming her wingman was away, then fed her destination coordinates into the flight computer.

Preparing for an unfriendly welcome.

Since the Georgians had no idea she was coming.

Caucasus Mountains, Georgia
Ten miles inside the border

More gunfire from the terribly inaccurate AK-47s on full auto sprayed their position. Acton was content to just wait it out as their enemy used up their ammo, but the choppers were getting louder, and he had no doubt they were Russian.

So they might be facing an even more massive enemy.

In fact, no matter what happened, they would be. Even if they eliminated these men that had betrayed them, they would still have to face Russian soldiers, and with three handguns and three mags each between them, there was no way that was going to end well.

He glanced over at Zorkin.

Should we surrender?

The idea went against everything he was raised to believe in, but he had to think about what was best, not his pride. And what was more important? Was it his life? His wife's? The Imperial Regalia?

There was only one thing of which he was sure.

Zorkin would happily die here, today. The man was in pain yet smiling, enjoying the firefight, enjoying the incredibly unbalanced odds. If Zorkin was the man Acton thought he was, he was a man who regretted surviving, a man who never thought the Cold War would end, who never thought he'd be tossed aside in the decade of peace Soviet bankruptcy had bought the world.

Zorkin probably thought he would die on the job, retirement not even a thought.

He knew this, because he knew how Kane thought.

228

Though he wondered if his former pupil thought differently now that he had apparently found love.

He glanced over at Laura.

It changes everything.

And he was determined to make sure she survived.

And that was more likely in the hands of the Russians than these criminals.

He rose and squeezed off two rounds, winging one of their attackers.

Inside Georgian Airspace
Passing 10,000 feet

Dawson surveyed the ground below, unable to make out anything beyond their target destination projected onto the visor of his helmet. Atlas and Niner below him continued to exchange barbs, Niner having positioned himself a couple of hundred feet above Atlas, threatening to keep his promise to land on him.

It helped pass the time.

He loved jumping out of perfectly good airplanes, especially from ridiculous altitudes, only minutes from entering the fray, if there was a fray to enter. If they were lucky they'd hook up with those already helping the professors, secure a position and wait for extraction, extraction he knew was already on its way.

His comm squelched.

"Zero-One, Control, come in, over."

"Go ahead, Control."

"We've still got those two choppers inbound. It looks like they don't know where the professors are and have been travelling up and down the mountain passes."

"That's good news."

"It was. It looks like they're about to get it right. If they stick to their pattern, the next pass is the right one, and they've got a ton of hardware sitting on the other side of the border, just waiting to cross when they get the word."

"Lovely. I'm surprised they're holding."

"It's our assessment that they don't want to risk whatever it is the professors have in their possession."

"ETA on those choppers?"

"We expect ten minutes. And there's more. It looks like there's some gunfire on the ground. Apparently the Russians are offering a five million ruble reward for their capture."

"Isn't that like fifty bucks, or something?" asked Niner. "If so, can we collect the reward?"

"One-One, you are more than welcome to present yourself to the Kremlin to collect."

Niner grunted. "I think I'll pass. But I do need the fifty bucks. Anybody want to take bets on whether or not I can actually land on top of the big guy?"

"I'll take a piece of that," said Spock.

Jimmy jumped in. "Me too. And I've got fifty that says you break something in the attempt."

"Now Jimmy, is that anyway to talk to a comrade during combat?"

"Kiss my pale white ass, you've said a lot worse to me."

"Zero-One, Control. Is it always like this?"

Dawson grinned. "You have no idea. We'll be boots on the ground in two minutes. How many hostiles?"

"There were twelve, but it looks like the professors have managed to take out four so far."

Dawson chuckled. "Knowing them, they'll have that thinned out some more before we get there."

Leroux laughed. "Knowing them, by the time you get there, you might not be needed."

Caucasus Mountains, Georgia
Ten miles inside the border

Acton popped his head up and aimed, squeezing the trigger twice, hitting his target center mass before dropping down. Their enemy was getting bolder as the chopper got louder, a sound he had finally made sense of. Over the past fifteen minutes the sound of the choppers had progressively got louder then quieter, and it wasn't until a few minutes ago that he had realized they were searching for them, the sounds actually from other passes through the mountains.

Though this time it sounded different.

This time it sounded like they were coming up the correct pass.

And would be here any second.

So they had to even the odds a little more.

And it also meant their betrayers probably sensed they were about to get robbed of their reward should the Russians arrive first and be forced to secure the situation.

He leaned out, squeezing off two shots, then stepped back, giving Laura room to fire two rounds of her own. She darted back into their alcove as a flurry of returned fire tore at the stone around them.

She smiled at him. "I think I got one."

He pressed against the rock as tightly as he could. "I think you just pissed them off."

Caucasus Mountains, Georgia
Eight miles inside the border

"Sir, a drone has spotted them, just ahead, but there's nowhere to put you down!" shouted the pilot over the din of the rotors. He pointed to a small flat area to their left, Dymovsky leaning over for a look. "We'll have to put you down there."

Dymovsky nodded. "Fine." He looked at the snow swept surfaces outside, immediately regretting what he was wearing. He eyed the properly equipped soldiers with him, debating whether to pull rank and demand one of their jackets.

Then I'd be everything they've come to expect from Moscow.

Filippov pulled a duffel bag from under his seat and unzipped it, pulling out a tightly rolled bundle. He handed it to Dymovsky. "Winter jacket. I brought it just in case."

This kid is good.

"You take it. You're the one who planned ahead."

Filippov produced a second one with a grin. "I planned for both of us."

Dymovsky chuckled, removing his thin overcoat and unrolling the compact jacket, quickly donning it as the helicopter landed. The doors slid open and the soldiers poured out followed by Dymovsky and Filippov, still handing supplies to his boss—gloves, hat and scarf.

This kid is very *good.*

The chopper lifted off as they headed toward the path nearby, cut through the mountains, the second chopper landing moments later. The captain commanding the troops walked over to him, pointing down the path. "They're this way, sir. My men will take point and bring up the rear. If there's any danger, hug the wall, it will cut down their field of fire."

Dymovsky nodded. "Very well, Captain. Let's hurry up, we're about to lose the light." He glanced over the edge of the narrow path, the drop several hundred feet.

I do not want to be standing on the edge of this in the dark.

Caucasus Mountains, Georgia
Ten miles inside the border

Dawson deployed his chute, the jerk a shock to the system, killing his momentum almost instantly, there a lot of it after almost 30,000 feet of free fall. He reached up and freed his toggles, testing his chute as he surveyed the area below, searching for a place to land near the location his visor indicated the professors were pinned down.

From up here there wasn't much he could do to help, and to try and swoop in and shoot their opponents from the air would be suicide, there simply no way to hug the side of a mountain with a nearly thirty foot wide canopy over your head.

"Zero-One, Control. Russian choppers have landed personnel, fourteen at last count, two miles north from your target location."

Dawson frowned, looking toward the north, not seeing the choppers, they probably holding back until the ground troops got into position, then they'd provide cover should it become necessary.

He surveyed the area. The canyons were tight which didn't leave a huge amount of maneuverability, though there was more than enough, especially when they had little to counter them with beyond a couple of sniper rifles.

Which just might be all they'd need if they could get a proper line of sight.

But shooting down choppers would take this to an entirely different level.

"If those troops get there before we do, that means we might be killing Russians. How does Washington feel about that?"

"They're monitoring, Zero-One. You're to proceed with the mission under your original parameters. Eliminate anything or anyone that threatens your safety or that of the professors."

Things must be bad in Japan.

"Roger that, Control." He scanned for a landing spot as close as possible to the professors.

"So we're killing Rooskies?" asked Niner. "Can someone please confirm that we're on the right side of the border? I really don't want to be blamed for starting World War Three."

"One-One, Control. You're confirmed well inside Georgian territory, over."

"Yeah, Control, but do the *Russians* realize that, or is this just the suburbs of their new Crimean resort?"

"One-One, our recommendation is you don't get caught, over."

Niner grunted. "Guys, I think Control is developing a sense of humor."

Dawson smiled, it true. He recognized the voice of the man they were dealing with, he green the first time they had worked with him, though he now showed much more confidence and comfort with his communications. He was a friend of Kane's and a man he knew he could trust to give him the best information available.

If he was dealing with Langley, Leroux was who he wanted to deal with.

And he was getting funny.

Dawson spotted a landing zone. "Bravo Team, there's a small plateau about one klick south-south-east of the target area, does everyone see it?"

Five confirmations quickly followed.

"Let's see if we can all set down there without breaking a nail."

Niner responded. "Atlas, you first. Remember, I'll be looking for something soft to land on."

"It'll be my fist shoved up your ass if you try it."

"Promises, promises."

Over Georgian Airspace

"Saber this is Gypsy One-Oh-Two. Permission to engage, over?"

Apocalypta—A-Poc for the syllabically averse—and her wingman screamed across the border into Georgian airspace, Georgian Air Traffic Control protesting loudly, jets already scrambling to intercept. The Georgian's aging fighters would be no match for their aircraft, but she had no desire to kill innocent pilots of a country that had no involvement beyond being the unwilling host to a minor skirmish between two massive militaries.

"Negative Gypsy One-Oh-Two, do not fire unless fired upon, over."

"Roger that, Saber, I highly recommend someone contact the Georgians again and remind them whose side we're on, over."

A-Poc's scope showed half a dozen so-called hostiles racing toward their position, though she doubted they had the balls to open fire, not on American fighters.

They have to know we'd give them a spanking that would make what the Russians did feel like a love tap.

"Riveter, let's hit the deck, see if they're willing to follow us into these mountains."

"Roger that," replied her wingman as they rapidly removed thousands of feet of comfort between them and the ground, the white-capped peaks of the Caucasus Mountains quickly nearing, the peaks soon over their heads. "This should be fun."

A-Poc laughed as she banked left then right, the canyon walls whipping past as they thundered toward their target area, the scope suggesting the Georgians were content to fly at altitude over the mountains and observe.

Exactly as I thought.

"I feel like I'm Clint Eastwood in Firefox!"

"Girl, how old are you?" laughed Riveter. "Independence Day, Will Smith!"

A-Poc rolled her eyes. "My God. I think I've been flying since you were a twitch in your daddy's jeans."

"Hey, don't hate the woman, hate that you came first."

She smiled, letting Riveter get the last word for the moment, instead concentrating on the terrain ahead.

And loving the greatest job in the world.

South Kuril Islands, Russian Federation
Japanese name: Chishima Islands

Captain Yamada cursed as an explosion ripped through the night sky, two flaming wrecks falling toward the ocean, it too dark to see if any parachutes had deployed. He raised his binoculars. "What the hell just happened? Who fired first?"

"I think they collided, sir!" replied his XO.

Then the horizon lit up, the Russian ships suddenly bright against the dark seas as missile after missile erupted from their launchers.

"Activate defenses and return fire! Everything we've got!"

He gripped his binoculars tight as he watched the Americans respond.

On the sea and in the air.

And so it ends?

All for a lie over seventy years old, to protect a bunch of old men who had probably done what they thought was right at the time, though seemed determined not to do so now.

I wonder what the Americans would think if they knew what this was truly about.

He had a feeling they wouldn't be here at all, and as the weapons systems of his country's destroyers opened up on the incoming ordnance, explosion upon explosion indicating their success and the destructive power of the incoming warheads, he wondered how long they would be able to hold.

"Sir, the Izumo has been hit!"

Yamada swung his binoculars to their starboard side, a massive fireball erupting from their sister ship, burning men highlighted against the intense orange and yellow of the flames that now engulfed the forward guns.

240

Someone jumped into the water, followed by another, their flaming bodies extinguished when they hit the water.

"Deploy rescue crews!"

"Yes, sir!"

He turned his attention to the battle, his ship rocking with each launch, with each shot fired from their mighty deck guns. The USS Fitzgerald had taken a hit, it partially aflame, and several Russian ships appeared to be fully involved. He stared at the skies, missiles streaking in the dead of night, fireball upon fireball indicating another brave young pilot meeting his maker.

All so Tokyo's elite could continue the lie.

Caucasus Mountains, Georgia
Ten miles inside the border

Acton spun toward Zorkin as the man yelped, suddenly gripping his shoulder, blood flowing over his fingers.

"You okay?"

Zorkin winced out a nod. "Yeah. Ricochet." He moved his hand and examined the wound. "I'll live, just a scratch."

Acton wasn't so sure 'scratch' was the right word considering the amount of blood that seemed to have flowed, though the pressure Zorkin was applying seemed to be stemming it.

But it also meant he was pretty much out of the fight if he wanted to maintain that pressure.

A roar from the enemy position erupted, the sound of footfalls crunching on snow clear as someone rushed their position. Acton leaned out and squeezed off two more rounds, another of their attackers dropping, another of his magazines empty.

One left.

The tight quarters and sustained AK-47 fire whenever they tried to take a shot, had proven effective in limiting their opportunities and their accuracy.

I guess suppression fire does work.

The sound of the choppers abruptly changed and he looked toward the thunder he could now physically feel, and cursed. Two imposing helicopters straight out of a Rambo movie were rounding the pass, an impressive array of weapons suddenly added to the mix as they slowed, turning toward their position.

"What now?" he shouted to Zorkin who had taken a glance at the choppers before returning his attention to their more immediate concern.

"We hold out! They can't land here!"

Acton stole a quick glance at Laura, whose eyes were wide and staring directly at the gunships. "They can open fire!"

Zorkin shook his head. "They want those relics you're carrying. They won't dare damage them."

One of the choppers turned slightly, repositioning itself, exposing one side. "Shit," muttered Acton as he saw an open door, there nobody in the back. "There's no one inside!"

Zorkin glanced over at him. "What?"

Acton pointed at the chopper. "There's no one inside, just the pilots!"

"They must have landed their troops somewhere else," said Laura. "Farther down the pass."

Acton agreed. "And they'll be here soon enough. Then it's over."

Zorkin glanced behind them, they about to have a second front opened up on them, there still six, at last count, in front of them. "We have a better chance of surviving if my people capture us!" he shouted, still gripping his arm.

Acton frowned. "Are you sure about that?"

Zorkin nodded. "Yes, your government knows you're here, you'll be safe."

"Eventually." Acton leaned out and fired two more precious bullets, the sound of someone crying out bringing a satisfied smile.

Make that five left.

He looked at Zorkin. "What about you?"

Zorkin shook his head. "I'm a dead man already. Don't concern yourself with me." He removed his hand from the wound and fired three rounds before ducking back down. "We hold until my countrymen arrive!"

Caucasus Mountains, Georgia
Eleven miles inside the border

Dawson flared his chute and came to a gentle landing, turning on his heel and pulling in the nylon canopy. As he began rolling it up, he checked for the others, spotting all five securing their chutes, no one seeming the worse for wear.

"Everyone good?"

Niner was the first to jog over, pulling off his helmet. "Yup."

"Find your soft landing spot?"

He grinned. "I did."

Atlas shrugged, rolling his shoulders. "The bastard landed right on top of me."

"I told you I would." He looked at Jagger. "And you were right, he wasn't as soft as I thought he'd be."

"Told you."

Niner started pointing fingers. "I'll be collecting my fifty bucks from each of you when we get back."

Dawson pointed to the north, in the direction the professors were supposed to be, the distinct sounds of gunfire and chopper rotors echoing through the valley. "Let's get a wiggle on. We're less than a klick out."

Niner smacked Atlas' ass. "Rock solid."

"As promised."

"Control, Zero-One. Any update on those Russian troops, over?"

"Zero-One, we're showing them less than five minutes from your target location. Your ETA?"

Dawson frowned. "Probably five minutes. What's the latest on the hostiles already at the location?"

"As expected, the professors have thinned them out. Looks like less than half a dozen actively in the fight."

Niner tossed a look over his shoulder. "I like those odds."

Dawson checked his watch. "Don't forget the dozen Russians."

"Okay, okay, I take it back."

Caucasus Mountains, Georgia
Ten miles inside the border

Acton spun as a roar from above drowned out the machine guns. He looked up to see someone dropping from overhead, his AK-47 at the ready, already belching lead at the mountainside over their heads. Acton pushed Laura to the side and jumped out from the alcove, twisting his body as he raised his weapon.

He emptied five shots into the man, the rounds tearing through his attacker's feet and lower extremities before he finally landed on him, slamming Acton into the hard ground, knocking the wind out of him.

And the AK-47 continued to fire.

Acton reached around, grabbing the man's arm, aiming the weapon away from where Laura was, but the man was impossibly strong, or Acton was impossibly cold, his hands like blocks of ice, all feeling in his feet lost long ago. Suddenly the man jerked to the left then immediately to the right, breaking Acton's grip. The Georgian bandit somehow managed to stand, stumbling backward before aiming his weapon directly at Acton's chest.

Laura calmly stepped forward, her Beretta extended. She pressed it against the man's temple and fired.

He crumpled forward, landing once again on Acton, this time unmoving.

The roar of more men charging their position had Laura whipping around, firing in groups of two as Acton struggled to get the man off him, he easily 250 pounds.

"I'm out!" shouted Laura, hitting the deck as the remaining men rushed toward them. Zorkin fired his final round, winging a man then futilely throwing his weapon at the horde.

It bounced off a head, slowing him for a split second.

And then they were on them, weapons aimed at all their heads. Acton raised his hands, still under their comrade. One of them sneered, raising his weapon, saying something Acton couldn't understand, though it seemed clear he was debating whether the reward was worth forgoing his desire for revenge.

Suddenly there was a loud thud, the man dropping to his knees, a gaping hole in his chest, a look of shock on his face as his soon to be lifeless hands reached for where his heart had once been.

His companions spun around, searching for the source, another hit, falling backward, blood splattering on the gray rock surrounding them. The final man started to fire blindly then had the sense to turn his weapon toward his prisoners.

His head disappeared in a red mist.

And the guns were finally silent.

Laura crawled over to her husband and together they rolled the dead blanket off him, he climbing to his feet, a wary eye on the bodies surrounding them and the choppers monitoring the situation.

With pilots who seemed little concerned with the new development.

"I wonder who we have to thank for that?"

Zorkin pushed himself to his feet, gripping his arm once again. "It could be the Russian troops deciding to save the tax payers five million rubles." He shrugged then regretted it. "Whoever it is, they have a clear view of our position."

Acton frowned, peering out into the near darkness. "So running isn't an option."

Laura stuffed her empty weapon in her belt, rubbing her hands together. "Without horses and supplies, we'll be dead by morning."

"Nobody move!"

They spun toward the voice, Russian troops suddenly rushing around the bend, weapons raised.

"I guess we know who our saviors were," muttered Acton, raising his hands once again.

A man stepped forward, clearly in charge, he and one other the only ones not in uniform. "Professor James Acton, Professor Laura Palmer and Citizen Viktor Zorkin, you are all under arrest!"

Caucasus Mountains, Georgia
Ten miles inside the border

"Nice shooting, gentlemen."

Dawson watched through his scope as the last of the professors' 'escorts' were eliminated, the three survivors looking about, probably trying to figure out who had just saved them. He turned his attention to the helicopters, still hovering, monitoring the situation.

They're probably trying to figure it out as well.

Niner lay prone on the ground about fifty feet to his right, his position giving him complete coverage, Atlas twenty feet farther on. "I would have to agree with that assessment," said Niner. "I *am* the best."

Atlas kept his eye pressed to his scope. "How that tiny body can hold such an inflated head, I'll never know."

"A lifetime of getting used to it. When you're this good, size doesn't matter."

Jimmy laughed. "You keep telling yourself that."

"Ouch! I do believe my manhood was stereotypically insulted."

"And you'd be right," rumbled Atlas.

"Trouble, BD," interrupted Jagger.

Dawson looked back at the trail as Russian troops rushed around the bend, weapons raised. "I see them."

"Looks like we're killing Russians today," muttered Atlas. "That can't be good."

Dawson chewed his cheek for a moment, surveying the area. Killing Russians was never good and best avoided, especially with two gunships, weapons bristling, covering the situation.

"What do we do, BD?" asked Jimmy. "Start shooting?"

Dawson shook his head. "No, if those pilots panic they could open up on the professors."

"Should we take them out?" asked Niner. "I've got a clear shot."

"Me too," added Atlas. "Our rounds will pierce those cockpits no problem at this range."

"No. I think we need to find a more peaceful solution."

And if that doesn't work, then *we start killing Russians.*

South Kuril Islands, Russian Federation
Japanese name: Chishima Islands

If I ever meet the inventor of the Phalanx system, I'll kiss him.

The computer-controlled system most of their new ships were now equipped with had made efficient work of most of the Russian missiles, only one of their ships having taken a direct hit. The Americans had made out worse, not from missile strikes but deck guns, the defense system not terribly effective on high-speed ballistic rounds.

It was the Russians though that now had his attention.

And he was smiling.

Every Russian ship had sustained significant damage, the combination of the American and Japanese arsenals simply too modern for most of the ships they faced, the Russian rearmament program not having finished its way through the Pacific Fleet.

Thank the heavens the Americans are on our side.

The battle hadn't lasted long, certainly not five minutes, more likely two or three before cooler heads had prevailed, the Russians begging for a ceasefire after they sustained a flurry of direct hits, they again claiming a misfire.

Right! From every ship? And multiple launches?

It was bullshit, but he had ordered his fleet to ceasefire the moment he confirmed the Russians had done the same. The Americans fired the last shot, destroying the missile in the air just before it made impact with the Russian flagship.

He redirected his attention to the skies, radar indicating the two air forces had separated, more than half the Russian planes downed, almost

251

half a dozen American planes lost. Rescue boats were in the waters from all sides, searching for downed pilots, his own crews having launched the moment the ceasefire seemed like it would hold.

People were dead.

Good people, from all sides, and everyone needed some time to let the adrenaline subside.

And let the politicians, now being informed of what had just happened, figure a way out of the mess they found themselves in.

Or war might be inevitable.

More ships from his own navy were already on their way, their attentions split between this engagement and an altercation with the Chinese. More American ships from the Seventh Fleet, along with additional air support, were on their way as well.

"Sir! The Hyuga is reporting a sonar contact!"

Yamada sighed at this new news from his XO. This was what he had feared the most. Submarines. He turned to look at the Hyuga to their port side. "I assume we have no idea who they are?"

"No, sir, but their bearing suggests they came from the north."

"Contact the Americans to see if it's one of theirs."

"Yes, sir!"

The last thing we need is to start dropping depth charges at someone trying to help us.
He frowned.

We might just lose the only thing keeping us alive.

Caucasus Mountains, Georgia
Ten miles inside the border

Acton aimed his weapon at the approaching Russians, stepping behind a large rock that had provided no cover from their previous problem, but excellent cover from the new arrivals.

Arriving from the north.

In the opposite direction of where their saviors had fired from only moments before.

Someone else is in this game. Someone who just might be on our side, not the Russians.

He just hoped it wasn't another rival group out for the reward.

Laura drew her empty weapon, the Russians not needing to know that little fact as he aimed his, the three remaining rounds not quite enough to finish off even those already visible, let alone the untold numbers around the bend, out of sight.

Zorkin simply shifted to the opposite side of his rock, his weapon already thrown at one of their attackers, it lying uselessly about twenty feet away.

"Drop your weapons or we will open fire," said the Russian in the lead.

Acton surveyed the situation. If they had ammo, they could potentially hold the pass until whoever had helped them arrived, though that could simply pull them out of one frying pan and toss them right into another, one with far worse consequences than possible arrest by the Russians.

Zorkin suddenly began a dash that turned into a stumble across the open space, weapons following him though not firing, the leader holding out his arms, motioning for everyone to take it easy. Zorkin joined them, gripping his hip.

"You okay?"

Zorkin nodded. "It's not broken, just bruised."

"So, what do you want to do?"

"Stall."

"For what?"

"For whoever fired those shots to arrive."

Laura frowned. "How do we know they're any more friendly than everyone else we've met on this trip?"

"Present company excluded, of course," added Acton with a wink at his wife.

"Those were sniper rounds. Georgian bandits don't have weapons like that."

Acton agreed. "And I didn't hear any Russian choppers farther south that could have dropped off a sniper team to take shots from that angle." He pointed at the blood spatter patterns. "Those shots definitely came from the south."

Zorkin smiled at him. "Very good, Professor. Perhaps you missed your calling?"

"What? Crime Scene Investigator?"

Zorkin chuckled. "No. Spy."

Acton rolled his eyes. "No thanks, I'll leave that to my students." He motioned toward the Russians, still holding their position. "So what are we saying here? If the Russians didn't shoot these guys, who did?"

"I'm not sure, but we've definitely got well-equipped friendlies in the area."

Acton and Laura exchanged excited glances. "Bravo Team!" they both hissed in unison.

254

Zorkin nodded. "Definitely some sort of Special Forces, probably American." He looked at Laura. "Bravo Team? As in Mr. White and his friends?"

Acton grinned at him. "So you *do* know them."

Zorkin nodded. "I've had the pleasure. And if they're here, we've got a chance at getting out of this alive and on the right side."

"Okay, so how do we make sure that happens?" asked Laura, eyeing the Russians who were inching forward.

"We buy them time." Zorkin glanced at their weapons, still pointed at the Russians. "Do either of you have any bullets?"

"I've got three rounds," replied Acton.

"I'm out," said Laura.

"Are you sure you've got three rounds?"

"Yes. I learned to count when I was potty training."

"Good boy." Zorkin motioned toward the advancing troops. "Put two rounds at his feet."

"Are you nuts?"

"Yes. But do it anyway."

Acton frowned. "Okay, you're the boss." He lowered his aim and prayed he hadn't lost count.

And squeezed twice.

The stone at the leader's feet was pulverized, dust and shards of sharp rock blasting up at the man's legs, Acton hoping the rounds didn't ricochet and set off what they were aiming to avoid.

An all-out gunfight.

"That's far enough!" shouted Zorkin, the leader holding out his arms, stopping the soldiers who Acton could tell clearly wanted to put an end to this. "In fact, let's have everybody back up a little."

Quick arm waves had them all back a few paces.

255

Zorkin seemed pleased. "Well, that worked."

Acton grunted. "Yeah, but for how long?"

"Hopefully long enough."

The Kremlin, Moscow, Russian Federation

"We insist you stand down before more get hurt," demanded Sasaki, glaring at his counterpart. Ivan Maksimov was no longer the friendly host, he fuming, the two delegations seated across from each other having tossed any pretense of friendship the moment the door had closed.

War was at their doorstep.

Someone had to blink.

And Sasaki's instructions just received were that it wouldn't be the Japanese.

The Americans are on our side.

"But for how long?" he had asked.

"Long enough. The Russians took a beating in the last exchange. They have to know that we and the Americans are committed. But it's important that they don't just withdraw. We need the Imperial Regalia returned. *That* is more important than avoiding war, and even more important than victory."

He had watched the reports from the embassy, the unfiltered, unconfirmed reports from the news organizations, chilling. A CNN crew happened to have been embedded on the USS Ronald Reagan and were pretty much broadcasting around the clock, the talking heads speculating as to why his country had reignited a conflict thought long over.

The Soviet-Japanese War, a forgotten war that had started *after* the surrender. Part of World War Two, yet not.

A precursor of what was to become the Cold War.

And now a powder keg about to ignite the next great war.

Unless he could somehow prevent it.

His Russian counterpart glared at him, slamming his fist on the table, the glasses and flower arrangements bouncing. "My government makes the same demand!" He held out a hand, lowering his voice suddenly. "We are willing to withdraw as a goodwill gesture, with the understanding you will do the same." He smiled slightly, it lacking any hallmarks of a sincere one. "Let this be settled at the negotiation table, among civilized men."

Sasaki said nothing, stifling his desire to suggest to the room that the only reason this offer was on the table was because of the pasting their navy had just taken, and the fact they were afraid of a true conflict with the Americans.

As he waited to speak, the crimson in the rotund man's cheeks increased as his rage built with the continued silence.

Sasaki finally spoke. "Not until what was taken from us is returned."

Maksimov leaned back in his chair, displaying his open palms. "It is my understanding that the items in question have been stolen."

Etsuko gasped, Sasaki holding out a hand under the table, touching her arm in an attempt to remind her of her duty to remain emotionless. It was a shock to him as well. A stunning revelation. It was at least confirmation that the Russians had the relics, though if they were stolen, *had* would be the right word. It at the very least meant the existence of the relics had been communicated to Moscow, his ploy of the open broadcast having worked.

Yet now they were stolen.

Stolen!

"Stolen? By who?"

Maksimov batted away the question with a flick of his wrist. "Who, is of no importance. Be assured we are in pursuit of the criminals." There was a pause, the first time the man appeared uncomfortable, Maksimov shifting in his chair. "There, however, remains a chance that we may not recover them." Etsuko stifled another gasp, Sasaki's jaw clenching. "In fact, they may even have been destroyed."

Sasaki felt the indignant rage build from within, his cheeks flushing, his hands gripping the arms of his chair. He glared at the man across from him. "Then, sir, I fear there may be no hope." He gripped his chair tighter, his knuckles turning white. "*War* may be inevitable."

Maksimov pursed his lips, meeting Sasaki's gaze, probably trying to ascertain whether there was a bluff to be called here. If the Americans hadn't so vigorously defended themselves just minutes ago, prompting the urgent call from the Russians for a new meeting, there would indeed have been a bluff to call. At least one worth calling, there no way the Japanese Navy could defeat the Russian Pacific Fleet.

Yet things had changed.

Dramatically.

"You would go to war over these relics?"

Sasaki nodded.

"I've been briefed on what they are. Your people have been lied to for decades. Why not continue the lie and save your country?"

Sasaki met the man's gaze. "It is a matter of honor."

A burst of air revealed the derision Maksimov felt for the word, a reaction Sasaki would expect from a posturing, arrogant fool. "Honor? Honor! You would go to war over *honor*? The very idea is ludicrous!"

Sasaki clamped down on his cheek with his teeth, controlling the reaction he so wanted to deliver as the tirade of disrespect continued.

And with each word, each insult, it proved to him just how desperate the Russians were to get out of the situation in which they found themselves. Their economy was collapsing. With the drop in oil prices and the economic sanctions due to the Ukraine situation, they no longer had the money to rebuild their military at the pace they had set for themselves, and they certainly didn't have the money for a sustained conflict that could see billions of rubles sent to the bottom of the ocean.

And it also proved to him that the Russians definitely didn't have the Imperial Regalia in their possession anymore, otherwise they'd turn them over.

"How can you possibly justify so many deaths over a matter of honor!"

Sasaki waited to make certain the onslaught of insults was over.

It was, the big man huffing on the other side of the table, his face red, beads of sweat on his forehead. He reached for a drink, Sasaki waiting for him to put the glass down so there would be no excuse for the man not to respond, should he feel the desire.

"When my people thought the Imperial Regalia were lost, they had assumed they were lost to the sands of time, to one day be recovered so none would be the wiser. We had faith in our gods and in our emperor. It was a lie or a deception in your mind, a necessity in ours, for the times after the war demanded stability, consistency, and to admit their loss may have sent our people into a spiral of despair rather than the vibrant renewal we did experience. Japan is what it is today *because* of the lie told back then.

"But now, with this new truth known, that not only were they not lost, but instead the men sent to protect them slaughtered illegally by your soldiers, my government can no longer standby and allow this atrocity to go unchallenged. And to add insult to the injury inflicted upon my people seventy years ago, you now have the unmitigated gall to not only confiscate but *lose* these relics our people hold so dear. These actions, both then and now, are unforgivable in our leaders' eyes."

Maksimov had remained remarkably quiet, though his response was delivered with a cold finality. "Then your leaders will die."

A slight smile emerged on Sasaki's face. "Don't be so confident, sir. I have just received reports, as I'm sure you have, that your navy took a beating from not only our ships, but the Americans."

Maksimov smiled. "That may be, but our submarines have arrived, and if you do not withdraw, they will blow your ships out of the water." He leaned forward. "You may have won the battle, but you *will* lose the war." He pushed back in his chair, flicking his wrist again. "Besides, you have more to worry about than us. The Chinese seem to be mobilizing for a serious territorial claim." He chuckled. "I think very soon your attentions will be divided, and you will have to decide what is more important to you. Islands that have not been yours for decades, or those that still are."

Sasaki shook his head. "You will find our resolve on this matter will not waver. This can all end if you return what is rightfully ours. If you had not stolen the Imperial Regalia, if you had simply allowed our people to take them back to Japan, all of this could have been avoided."

Maksimov leaned forward, jabbing a finger in the air at him. "No! This is *not* our fault. *Your* people trespassed, *not* ours. Our people confiscated items found on *our* land, not knowing what they were. Instead of informing us of what they were, you instead sent warships into our territory, blockading islands belonging to *us*. And instead of admitting the true purpose to your indignity, you instead lie to the world, tricking the Americans into supporting you." He shook his head. "No, sir, *you* are in the wrong here, not us, but your pride won't let you see it."

The sad thing about what Maksimov said was that he was absolutely right. Japan had violated their territory, and his government had responded with force and a lie. If the truth had simply been told, the Russians might very well have returned what they had taken. He had been there. He could attest to the fact the Russian commander on the scene had *no* idea what he had just seized.

If Tokyo had simply told the truth, this may all have been avoided.

Yet they hadn't. Pride, honor, tradition, showing their ugly side.

But with the apparent theft of the relics, the Russians, despite knowing they had something of importance to his people, having treated them so cavalierly to leave them vulnerable, had changed the equation.

Yes, his government had created the situation, but the Russian government, through its negligence, was perpetuating it.

And if the Imperial Regalia were indeed possibly destroyed as his counterpart had suggested, he feared what the response might be.

He stared at Maksimov, revealing none of his thoughts, he still having a job to do. "I am afraid I am but the messenger here. But you confuse pride and honor. This is a matter of *honor* for our country, our emperor, and our way of life. A crime was committed by your country at the end of the war, and a mistake was made by us as a result. We lied to our people, and that was dishonorable. To admit that lie now, after an emperor has been sworn in, presenting replicas as evidence he is the rightful heir, would bring shame and dishonor to our entire nation and those prominent families that control much of what the outside world does not see." He leaned forward. "So you see, sir, my government cannot back down. Not without the Imperial Regalia returned." He lowered his head slightly, staring into Maksimov's eyes. "I highly recommend, should you desire peace, you recover our property. Intact."

Caucasus Mountains, Georgia
Ten miles inside the border

Dymovsky glanced down at his feet, his pants and shoes covered in rock dust, his eyes and nerve endings telling him he hadn't been hit by the shots fired at him by Professor James Acton. When he had read the man's file, he had assumed his exploits were overblown, though surveying the scene seemed to suggest otherwise. Almost a dozen Georgian bandits were dead, none by Russian government hands, one even missing a head somehow.

He glanced at Zorkin who he had no doubt was responsible for the order to fire the two shots. He was bleeding from the shoulder, the amount of blood suggesting it wasn't superficial. He wasn't a threat anymore, and if all these professors had were two handguns and a questionable amount of ammo, then something more was going on here.

They're stalling.

But why were they stalling?

Filippov stepped up behind him, whispering in his ear. "The lead pilot just reported he thinks there's at least one sniper in the area."

Dymovsky's eyebrows rose and he turned his head slightly toward his partner. "Are you sure?"

"I can only report what I was told, but"—he nodded toward the man with a missing head—"the evidence certainly suggests it."

Dymovsky surreptitiously scanned the path that stretched ahead of them, bending slightly to the left, no one evident. His eyes began to follow a ridgeline over their heads when his satellite phone vibrated in his pocket.

He frowned and turned, stepping around the bend so the Russian speaking Zorkin couldn't overhear what was said. "Dymovsky. Go ahead."

"This is Deputy Minister Maksimov. Report!"

Dymovsky frowned, it clear his belligerent puppet master was in a foul mood. He could only assume things weren't going well in the Kuril's or the negotiation room. "Sir, we have the professors and Zorkin."

"Oh, thank God! So you have the relics?"

"Not yet, sir."

"Not yet! I thought you said you had them!"

The shouting was so loud it was causing half of what he said to be transmitted as static.

The louder you talk, the less likely it is I'll hear you, you ass!

"We have them trapped and I'm about to begin negotiations for their surrender."

"Forget negotiations. Just kill them and take what they stole."

"Sir, killing American and British citizens is, I believe, highly inadvisable."

"Nonsense. You're in Georgia. Kill them, make it look like the Georgians did it, and get the hell out of there and back to Moscow. We need those ridiculous trinkets the Japs are so enamored with or there could be war!"

"So we're returning them now?"

"Yes. They've offered to withdraw and cede the islands to us. We're happy with that result."

Bullshit. You're scared of how much a conflict in the Pacific could cost the Federal Treasury, and have figured out a way to make it look like you won.

And it was true. If the Japanese received whatever it was they were after in a private settlement, then there was no reason to think they'd admit publicly what this had all been about. They would withdraw, cede the islands, and it would look like Mother Russia had won without conceding anything.

And the Japanese would be the aggressors, their friendship with the United States perhaps strained for some time.

"What are these relics that they want? Why are they so important?"

"That is not your concern. All you need to know is that it is *absolutely essential* that we retrieve these relics, *intact*, as quickly as possible. Now kill those damned professors and that traitor Zorkin, and get me my relics!"

The call ended and Dymovsky shook his head, jamming his phone back in his pocket. Filippov looked at him. "Learn anything new?"

Dymovsky smiled at him, the young man discovering quickly that men in their position rarely knew the whole truth. "Not much, except that Moscow isn't after the professors at all, only some relics that they possess that belong to the Japanese."

Filippov's eyebrows narrowed. "Why would they steal Japanese relics?"

"I don't think they did for a second. I think Orlov gave them to the professors so they could get them back to the Japanese, but the plan was interrupted. If the Kremlin hadn't discovered they were missing, the professors would have been on their plane and long gone, and Comrade Zorkin would still be sipping his dinner in his apartment, none the wiser."

"So they're not the bad guys?"

"Perhaps to the world at large, no, but to Moscow? Yes. And if we are being completely honest with ourselves, Moscow seems to want to return these relics, and if they still had them, they would. The professors having them could actually cost more lives."

Filippov frowned. "They may be to blame with *that* logic, but I've been around enough to know that we live in a country where no one trusts anybody. If we didn't constantly live in fear of the wrong thing being done, Orlov would never have felt the need to contact the professors, he would have trusted that his government would have done the right thing. Instead, because of the environment we live in, he did what he thought was best because he couldn't rely upon our leaders to act in their people's best interest."

Dymovsky smiled, patting the young man on the shoulder. "Son, with thinking like that, you're either going to go very far, or be dead very soon."

Filippov grinned. "Let's hope we both live long enough that we rise past our enemies and see *them* buried rather than us."

Acton watched the leader's whispered conversation, not missing the man's eyes surveying the area ahead before a quick departure, a phone making an appearance. He glanced at the choppers, still hovering, their rotors loud, the wind forcing the biting chill deep into his bones.

I'm going to lie on that beach for a month when we're out of here!

He frowned as a soldier stepped forward half a pace.

If we get out of here.

With their commander out of sight, the mice appeared ready to play.

And with one bullet between them, he had only one play left.

He lifted the bag holding the Imperial Regalia and pointed his gun at it.

"If anyone takes another step, I'll destroy them!"

They kept advancing.

Maybe they have no idea why they're here!

He groaned inwardly.

Boys, if you're anywhere near here, now would be a good time to show up.

Dymovsky heard the professor shout and he blanched as he and Filippov exchanged horrified glances. "No!" shouted Dymovsky as he elbowed his way around the bend and back to the front. "Everyone back!" He rounded the turn and found three of his soldiers within feet of the professors, Acton with his Beretta pressed against a canvas bag that clearly contained the keys to stopping what could soon become a costly, bloody war.

"One more step and I put a bullet through the mirror!" shouted Acton. It was unfortunate for the man that Dymovsky had read his file. This was a devotee to history and there was no way he was going to destroy a precious relic simply to save his own life.

The bigger concern however was that the relics could be damaged should the situation continue.

"I said everyone back!"

The men stopped their slow advance, beginning to fall back equally slow. He stepped in front of them, his hands raised slightly, defusing the situation. Acton seemed to visibly relax, the man's eyes now focused on Dymovsky instead of the soldiers.

Dymovsky urged them all further back, retreating himself to force the issue. He couldn't risk someone accidentally firing and hitting the relics, and at this moment there were too many guns squeezed into too small an area.

He looked at the professor. "We seem to be at an impasse, Professor Acton."

"It would appear so."

"You have what I want, yet you know I can't risk them being damaged or destroyed."

"Then why don't you just goosestep—"

"James!"

"—back to Moscow and leave us be?"

Dymovsky smiled slightly at Laura Palmer's admonishment of her husband. "I have my orders."

"What are your orders? To recover the relics intact?"

"Yes."

"But why? What do you want to do with them?"

"My government wishes to return them to Japan so peace can be restored."

Acton smiled. "Then why not let *us* do that?"

Dymovsky frowned. The professor was right. If peace were indeed the ultimate goal then it wouldn't matter who returned the relics. But Moscow was insistent he recover them, even though they knew who currently possessed them, and couldn't possibly believe that these people had any intention other than returning the relics themselves.

It's all to save face.

Just as with the Japanese, his own government was willing to risk war, all so that *they* could be the ones to return them. If these professors returned them, then the credit would go to *them* for preserving the peace, and Russia may even lose its claim to the islands should the Americans demand reparations for the skirmishes that had already occurred.

No, his government wanted to be the ones to return them so they could secure their claim on the islands and embarrass the Japanese into submission, knowing they couldn't admit as to why any of this had occurred.

Both sides were arrogant and misguided. *Both* were trying to save face, one for lies told over seventy years ago, one for unchecked arrogance and provocation today.

And if neither backed down, they could end up destroying each other.

But what's the surest way to peace?

If the professors returned the relics, he had no doubt that peace would be restored, and it would eliminate his government from the equation, preventing any more provocation on their part. The risk was that the professors, at the moment, appeared to have no way to get out of here with the relics except on foot.

And they appeared quite ill-equipped to accomplish even that.

They'll be frozen to death by morning.

He couldn't risk it.

"I'm afraid, Professor Acton, we remain at an impasse."

"Perhaps I can help sway opinions."

Dymovsky spun around, looking up to see four soldiers, clearly special forces by their equipment, staring down at them from a ridge above, weapons aimed at him and his team.

"Everyone drop their weapons, nice and slow."

Dawson kept his weapon trained on the most nervous looking Russian in his arc. He wasn't worried about the leader; he didn't have a weapon in evidence, though he was sure there was probably one tucked away in a shoulder or hip holster somewhere.

Something jerked to his left and Spock fired, the soldier crying out as he was hit in the shoulder. A deliberate flesh wound. If Spock had wanted the man dead, he'd be dead.

Dawson stared at the leader. "The next one dies."

The leader smiled, nodding toward the captain in command who raised a radio.

"Now."

The choppers immediately adjusted their position, their weapons now aimed directly at Dawson and his men.

Let's hope timing is everything.

"Bogies in sight." A-Poc banked to the left, her Heads Up Display indicating a lock on the first helicopter. "I've got tone." She flicked her thumb, selecting her sidewinder missiles. "Fox Two." She fired, calmly turning her attention to the second target as the missile streaked from her weapons pod toward the doomed airframe hovering ahead.

"Second bogie in sight. I've got tone. Fox Two." She squeezed, the missile dropping, the propellant igniting, racing toward its target. As the first helicopter erupted in a ball of fire, the second banked hard to the left, its pilot recognizing what was happening, the only result the exposure of its belly to its enemy.

The second missile found its target, the threat to the ground forces eliminated as A-Poc and her wingman blasted past, her eyes already on the twisting corridors of their chosen route, the Georgians still apparently content to observe from above.

"Saber this is Gypsy One-Oh-Two, two bogies splashed. Where are those Georgians, over?"

"Gypsy One-Oh-Two, Georgian Air Force is returning to base. Change course immediately, you're about to violate Russian airspace, over."

A-Poc flattened out then pulled up hard, gaining altitude to clear the mountain tops, then flipped it hard to the left, pulling enough gees to impress an astronaut as she banked sharply, her HUD indicating she had stayed outside of Russia, her jet wash probably guilty of violating it. She checked for her wingman and smiled, spotting her on her wing.

"Gypsy One-Oh-Two returning for another pass."

She pushed forward on her stick, plunging back toward the canyons below.

Best. Job. Ever.

Acton's jaw lay open as he watched the helicopters drop from sight, the jets shaking the ground as they thundered past. He leaned out to see the Delta Force members overhead covering the Russians, Russians who suddenly seemed far less confident in their control of the situation.

And he sensed panic in the eyes of some of them.

Panic that could trigger a disaster that might kill them all.

Then he had an idea.

He handed his gun to Zorkin and stepped out slowly from behind the rock they had been using for cover, his hands up, the canvas bag containing the relics slung over his shoulder. "Perhaps I can suggest a solution?"

The leader, who appeared just as shocked as anyone else at the unexpected turn of events, snapped his jaw shut. He and several guns turned toward Acton, prompting him to extend his hands further out from his sides.

"What do you propose?"

"Come with us."

The man's eyebrows shot up. "What?"

"Come with us. *You* come with us and we'll hand the relics over together. Hell, *you* can hand them over yourself as a representative of the Russian government. I don't care. I just don't trust that Moscow will actually do it. *You* come with us, send your men back, and we'll deliver these to the Japanese together and stop whatever the hell is going on over there."

The man's head slowly bobbed.

It was a crazy, brilliant idea. Dymovsky eyed the professor, casting a quick glance overhead at the soldiers. If those were all Acton had on his side, the odds, if not the high ground, were in his favor, though he had the distinct impression there were more hidden somewhere, perhaps the snipers the dead pilot had referred to.

Though numbers weren't everything.

High ground, held by what were probably Delta Force or Navy SEALS, would trump his superior numbers any day.

Yet Acton's solution was an interesting one. He could order his men back and use whatever means of extraction the American soldiers had

271

already planned, probably already en route. It would save all their lives, and get the relics back in the proper hands, saving even more.

"That *is* an idea."

"Comrade, no!"

He spun toward the captain in charge of the ground troops, the man's AK-74 rising, its aim shifting from the suspects to Dymovsky.

And he knew he was going to die, the rage in the man's eyes clear.

He was about to fire.

A shot rang out from overhead, the captain spinning around, his finger squeezing, bullets spraying from the barrel of his weapon, lead ricocheting off the rock face before finding flesh.

Filippov didn't get a chance to cry out, he caught in the face with three rounds, his body collapsing forward, toppling over the edge and falling out of sight.

And the shots continued until the magazine was at last emptied, the final rounds finding one more soft target.

Dymovsky's stomach.

Chaos erupted.

All of the soldiers turned their weapons on the Americans above.

Americans who simply stepped back, out of sight.

"Cease fire!" he gasped as he collapsed against the rock face.

But his order went unheeded.

Dawson stepped back, there no point in getting shot or shooting back. The thunder of Niner's sniper rifle belching lead at the Russians was enough for him to know the fight would be soon over, the talented operator and his spotter, Jimmy, having a clear view of the entire proceedings less than a mile away.

His only concern now was the professors.

And there were too many panicking and dying Russians ten feet below him to let this continue for too long.

"Grenades!"

He pulled one off his ammo belt, the others doing the same. Pulling the pin, he counted to two then tossed it over the edge, making sure it was around the bend so the professors and Zorkin would be shielded by the rock face.

The blasts were deafening, the screams horrific, but the gunfire stopped. He stepped over to the ledge and looked down at the carnage below. Not a soldier was left standing, and those that remained intact were either dead or writhing in agony.

He sighed.

They had their chance.

And they squandered it.

He took no pleasure in killing these men. They had done nothing to harm anyone, at least not here, not today. And now thanks to poor training or poor leadership, they were dead or dying.

And his team remained intact, not a scratch on them.

"Cover me."

He handed a rope to Atlas who took a grip on it, Dawson lowering himself to the path below, his weapon on the Russian troops just in case anyone decided to make a last stand.

No one did.

He looked up. "Get down here and see what you can do for them." He activated his comm. "One-One, Zero-One. Position secure. Get here on the double, over."

"Roger that, Zero-One," replied Niner.

Dawson heard familiar voices around the bend.

"Are you okay?" asked what sounded like an older man, clearly Zorkin.

273

"Yes, I think so," replied Laura. "James?"

"Yeah, though I think I shit my pants," said Acton. "How's your shoulder?"

Zorkin grunted. "It's just a flesh wound."

"Well, you're bleeding all over yourself, so you might want to rethink that bravado and let me take a look at it."

Dawson rounded the bend, smiling at the source of the banter. "Good to see you all again."

"BD!" Laura rushed forward and gave him a hug as Atlas rounded the bend. "Atlas!"

"I heard sugar was being dispensed," rumbled Atlas, giving Laura a quick hug.

Acton shook their hands. "Thank God you're here."

"Let's try meeting on a beach next time," said Dawson, looking around. "It's too damned cold here."

"We *were* on a beach. It was nice." Acton shivered. "And warm."

Dawson spotted a bag slung over Acton's shoulder. "Is that them?"

Acton nodded. "Yes. Now can we get the hell out of here before the jewels start clinking?"

Dawson chuckled, turning to Atlas. "Stick out a thumb, find us a ride."

"Consider it done," replied Atlas, stepping away, contacting Control as Jagger and Spock began to quickly disarm the Russians, tossing their weapons over the edge of the path.

Acton glanced up as two jets slowly circled overhead. "They saved all our asses, I think."

Dawson agreed. "Yup. Sometimes flyboys are handy to have around."

The thunder of helicopters that had been approaching for the past couple of minutes was finally noticed by Acton. He looked about. "Are those Russian?"

Dawson shook his head. "No, that's our ride home."

Acton nodded toward the Russians, the rest of the team doing what they could to treat the wounded and make the dying more comfortable. "What about them?"

Dawson frowned. "We'll have to leave them," he said as Niner and Jimmy arrived from the southern end of the path. "But I don't think any of them are going to be alive much longer."

Niner grinned at them. "Hiya, doc, how are things? Been up to anything interesting lately?"

Acton smiled, shaking the new arrivals' hands. "Oh you know, the usual. Catching a little sun, enjoying my vacation."

Niner made a show of shoving past him, his arms extended. "Laura, baby, how are you?"

Laura laughed, giving him a hug then pushing him away good-naturedly. "Now, Niner, you know we can't be doing that in front of my husband."

Niner smacked Acton's ass, causing him to flinch in surprise, giving Dawson a look that had him stifling a laugh. "I think the doc likes it. Makes him realize how lucky he is."

"Next time you spank my ass, Niner, it better be on a football field or after a fine meal."

Niner grinned, about to say something, Dawson cutting him off. He motioned toward Zorkin. "See what you can do for him."

Niner became all business, he and Jimmy immediately heading for the elderly Russian sitting on a rock, still gripping his arm. Spock rounded the bend, shaking his head slightly.

None of this was necessary.

Dymovsky watched the friendly banter between the professors and the American soldiers, it clear they knew each other. Which meant this must be the Delta Force team referred to in the files he had read.

He looked over to where Filippov had fallen over the edge, he about the only person who had ever been truly friendly to him in years—at least at the office. He had friends outside of work, he had family.

Yet as the blood oozed from his stomach, as the pain racking his body slowly eased as he became weaker from the numbing effect of the cold rock, he realized the finality of his situation.

He would die today, along with so many others, a failure.

The Kremlin would blame him for what had happened, quite likely concocting a story where he had planned the fiasco with Orlov, letting the professors escape with the stolen Japanese relics in order to collect some sort of reward.

Or they might just go with the incompetence route.

It had worked before, he blamed for the Brass Monkey near-disaster.

As long as their Napoleonic leader shared none of the blame.

He looked up as Professor Acton knelt down beside him. "Can I get you anything?"

Dymovsky shook his head. "N-no. I-it doesn't actually hurt that much."

Acton glanced over at one of the American soldiers. "Can you do anything for him?"

A slight shake of the head was the response.

Acton seemed genuinely disappointed.

"I-it's okay. It's not your fault. A-and I'd rather d-die quickly."

"Can I ask you something?"

Dymovsky nodded.

"Why?"

"I-I had my orders."

"I know, but was all this worth it? Look at how many people died."

Dymovsky smiled weakly. "If you r-return them and stop the war, then yes."

"But you and your men?"

"We-we died pursuing you. I-if I hadn't done my job, th-then you might not have tr-tried so hard to get out." He smiled slightly, looking past Acton as a freshly bandaged Viktor Zorkin stepped over.

Zorkin knelt down beside them, putting a hand on Dymovsky's shoulder. "You were a good adversary. I enjoyed the chase. Even if you were working for a government I no longer believe in."

Dymovsky nodded slightly, saying nothing.

"What will happen to my friends?"

Dymovsky closed his eyes, picturing the young man whose only concern was helping his father, and the old couple, who cared only for who would tend their beloved animals. "I'm afraid this incident will be w-wiped from the records."

Zorkin frowned. "So they're all going to die."

Dymovsky nodded. "Y-yes, I fear so."

A sudden jolt of pain shot through his body and he gasped, his eyes opening wide as a blinding white light overwhelmed his vision, his adversaries washed away.

And it was over.

Zorkin leaned forward, closing the man's eyes, the American professor sighing, patting the man on the shoulder. He was dead, but that was the life of one who served, whether it was as a soldier, a spy, or a law enforcement officer—you could die at any time.

And this man had died honorably, doing his duty for his country, however misguided it may have been. He had done nothing to deserve this,

277

and in fact had tried to defuse things, ready to join them in handing over the relics.

No one should have died.

Instead, due to the actions of one out of control soldier, too many had given their lives for no good reason that he could think of. And unless he took action, more good people would die.

And that was unacceptable.

The Delta leader walked over. "Okay everyone, we've got more Russian choppers heading here so we've gotta book. On the double, people. Company's arriving and they're not invited."

Diyarbakir Airbase, Turkey

Sasaki walked briskly across the tarmac, toward a hangar nearby, its massive doors partially opened. Apparently a call had been received by his government only hours before, indicating the Americans had recovered property belonging to the Japanese people, it all very hush-hush, nothing specific going out over the airwaves, encrypted or otherwise.

But there was only one thing they could possibly be referring to.

He had been immediately dispatched as he was the only person currently in the region privy to the secret, cancelling a meeting with Maksimov at the last minute, much to the surprise of his counterpart, Etsuko giggling as she related the indignant rage he had expressed at the news.

And at the news being delivered by an underling.

Part of him had wondered if the Russians would do anything foolish like try to shoot them down or force them to land, though it was a small part. The Russians were arrogant, but not stupid. An action like that would be unprecedented, at least in modern relations between civilized countries.

Though nothing would surprise him in this day and age.

The news was tense in the Chishima Islands, the standoff continuing, all three sides licking their wounds and holding their positions, no further incidents having occurred since the few minutes of lunacy that had put the world on the brink.

But until the Imperial Regalia were officially reclaimed, hostilities could again break out with the twitch of a gunner's nervous finger.

As he stepped through the doors, the bright sunshine outside leaving him momentarily blind as he entered the dim hangar, he prayed to all that was holy that what he was about to see were the cause of so much pain and destruction.

And that they were intact after seventy years unprotected.

His eyes adjusted and he saw a congregation standing in the middle of the hangar. Six heavily armed soldiers, all in black, appeared to be securing an invisible perimeter, at the center of which stood a table with a man and woman of European descent.

"I am Arata Sasaki, Japanese Foreign Ministry, I understand—" He froze, his jaw dropping as his eyes moved from the smiling Europeans to the table. His knees nearly buckled as he immediately recognized what they were. "Y-you found them!"

"Yes," replied the man.

"How?" He ran his hands over the air above the precious relics, not daring to actually touch them lest his eagerness destroy what had survived so much.

"It took some effort," replied the woman.

He looked up at them, finally. "Are they authentic?"

The man nodded. "My name is Professor James Acton. This is Professor Laura Palmer. We're both professors of archaeology, and we believe they are indeed genuine."

Sasaki sighed, closing his eyes for a moment. He opened them, beaming a smile at the two professors. "Thank you. On behalf of the Japanese people and my government, we thank you."

Acton bowed slightly. "You're welcome. But I do have a question."

"Anything!"

"How did the Russians come to find them in the first place?"

Sasaki dropped his head in shame, bowing apologetically. "I am afraid that is the one question I cannot answer."

Acton looked at the other professor. "I had a feeling you'd say that. Don't worry about it."

Sasaki rose. "Thank you for your understanding." He reached into his pocket, retrieving his phone. "Excuse me, but I have a call to make." The two professors bowed slightly and he turned away, walking quickly toward the still open doors of the hangar.

"Sasaki, is that you?"

"Yes, sir."

"Report."

"I have them!"

South Kuril Islands, Russian Federation
Japanese name: Chishima Islands

"Sir, we've been ordered to assist against the Chinese at Senkaku."

Yamada turned, his eyes slightly wide. "What? Confirm those orders."

Nakano bowed. "I already have, sir. It would appear that some sort of peace agreement has been reached with the Russians. We are to assist at once with the Chinese situation."

"And the islands?"

Nakano shook his head. "There's nothing mentioned in the message, sir."

Yamada frowned, peering through his binoculars at the Russian ships in the distance, most of the fires out though smoke still billowed from the worst hit.

Then one turned, the disabled ship following, a towline evident.

And the others joined them.

Thus ending the most intense skirmish his country had been in since the war.

I wonder what the historians will call this when they write about it.

He turned, staring at the tiny islands behind them, islands that the world thought had been at the root of all this, and wondered if the truth would ever be told.

Or was there never enough time to pass before the shame of an emperor could be revealed.

Over Spanish Airspace

Acton rested his head against the seatback, his eyes barely open. Laura sat beside him, the half-dozen members of Bravo Team spread across her private jet.

Their *private jet.*

He still had a hard time fathoming just how rich she was, and now *he* was. He could never think of it as *his* money though she had given him joint access to everything.

God, I love that woman!

It wasn't the money, not by a longshot, it was her. She was incredible. The smartest, bravest, most beautiful woman he had ever met. A woman that had been through so much since she had met him, and despite all the danger and heartache, had stuck by his side.

Remarkable.

He had thought about things long and hard at times, especially before proposing. She always liked to say that it wasn't his fault that these things had happened to them, though he had come to the conclusion it was.

For the most part.

The Triarii, responsible for so much of their pain, would never have been in her life if he hadn't contacted her. They wouldn't have met Martin Chaney, a member of that organization that had then introduced them to his contacts at the Vatican, and they never would have become involved with Bravo Team.

It *was* all his fault.

And one of these days he would get her killed.

And every day it tore at his heart.

Yet there was nothing he could, or would, do about it, for he knew if he did end it, end them, it would break her heart just as surely as if he had stabbed it with a dagger of betrayal.

He stared at her, a smile on his face, a hint of tears in his eyes.

"What's wrong?"

"Nothing. Just thinking how much I love you."

She leaned over and gave him a long, slow, kiss. "I love you too." She pulled back a few inches, staring into his eyes. "We're safe. Stop worrying about me."

His smiled spread. "You know me too well."

She punched him in the shoulder. "I'm a big girl. Don't make me kick your ass. I just want to get back on that beach and banish the cold from those mountains out of my bones."

His smile broadened. "God, you're great."

"Bloody right I'm great." She poked him. "And so are you, so get over yourself."

He chuckled, deciding she was right. "So, do you think Greg and Sandra noticed we were gone?"

She shrugged. "Not sure, but I do know when I called her there was some giggling going on, so I have a funny feeling they didn't mind the alone time."

Acton smiled, his eyes watering with the thought of how great it was that his best friend was still with them, how he had survived being shot twice, quite likely by one of the six men on this plane with them, then fought back, surviving against the odds, regaining his ability to walk, now healthy enough to travel across the world to lay on a beach and make love to his wife.

Life is good.

He frowned. "I'm concerned about Viktor."

Laura nodded. "Me too. He's too old to do what he's planning on doing. Whatever that is."

"I don't know about that," replied Acton. "That old bastard got us out of Russia and halfway through the mountains, took a bullet, and was still as feisty as ever when we left him in Turkey."

"This is true. I hope he's able to help Arseny and his boy. He was such a sweetheart. And Darya and Boris. They were just precious."

"He'll figure out a way. Somehow."

Acton leaned back, closing his eyes for a moment, thinking about how he wished he could have gone with Zorkin to help clean up the mess they had left behind. If they hadn't have agreed to go to Moscow, Orlov's son wouldn't have become involved, the old couple wouldn't have become involved, and Zorkin wouldn't have become involved.

But if Orlov hadn't called them then none of this would have happened, so it was actually *his* fault.

Acton mentally kicked himself.

The man was trying to do the right thing.

He sighed.

And was probably dead for his efforts.

Though at least the relics were in the proper hands. Dawson had informed them just a short while ago that satellite imagery showed the Russian Air Force and Navy being recalled, and their Eastern Military District standing down. The Japanese Navy had redeployed to push back the Chinese, and the bulk of the US Seventh Fleet was moving to join them, a few ships left behind to make sure nobody acted up until formal agreements could be signed, and with the combined navies steaming southwest, the Chinese were pulling out, claiming a naval exercise.

The conflict was over.

Though not before an apparent flurry of suicides among high-ranking Japanese politicians and captains of business, the press wildly speculating as to the cause, the going theory that they had somehow been responsible for the unwinnable conflict.

A conflict recognized as too great a danger to be allowed to continue by a brave Russian citizen who had realized he couldn't trust his government to do the right thing, and instead had made a single phone call to a man he barely knew, a man he trusted more than those he had worked with for years.

Acton opened his eyes, watching the Delta team laughing and joking around.

And thanks to these brave souls who had once again risked their lives.

A risk no one would ever know about.

Dawson walked down the aisle, stopping by Atlas' seat. "Just got off the phone with Maggie. Looks like there might be trouble on the home front."

All the joking and kidding around immediately stopped, everyone turning to their friend, Acton sensing something was terribly wrong.

"What?" asked the proud warrior, his voice giving the first hint of trepidation Acton had ever heard from it.

Dawson said nothing, just reaching out and putting a hand on the big man's shoulder.

Atlas muttered a curse. "It's Vanessa, isn't it?"

Dawson nodded.

Atlas sighed. "I had a feeling." He looked up at Dawson. "What do we know?"

"Apparently she broke down then ran out of Maggie's apartment saying she couldn't take it."

Atlas' face sagged and Acton felt for the big man, his chest tightening as one of the toughest men he had ever known began to slowly deconstruct in front of him. "I-I guess it wasn't meant to be."

Niner rose from his seat, switching to the one next to Atlas. He put a hand on his friend's shoulder and squeezed. "I'm really sorry, man. I know you really like her."

Atlas tossed his head back against the seat, sighing loudly. "I loved her, man." He squeezed the armrests, Acton for a moment wondering if they could take the pressure.

He let go.

"Shit, this sucks!" Atlas leapt to his feet and began pacing back and forth, everyone giving him his space.

Laura leaned over to Spock. "What's going on?"

"Before we left, his girlfriend was read-in on what he does for a living," explained Spock. "She'd accused him of lying about something then accused him of being part of Delta and threatened to leave him if he didn't tell her the truth."

"Oh, that poor dear!"

"You don't normally get to tell people what you do, but BD got the clearance since they were talking marriage, so Atlas told her. She seemed okay with it at first, all proud like, but I guess things went up shit's creek after we left."

Laura nodded then rose, walking toward the big man and taking him by both arms, looking up into his eyes.

He seemed confused as to what to do, the desire to pace obvious, the fact he'd bowl her over equally so.

"What's your real name?"

"Leon."

She smiled. "Leon, don't lose hope yet. When you get back, sit down and talk with her. Find out what the problem is. If you love her, and she loves you, then you'll figure this out. She's just panicking now because she found out this big, scary secret, and the man she loves isn't there to talk it over with her. Once you two get some time together, I'm sure everything will be fine."

Atlas sighed, dropping his chin to his chest, nodding. "We'll see."

She patted his cheek. "Yes, we will."

An announcement over the PA had them all sitting in preparation for landing in Portugal, Acton and Laura planning on continuing their vacation while she let them use the plane to get back home. Atlas sat, his friends continuing to reassure him, as Laura buckled in beside her husband.

She took his hand, gripping it tight???. "I've never seen him so sad before."

Acton agreed. "I know. But it must be tough for these women. Until they're about to get married, they have no idea what their future husbands do. To then have to decide whether to continue forward, knowing your husband puts himself in harm's way every day, has to be an almost impossible thing to wrap your head around."

"I guess it's no different than marrying a police officer."

Acton shook his head. "I don't know about that. When someone dates a cop, they know they're a cop and they're obviously fine with it since they stick with them. In this case, you think you're dating a soldier, so, yes, there's a small chance he could die in combat or training, but to find out he's Delta? Christ, I don't know how these guys do it. How they're *wives* do it."

"They're incredible women."

Acton grunted. "They must be." He leaned over and gave her a peck. "Just like you."

"Aww, you're looking for something," she said, poking him in the chest.

"And I'm too damned tired and sore to participate. I'll just lie there, okay?"

Acton laughed. "There's no right answer for that one, is there?"

Abbotts Park Apartments, Fayetteville, North Carolina

Butterflies.

Atlas couldn't believe he had them, but he did. When they landed he had immediately called Maggie, actually beating Dawson to the punch. "Tell me everything you know."

And what he was told was heartbreaking, no one having been able to reach Vanessa since she ran out. Maggie did report that after many unanswered phone calls she had gone to the apartment last night and a shouted "go away" had been the response to her knock.

"At least we know she's alive," he had murmured.

"Go and talk to her. Don't take no for an answer. Talk through the door if you have to, rappel down to her balcony, but whatever you do, don't let that girl wallow in self-pity any longer. She needs to talk to someone, and that someone is you."

"Funny, I heard something just like that recently."

Maggie laughed. "Not from those testosterone junkies you hang out with."

He chuckled. "No, Laura Palmer."

"I knew it had to be a woman. And a *smart* woman at that."

"Thanks, Maggie."

"Let me know how it goes."

And he was about to find out.

Flowers in one hand, chocolates in another, and a fine bottle of red wine tucked under his arm.

All the things he could think of, besides himself, that might cheer up the woman he loved.

He knocked.

Nothing.

He tried again, keeping it gentle.

"Vanessa, it's me."

A door across the hall opened and her nosy neighbor stood in her door, arms crossed. "Booyee, are *you* in trouble! What the hell you been doing to that girl that's got her crying so much? I told her you'd be nothin' but trouble. Imagine, datin' an army man, especially after what happened to her daddy!"

The click of the deadbolt on the other side of Vanessa's door signaled the end, he hoped, to the unwarranted berating he was getting from a woman whose only claim to fame was four husbands and four child support checks.

The door opened and Vanessa glared at the woman. "You mind your own business and leave my man alone!" She grabbed him by the arm, pulling him inside before slamming the door shut and locking it.

"Hi, babe, how are you?"

She crossed her arms, one foot out front, tapping as she stared at him, saying nothing. She nodded toward the flowers. "Those for me?"

Atlas had honestly forgotten he had been holding them. "Oh, um, yes." He held them out to her.

She grabbed them, took a look and tossed them on the table. "Beautiful."

She might as well have been reading the word from a dictionary. She flicked her wrist at the chocolates. "And those?"

"Uh huh." He handed them over.

She tossed them on the table.

"And that?"

He gripped the bottle of wine. "Umm, maybe I better hold on to this?"

He flashed a toothy grin, scrunching his shoulders slightly as he tried to feel her out.

She melted, falling into his arms and squeezing him tight. "Oh, gawd, did I miss you."

"Me too, babe, me too. But I'm home now."

She pulled him to the couch and they sat down. She nodded toward the television, CNN on mute, a report on the Japanese situation playing. "You had something to do with that, didn't you?"

He smiled slightly. "You know I can't tell you."

She leaned closer to him. "You know I can tell when you're lying, don't you?"

He leaned away from her. "How?"

She continued pressing forward, slowing crawling up his body. "You just look guilty."

He lay back on the couch. "Huh, never been a problem before."

She lay atop him, her lips inches from his. "I guess you love me."

He smiled, gazing into her eyes. "I guess I do." She leaned in for a kiss but he took her by the shoulders and held her in place. "Do you think you can love this life I'm offering you?"

She smiled. "Absolutely."

Ebiso District, Tokyo, Japan

Jiro Sato lay on his bed, gasping for breath, Keiko lying beside him, her chest heaving.

"Oh my, that was, I mean, you were, I mean." He stopped. "Oh my."

"Glad you enjoyed yourself."

Butterflies formed instantly, his chest tightening. "Umm, you didn't?"

"Are you kidding me? Were you not in the room?"

He grinned at the ceiling.

"I want to do it again."

He turned his head toward her. "I never want to stop!"

She giggled, rolling on top of him, the sheet falling off her shoulders revealing the most incredible sight he had ever seen, and hoped to ever see again.

That this was love, there was no doubt.

And with what they had just done, he was pretty sure the feeling was mutual.

"You have to meet my mother."

Keiko placed a finger on his lips. "*Never* mention your mother when we're having sex."

His eyes widened in horror. "Oh, um, yeah. Forget I said that."

Someone knocked on the door.

"Ignore it."

"Never answering the door again."

Keiko moaned. "Never leaving the bed again."

The knock became more urgent.

Keiko stopped, her shoulders slumping. "Get it. And tell whoever they are that they ruined a perfectly good lay." She rolled off and he got up from the bed, quickly wrapping a robe around himself, slipping his feet into a pair of slippers, the knocking continuing.

He peered through the peephole and his eyes widened in shock.

He opened the door. "Umm, what are *you* doing here?"

Deputy Minister Sasaki bowed. "May I come in?"

"O-of course!"

Jiro stepped backward, Sasaki entering, a security detail remaining outside in the hall. Sasaki looked at him. "I hope I'm not interrupting anything."

Jiro glanced toward the bedroom to see the door closing.

Something Sasaki apparently hadn't missed.

"Oh, I'm terribly sorry," he said, smiling.

"What can I do for you?"

"I thought you deserved to know that the Imperial Regalia have been recovered, and have already been delivered to their sanctuaries."

The revelation was almost cathartic, his muscles relaxing, a sigh escaping as his eyes closed, the weight of seventy years of shame abruptly lifting from his shoulders, a weight no young man should ever have been forced to bear, and now, with the shame and dishonor gone, a weight his children would never need to share.

It's over.

"Thank you for telling me."

Sasaki bowed slightly. "It was my duty and honor. If it weren't for you, we never would have recovered the Imperial Regalia. The Japanese people will never know what happened, but if they did, they would thank you."

"Um, ah, thank you." He bowed.

Sasaki bowed deeply, holding out a rolled up scroll with a wax seal in the center, the symbol of a chrysanthemum pressed into it.

His eyes widened.

"And His Majesty would like to thank you as well."

Jiro fainted.

Butyrka Prison, Moscow, Russian Federation

Orlov sat on what might loosely be described as a bed, the mattress paper thin, the slats underneath spaced so far apart, he feared his large frame might fall through, the threadbare sheet probably providing more support.

His entire body ached.

And he was terrified.

The interrogation had been intense and painful the first day, all manner of threats made, all manner of methods used.

He had talked.

Oh God, had he talked.

He was never a brave man, never a man who should have been subjected to anything like he had been.

And he had talked.

Repeatedly.

Yet the interrogations, the torture, had continued.

The same questions.

The same answers.

And repeated again.

Until it had stopped.

There had been no explanation, nothing. He had been taken back to his cell, barely able to walk, then left alone. He received his meals through a slot in the door, and that was it.

He asked nothing, asked for no explanations and no favors, terrified of what the response might be.

He just sat.

Healing.

And worrying about his wife and son, he having betrayed them both with his pathetic weakness.

"Open three-oh-two!"

The locks clicked and Orlov's heart raced as he rose, standing on the line he had been instructed to, his entire body shaking as he prepared for another beating.

The door opened and an impossibly old man stepped inside.

His eyebrows rose. "A-aren't you a little old to be a prison guard?"

The man smiled. "Who said I'm a prison guard?" He leaned forward. "Do everything I say, when I say, and you'll see your son shortly."

Orlov's jaw dropped. "Wh-who are you?"

"Viktor Zorkin, pleased to meet you." The man extended a hand then motioned toward the door. "Now let's go, I have some more friends to collect."

THE END

ACKNOWLEDGEMENTS

The idea for this book came from an article my dad sent me about missing historical artifacts. In it was mentioned the theory that the Imperial Regalia might actually be among them. The very idea intrigued me and I actually stopped writing the Delta Force Unleashed thriller I was writing, switching my attention to this new idea. It dealt with an area of the world I hadn't covered before, and quite frankly, fascinated me.

Hopefully it did you too.

I'd like to take a moment to thank Greg "Chief" Michael for his invaluable advice on the naval scenes. He helped verify and correct a lot of my terminology and tactics, assisting me greatly. Any errors are this author's alone, and I will cover my ass by suggesting they can all be chalked up to poetic license.

I'd also like to thank my dad for all the research, and Brent Richards and Ian Kennedy for some military terminology help, and as always my wife, daughter, mom and friends.

And here's a question. Did you get as hungry reading the biscuit scene as I did writing it? Man, my stomach was grumbling like crazy! Okay, now I have to Google where I can get fresh biscuits near here.

Another special mention to the winners of an impromptu "name that character" contest held on Facebook. Chariya "Apocalypta" Em was the winner, and Richard's nomination of Rosie "Riveter" Bugnet also made it in as a last minute addition. Thanks to all who participated. If you want to join in the fun (yes, fun!) follow me on Facebook today. Details are on my website.

To those who have not already done so, please visit my website at www.jrobertkennedy.com then sign up for the Insider's Club to be notified of new book releases. Your email address will never be shared or sold and you'll only receive the occasional email from me as I don't have time to spam you!

Thank you once again for reading.

ABOUT THE AUTHOR

With over 500,000 books in circulation and over 3000 five-star reviews, USA Today bestselling author J. Robert Kennedy has been ranked by Amazon as the #1 Bestselling Action Adventure novelist based upon combined sales. He is the author of over twenty-five international bestsellers including the smash hit James Acton Thrillers. He lives with his wife and daughter and writes full-time.

Visit Robert's website at www.jrobertkennedy.com for the latest news and contact information, and to join the Insider's Club to be notified when new books are released.

Available James Acton Thrillers

The Protocol (Book #1)

For two thousand years the Triarii have protected us, influencing history from the crusades to the discovery of America. Descendent from the Roman Empire, they pervade every level of society, and are now in a race with our own government to retrieve an ancient artifact thought to have been lost forever.

Brass Monkey (Book #2)

A nuclear missile, lost during the Cold War, is now in play--the most public spy swap in history, with a gorgeous agent the center of international attention, triggers the end-game of a corrupt Soviet Colonel's twenty five year plan. Pursued across the globe by the Russian authorities, including a brutal Spetsnaz unit, those involved will stop at nothing to deliver their weapon, and ensure their payday, regardless of the terrifying consequences.

Broken Dove (Book #3)

With the Triarii in control of the Roman Catholic Church, an organization founded by Saint Peter himself takes action, murdering one of the new Pope's operatives. Detective Chaney, called in by the Pope to investigate, disappears, and, to the horror of the Papal staff sent to inform His Holiness, they find him missing too, the only clue a secret chest, presented to each new pope on the eve of their election, since the beginning of the Church.

The Templar's Relic (Book #4)

The Vault must be sealed, but a construction accident leads to a miraculous discovery--an ancient tomb containing four Templar Knights, long forgotten, on the grounds of the Vatican. Not knowing who they can trust, the Vatican requests Professors James Acton and Laura Palmer examine the find, but what they discover, a precious Islamic relic, lost during the Crusades, triggers a set of events that shake the entire world, pitting the two greatest religions against each other. At risk is nothing less than the Vatican itself, and the rock upon which it was built.

Flags of Sin (Book #5)

Archaeology Professor James Acton simply wants to get away from everything, and relax. A trip to China seems just the answer, and he and his fiancée, Professor Laura Palmer, are soon on a flight to Beijing. But while boarding, they bump into an old friend, Delta Force Command Sergeant Major Burt Dawson, who surreptitiously delivers a message that they must meet the next day, for Dawson knows something they don't. China is about to erupt into chaos.

The Arab Fall (Book #6)

An accidental find by a friend of Professor James Acton may lead to the greatest archaeological discovery since the tomb of King Tutankhamen, perhaps even greater. And when news of it spreads, it reaches the ears of a group hell-bent on the destruction of all idols and icons, their mere existence considered blasphemous to Islam.

The Circle of Eight (Book #7)

The Bravo Team is targeted by a madman after one of their own intervenes in a rape. Little do they know this internationally well-respected banker is also a senior member of an organization long thought extinct, whose stated goals for a reshaped world are not only terrifying, but with today's globalization, totally achievable.

The Venice Code (Book #8)

A former President's son is kidnapped in a brazen attack on the streets of Potomac by the very ancient organization that murdered his father, convinced he knows the location of an item stolen from them by the late president. A close friend awakes from a coma with a message for archaeology Professor James Acton from the same organization, sending him on a quest to find an object only rumored to exist, while trying desperately to keep one step ahead of a foe hell-bent on possessing it.

Pompeii's Ghosts (Book #9)

Two thousand years ago Roman Emperor Vespasian tries to preserve an empire by hiding a massive treasure in the quiet town of Pompeii should someone challenge his throne. Unbeknownst to him nature is about to unleash its wrath upon the Empire during which the best and worst of Rome's citizens will be revealed during a time when duty and honor were more than words, they were ideals worth dying for.

Amazon Burning (Book #10)

Days from any form of modern civilization, archaeology Professor James Acton awakes to gunshots. Finding his wife missing, taken by a member of one of the uncontacted tribes, he and his friend INTERPOL Special Agent Hugh Reading try desperately to find her in the dark of the jungle, but quickly realize there is no hope without help. And with help three days away, he knows the longer they wait, the farther away she'll be.

The Riddle (Book #11)

Russia accuses the United States of assassinating their Prime Minister in Hanoi, naming Delta Force member Sergeant Carl "Niner" Sung as the assassin. Professors James Acton and Laura Palmer, witnesses to the murder, know the truth, and as the Russians and Vietnamese attempt to use the situation to their advantage on the international stage, the husband and wife duo attempt to find proof that their friend is innocent.

Blood Relics (Book #12)

A DYING MAN. A DESPERATE SON.
ONLY A MIRACLE CAN SAVE THEM BOTH.

Professor Laura Palmer is shot and kidnapped in front of her husband, archaeology Professor James Acton, as they try to prevent the theft of the world's Blood Relics, ancient artifacts thought to contain the blood of Christ, a madman determined to possess them all at any cost.

Sins of the Titanic (Book #13)

THE ASSEMBLY IS ETERNAL. AND THEY'LL STOP AT
NOTHING TO KEEP IT THAT WAY.

When Professor James Acton is contacted about a painting thought
to have been lost with the sinking of the Titanic, he is inadvertently
drawn into a century old conspiracy an ancient organization known
as The Assembly will stop at nothing to keep secret.

Saint Peter's Soldiers (Book #14)

A MISSING DA VINCI.

A TERRIFYING GENETIC BREAKTHROUGH.

A PAST AND FUTURE ABOUT TO COLLIDE!

In World War Two a fabled da Vinci drawing is hidden from the
Nazis, those involved fearing Hitler may attempt to steal it for its
purported magical powers. It isn't returned for over fifty years.

And today, archaeology Professor James Acton and his wife are
about to be dragged into the terrible truth of what happened so
many years ago, for the truth is never what it seems, and the history
we thought was fact, is all lies.

The Thirteenth Legion (Book #15)

A TWO-THOUSAND-YEAR-OLD DESTINY IS ABOUT TO
BE FULFILLED!

USA Today bestselling author J. Robert Kennedy delivers another
action-packed thriller in The Thirteenth Legion. After Interpol Agent
Hugh Reading spots his missing partner in Berlin, it sets off a chain
of events that could lead to the death of his best friends, and if the
legends are true, life as we know it.

Raging Sun (Book #16)

WILL A SEVENTY-YEAR-OLD MATTER OF HONOR
TRIGGER THE NEXT GREAT WAR?

The Imperial Regalia have been missing since the end of World War
Two, and the Japanese government, along with the new—and
secretly illegitimate—emperor, have been lying to the people. But the
truth isn't out yet, and the Japanese will stop at nothing to secure
their secret and retrieve the ancient relics confiscated by a belligerent
Russian government. Including war.

Available Special Agent Dylan Kane Thrillers

Rogue Operator (Book #1)

Three top secret research scientists are presumed dead in a boating accident, but the kidnapping of their families the same day raises questions the FBI and local police can't answer, leaving them waiting for a ransom demand that will never come. Central Intelligence Agency Analyst Chris Leroux stumbles upon the story, finding a phone conversation that was never supposed to happen, and is told to leave it to the FBI. But he can't let it go. For he knows something the FBI doesn't. One of the scientists is alive.

Containment Failure (Book #2)

New Orleans has been quarantined, an unknown virus sweeping the city, killing one hundred percent of those infected. The Centers for Disease Control, desperate to find a cure, is approached by BioDyne Pharma who reveal a former employee has turned a cutting edge medical treatment capable of targeting specific genetic sequences into a weapon, and released it. The stakes have never been higher as Kane battles to save not only his friends and the country he loves, but all of mankind.

Cold Warriors (Book #3)

While in Chechnya CIA Special Agent Dylan Kane stumbles upon a meeting between a known Chechen drug lord and a retired General once responsible for the entire Soviet nuclear arsenal. Money is exchanged for a data stick and the resulting transmission begins a race across the globe to discover just what was sold, the only clue a reference to a top-secret Soviet weapon called Crimson Rush.

Death to America (Book #4)

America is in crisis. Dozens of terrorist attacks have killed or injured thousands, and worse, every single attack appears to have been committed by an American citizen in the name of Islam.

A stolen experimental F-35 Lightning II is discovered by CIA Special Agent Dylan Kane in China, delivered by an American soldier reported dead years ago in exchange for a chilling promise.

And Chris Leroux is forced to watch as his girlfriend, Sherrie White, is tortured on camera, under orders to not interfere, her continued suffering providing intel too valuable to sacrifice.

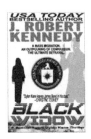

Black Widow (Book #5)

USA Today bestselling author J. Robert Kennedy serves up another heart-pounding thriller in Black Widow. After corrupt Russian agents sell deadly radioactive Cesium to Chechen terrorists, CIA Special Agent Dylan Kane is sent to infiltrate the ISIL terror cell suspected of purchasing it. Then all contact is lost.

Available Delta Force Unleashed Thrillers

Payback (Book #1)

The daughter of the Vice President is kidnapped from an Ebola clinic, triggering an all-out effort to retrieve her by America's elite Delta Force just hours after a senior government official from Sierra Leone is assassinated in a horrific terrorist attack while visiting the United States. As she battles impossible odds and struggles to prove her worth to her captors who have promised she will die, she's forced to make unthinkable decisions to not only try to save her own life, but those dying from one of the most vicious diseases known to mankind, all in the hopes an unleashed Delta Force can save her before her captors enact their horrific plan on an unsuspecting United States.

Infidels (Book #2)

When the elite Delta Force's Bravo Team is inserted into Yemen to rescue a kidnapped Saudi prince, they find more than they bargained for—a crate containing the Black Stone, stolen from Mecca the day before. Requesting instructions on how to proceed, they find themselves cut off and disavowed, left to survive with nothing but each other to rely upon.

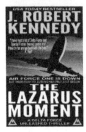

The Lazarus Moment (Book #3)

AIR FORCE ONE IS DOWN.
BUT THEIR FIGHT TO SURVIVE HAS ONLY JUST BEGUN!
When Air Force One crashes in the jungles of Africa, it is up to America's elite Delta Force to save the survivors not only from rebels hell-bent on capturing the President, but Mother Nature herself.

Available Detective Shakespeare Mysteries

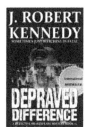

Depraved Difference (Book #1)

SOMETIMES JUST WATCHING IS FATAL

When a young woman is brutally assaulted by two men on the subway, her cries for help fall on the deaf ears of onlookers too terrified to get involved, her misery ended with the crushing stomp of a steel-toed boot. A cellphone video of her vicious murder, callously released on the Internet, its popularity a testament to today's depraved society, serves as a trigger, pulled a year later, for a killer.

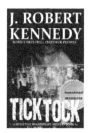

Tick Tock (Book #2)

SOMETIMES HELL IS OTHER PEOPLE

Crime Scene tech Frank Brata digs deep and finds the courage to ask his colleague, Sarah, out for coffee after work. Their good time turns into a nightmare when Frank wakes up the next morning covered in blood, with no recollection of what happened, and Sarah's body floating in the tub.

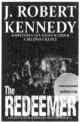
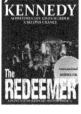

The Redeemer (Book #3)

SOMETIMES LIFE GIVES MURDER A SECOND CHANCE

It was the case that destroyed Detective Justin Shakespeare's career, beginning a downward spiral of self-loathing and self-destruction lasting half a decade. And today things are only going to get worse. The Widow Rapist is free on a technicality, and it is up to Detective Shakespeare and his partner Amber Trace to find the evidence, five years cold, to put him back in prison before he strikes again.

Zander Varga, Vampire Detective

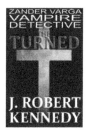

The Turned (Book #1)

Zander has relived his wife's death at the hands of vampires every day for almost three hundred years, his perfect memory a curse of becoming one of The Turned—infecting him their final heinous act after her murder.

Nineteen year-old Sydney Winter knows Zander's secret, a secret preserved by the women in her family for four generations. But with her mother in a coma, she's thrust into the frontlines, ahead of her time, to fight side-by-side with Zander.

Made in United States
Orlando, FL
11 May 2023

33048360R00193